SOULMATES
A METAPHYSICAL LOVE STORY
SARAH FAETH SANDERS

Duck & A Rabbit

Press

DUCK & A RABBIT PRESS

This book contains the following content, which some readers may find difficult to read: domestic abuse, mental/emotional abuse, religious trauma, family estrangement, unwanted pregnancy, abortion, and illicit drug use. In two instances, a character makes fatphobic comments. This book has a happily ever after, and was written with immense hope and love for its readers.

For more information or to know which sections to skip to avoid sensitive content, please feel free to contact the author directly.

To Mom and Dad.

What you are about to read is part of a grand tapestry of stories.

There are many I could tell you, and I will, but this particular story is one of my favorites. It happens to be plucked from the very time and place in which you exist now. Perhaps it will be useful to you.

The main character in this story, and all the stories I will tell, has been of interest to me for a very long time. Her journey, you see, is a fascinating case study on the evolution of the soul. I am deeply interested in such a journey, having spent much of my own existence trying to understand the nature of the universe.

And how is it that one comes to understand the nature of the universe? Through stories, of course.

But to tell her story, I must also tell the story of her soulmate. We will start our story just before our characters' lives begin.

The being existing on the left (if there is such a thing in space) is the color purple, but you would not know this, as she is currently invisible to the human eye. Her name sounds like the taste of strawberries and the sting of saltwater on one's skin. We will call her A.

The being on the right is teal. Also, invisible. His name lies somewhere between the call of a purple finch and the feeling of worn leather. We will call him Z.

A and Z have been with one another for thousands of years. It is difficult to explain precisely what this means to a reader whose only remembered experience of time has been linear, but I will do my best.

From time to time (and here is yet another instance where time as a descriptor falls short), one or both of them will experience a strong pull. Some current of time or space will tug them into an incarnate form, often in response to a need for growth. On the other side of each incarnation is a lesson learned, a desire met, or a truth realized.

And in each life they live, they search for each other.

A and Z are enjoying the presence of two other beings, friends from many lifetimes and soulmates themselves.

One of these beings often fluctuates between bright purple and grey. His name is pronounced using a blend of "ohm" and the clanging of a cymbal. We will call him T.

T is revolving around a mustard yellow being, whose name changes depending on who is addressing them. T knows them as the shock of a battery against his tongue, though at the moment, he has no tongue. We will call them Y.

The energy between A and Z is similar to a magnetic wave, while the energy between T and Y resembles a chemical reaction. While A and Z's connection is like the pull of a flower to a wandering bee, T and Y are extremely difficult to separate once they've been together.

In the course of their existence, these beings have changed despite their familiar patterns, evolving alongside the universe itself. Both *it* and *them* began as scattered, ruthless, fickle kinds of things. Ever so slowly, they grew more aligned, more aware, and more inclined in the direction of pure, uninhibited love. For this, truly, is what it means that the universe is expanding.

The cohort is drifting together somewhere near Earth. They often find themselves here, for they enjoy many memories on this planet. They all agree: there is almost no better place to stretch one's perspective than on the small blue marble. For though it is dying, the life upon it tends to thrive in unexpected ways.

A and Z are dancing around each other, their edges brushing against one another as they go. As they twirl, they borrow bits of starlight, sending them to one another as if they are blowing kisses.

As they spin, A feels the slightest shift in her awareness. She is slipping away.

Come with me, she calls to him.

He is already reaching for her, determined not to part.

With that, the soulmates speed toward Earth like two pieces of a star. They encircle one another, gracefully, violently, as they go, each trying desperately to remember the other for as long as they can.

Beside them, T and Y rush toward the earth in an explosion of light and color as they fight against the force that threatens to tear them apart. Refusing to separate, they erupt and are consumed by the passion of their refusal, finally and resoundingly synthesizing into a singular form just before landing.

A and Z hold on to one another as long as they can, but the inertia of the fall threatens to fling them onto opposite corners of the earth.

Hold on, they tell one another. *Stay with me.*

In an instant they are pushed out of one another's sight, each of them batted around by the multitude of souls who throng to the entrance of this world, hurdling chaotically toward their destinies.

PART ONE

1

Audrey Anderson sat on a bench outside her freshman dormitory, reading. She wore a long floral skirt and a simple gray tank top. Her bright red hair was piled on top of her head in a bun, her green eyes laser-focused on the book she held.

Despite it being nearly 8 pm, it was still warm outside in Azusa, California. It was mid-September, and Audrey had just moved into her dorm room six days ago. Tonight was the final night of orientation activities. Most of her fellow classmates were at a giant outdoor mixer event. She could hear the music from the upperclassmen's skits from where she sat, punctuated by laughter and loud applause.

Why was she here, reading *Whistling in the Dark* by the light of a lamp post, instead of socializing with her fellow Cougars? The answer to that was both simple and complicated.

The simple answer was that she was waiting for a call from her boyfriend, Paul.

He called her every night at 8 o'clock. He was a freshman too, but at another private university about thirty minutes away. The two of them had been dating for over a year, having attended the same church and high school in Redding, California.

The complicated version had to do with the person Audrey—you and I know her as A—had molded herself to be to adapt to the life she was given. It was in the twisting involved in making a phoenix fit inside a chicken egg. The phoenix being Audrey, the egg being the life of an evangelical woman, raised in an evangelical home.

Yes, A happened to be born into one of humanity's most peculiar traditions: American evangelicalism. It was a relatively short-lived phenomenon in the grand scheme of things, this belief system, but an impactful one nonetheless. This belief system channeled every ounce of Audrey's considerable passion and intelligence into maintaining a highly specific ideal of womanhood, created by a handful of Jewish and Hellenistic men in the first few centuries of the "modern" age.

These particular men, in the centuries since, have been profoundly disappointed by the unintended consequences of their actions. Believe me, I've discussed it with them many times.

Audrey was now busy dealing with said consequences herself. Namely, Paul.

She had already cut short her call with Paul last night in order to go to an Alpha group meeting. Alpha groups were university-assigned cohorts of freshmen, each led by an upperclassman who was supposed to guide them through the ins and outs of their first year of college.

Her group had gone together to Donut Man, a local legend for students of Azusa Pacific University, and a supposed rite of passage. Audrey spent the entire outing checking her phone, anxious about the time. When she got back to her dorm room at 10:30 and called Paul back like she'd promised, his tone was short and impatient. She shrunk, apologetic, at his voice.

"It just makes me uncomfortable that you're out late with a bunch of guys," he said after she'd apologized for the third time. "It's not that I don't trust you. I just don't trust other people."

Actually, it was three boys and four girls, she thought. But she wouldn't say that out loud.

Did Audrey know that Paul's comments were a blatant form of manipulation? Did she realize that one's own insecurities were not a basis for restricting the freedom of a loved one?

Yes. Somewhere. Deep, deep down in her heart, in a place that rarely saw the light of day, she knew.

On the surface, however, Audrey accepted the idea that Paul's brain was simply wired differently than hers. His jealousy was a mere symptom of his genetic coding. He just needed a bit more encouragement. A bit more support. Something to buoy his ego. And it was her role to provide that for him.

"Believe me, I wish I had been here talking to you instead," she said. "You should *see* these people they have me in an Alpha group with. One of them, I think his name is Trevor or something, smelled like he had hard-boiled eggs in his pockets."

Paul chuckled quietly at this.

When all else fails, insult the person he's jealous of.

"And another one of the guys was wearing a Slipknot t-shirt. Like, I thought we were at a Christian university? What the *heck* are you wearing, dude?"

Remind him he is spiritually superior to them.

"A couple of the girls I like though. Samantha seems really nice. Her family are ex-Mormons. And Erin is engaged to someone from Redding. Small world, right?"

Remind him there were girls there, too. Nice girls. Safe girls.

"But one of them was practically hanging out of her shirt. Of course, she spent most of her time flirting with the boys."

Audrey isn't paying the boys any attention. And they aren't paying any attention to her. Cleavage Girl has that front taken care of.

Paul listened quietly, then said, "It's good you're making friends, baby girl. Just be careful, okay?"

Crisis averted.

"I will, babe," she said. "You know me."

So, here she was, being careful. Reading a book. Waiting for his call.

"Audrey!"

Audrey looked up to see one of her Alpha group members running toward her. Erika. *Cleavage Girl.* Audrey felt a pang of regret for what she'd said about her the day before. In truth, she liked her a lot. She was loud, and funny, and immediately sucked all the tension from any space she happened to be in.

"Hey!" Erika said as she got closer. "What are you doing over here by yourself? There are like four of us from the group over there together." She jutted her chin in the direction of the mixer. "You should come!"

"Oh, it's okay," Audrey said. "I'm a little tired, and I'm waiting for a call anyway." She waved her phone at her pathetically, as if to prove it.

"Come on, you sure?" Erika said, her face frowning with concern. "We won't ever be freshmen again! *Come oooon!*"

Audrey smiled, trying to paint the honest regret on her face for Erika's benefit. "I know," she said. "Really though, it's okay. I'm good. I'd rather just read and go to bed."

"Okay," Erika said doubtfully. "Suit yourself. If you change your mind, we're near the back, on the left side. I'll see you at the next Alpha meeting!"

Audrey smiled and nodded as Erika jogged away. Then she let out an audible sigh.

If she was being honest with herself, she was miserable. She missed Paul. She missed her friends back home. She missed her church, and her parents, and her little brother, and her cat. She missed the comforting predictability of Redding. No one there so much as dared to disagree over football teams, let alone basic theological tenets.

A few days prior, on her way to the Dining Hall, Audrey overheard two students talking about *cultural relativism.* It was a term uttered like a curse at her church, spit from one's mouth like it was foul. But here, it was apparently a regular topic of conversation. For some reason, it made her feel scared.

There was her roommate, though. Kara. She was calm, soft-spoken, and constantly reading the Bible. In fact, she was probably in their room reading her Bible right now, getting ready for bed. Like a normal, healthy person.

Audrey's phone buzzed. It was Paul.

"Hey," she said into the receiver after the first ring. "How are you?"

"Hey, baby girl," he said. "I'm good, how are you?"

"Good, just reading. What are you doing?"

"I'm waiting on Travis and Ezekiel," Paul said. "We heard about this hike you're supposed to do at night, I guess it's really cool. We're gonna go check it out as soon as Ezekiel is ready."

"Oh," Audrey said. "That sounds cool."

"Yeah, it's gonna be awesome," Paul said. Then he laughed, seemingly at something happening in the background.

"So you like those two? You're becoming pretty good friends?"

"Yeah," Paul answered. Audrey heard a male voice in the background, then Paul laughed again.

"That's good," she said. "I'm glad you're making friends."

"Yeah," Paul said absently. "What are you doing?"

"Reading," she said again. "You know, I think you'd really like this book, actually. It's a bunch of short chapters, each about a different topic. There's this one entry on boredom that blew my—"

Paul laughed again, making Audrey pause.

"You know what, Audrey, I'd better just let you go," he said quickly. "I think Ezekiel's almost ready anyway."

"Oh, okay," Audrey said. "Have fun, babe. I love you."

"Love you!" Paul said cheerily, and hung up.

Audrey put her phone down next to her and sat in silence for a few minutes, thinking.

Only a few months ago her life made perfect sense. She was just about to graduate at the top of her class with honors. She was well-liked at her small Christian high school. She had a tight-knit group of friends, but was acquainted with at least a few people from all the major cliques.

She was the best debater on her school's forensics team, widely hated by other districts for both her debate skills and her propensity to steer every mock Congress session toward the topic of abortion. She spent her weekends in church, and her summers on mission trips to Tijuana and the Tenderloin district, sharing God's love with all the poor sinners. She sang in the church choir and did the "O, Holy Night" solo every year at the Christmas service because she was so good.

And to top it all off, she had the perfect boyfriend. He was tall, towering over Audrey, who was 5'3", by 11 inches. He had blue eyes, dark brown hair that popped against his pale skin, and a smile that made her stomach do backflips. Everyone in her family loved him. Their parents were good friends with each other, and their little brothers even played together from time to time.

He also made her laugh occasionally, and he supported her dreams of singing on stage. Well, sort of. He suggested she become the full-time worship leader at his church after he became a pastor post-graduation. And she supposed that would likely come with a stage.

On top of all that, Paul checked all the boxes of the "future husband" checklist she made in tenth grade at one of her youth group's annual "purity nights" for girls. He was tall, handsome, ambitious, he said and did romantic things, and his religious beliefs mirrored her own exactly.

Taken together, everything led Audrey to believe Paul was her soulmate. After attending a purity night once a year since she started growing breasts, she knew this was basically what she could expect from the man God chose for her: some generally good qualities, and "equally yoked" with her. Besides, even though what she and Paul had done wasn't *technically* sex, she was pretty sure they still *had* to marry each other now.

An eruption of laughter from the lawn lifted Audrey from her thoughts. She sighed. She could already feel some of the closeness between her and Paul fading. She tried to believe she was overreacting. It was a big week for both of them. Settling into new schools would be a serious adjustment. Everything would feel normal in a few weeks when they could see one another again.

At least, that's what she told herself. The truth is, very little would ever feel "normal" for young Audrey again.

2

Audrey rubbed her eyes, willing them to see the paper in front of her with renewed focus. It was nearly eight weeks into her first semester of college, and midterms were just around the corner. She sat in a cozy coffee shop about ten minutes from campus, studying.

The chiming of a bell behind her told her someone had just walked in; a chill swept across her from the open door, but she didn't look up from her notebook as they walked past her and into the back—an employee headed to clock in.

Audrey hummed a tune softly under her breath—a vocal warmup that always stuck in her head. She had already settled on a major in music composition, with a focus on vocal performance. She was minoring in graphic design, a backup that satisfied her creative spirit and had "work from home potential" written all over it. But she was already in love with the music program despite only being in one music-related class so far.

Secretly, she still dreamed of singing on stage—and *not* in a church. (Scandalous, I know.) One of APU's graduates had, according to rumors, gone on to sing backup vocals for Nicki Minaj. Thinking about such a prospect made Audrey feel delightfully wicked. She liked to imagine herself in such a scenario—going on tour, surrounded by music all the time. Lately, when it popped into her head, she tried to put it away. Best to not think too far into the future.

After all, God had already laid a path out before her. She need not make any concrete plans just yet. And there was always Paul to think of.

The rest of her courses were undergraduate requirements, mostly Bible classes. Currently, she was going over her notes for "Christian Life, Faith, and Ministry," a requirement for all APU freshmen. Her instructor was Professor Bowman, one of three professors who taught the class each semester. She was beginning to understand he had a reputation on campus, along with a handful of other professors, for being quite bold about his theological perspectives.

It was a reputation well-earned. After each class with him, Audrey felt strangely light and heavy at the same time. It was similar to the feeling she had after a long run when her runner's high had already kicked in and she was willing herself to slow down even though her legs didn't want to. There was a sort of exhaustion just below the surface, but it felt like fuel.

The notes from her most recent class were making her head ache, and not just because the margins were filled with tiny pencil caricatures of her classmates. She had quickly come to feel like a fool, exposed to the vast diversity of perspectives under the umbrella of Christianity after 18 years in the dark. In her home church, it was not just other religions that were scorned as being spawned from the devil himself. Even traditions like Catholicism were deemed dangerous aberrations from the will of God. Minor denominations' beliefs were never even acknowledged. It was like they didn't exist.

Yet here was a man who not only claimed to be a devout Christian, but who'd recently spent six weeks meditating at a Buddhist monastery. That such a thing was possible without earning a ticket straight to hell was brand new information to Audrey.

Audrey's mind was expanding. New ideas were filling in the cracks that emerged as fast as she could absorb them. It was invigorating, like dry ground eagerly soaking up the rain. But it was painful, too. Like the stretch of one's stomach after a large meal when they have been starving too long.

The foundations of Audrey's belief system were swaying beneath her. But like an animal who's always lived in a cage, she didn't consider going through the open gate to flee. Instead, she danced around the fissures that appeared, trying not to fall in.

Audrey sighed, her mind muddled. She needed a break.

She got up and walked toward the counter to peruse the specials on a small laminated menu. An hour or so ago she started off with green tea, but it just hadn't hit the spot.

"Hi, can I help you?" said the barista behind the counter, a young woman with curly blonde hair. *Sam*, read her name tag.

"Hi," Audrey said, stepping closer. She pointed to a drink on the menu called *Cherry Bomb*, a cherry amaretto latte. "How's this one?" she asked.

"It's good," the barista said. "Very sweet."

"I'll try it," Audrey said, nodding. "A medium, please."

After paying, Audrey stepped to the side to let the girl behind her pay for a poppyseed muffin. There were only a handful of other customers in the shop, all college students. They sat at their tables, headphones in, staring at their laptops. A few had their heads bent, squinting at their books.

The coffee shop was relatively small, but in a cozy sort of way. Exposed brick lined the walls. The layout was strangely interrupted by the counter and the front entrance so that the shop had many small corners, each stuffed with eclectic furniture. A small bookshelf sat just by the door with books available to read. The shop was decorated with photographs and sculptures that reflected its name—Windmills. It was enough to justify a theme but stopped short of tacky.

Today was the first time Audrey had chosen this particular coffee shop. She was burnt out on Starbucks, and the campus coffee shop was constantly crowded. She had actually planned on studying at a larger cafe just down the road, but she liked the look of this place when she passed by. She immediately felt comfortable upon walking in, the dark colors and warm smells enveloping her in a cheery, caffeinated hug.

In fact, she wouldn't mind working at a place like Windmills. She'd been considering getting a part-time job, a plan her parents insisted wasn't necessary, as school was supposed to be her job. Paul complained it would only take more of her time away from him. But those were the same reasons they'd used when she wanted a job during high school, too.

Audrey turned on her heels to the barista, who had just handed Muffin Girl her receipt.

"Are you guys hiring by any chance?" she asked.

"Actually, yeah," Sam started. But before she could finish, a voice cut in behind her.

"Are you thinking of applying?"

It came from the employee who walked in earlier. He was still tying his apron, a curious smile on his face.

Audrey froze. She felt a strange shift inside her when he spoke, like the feeling one gets when one steps from dry land onto a boat. And now, looking at him, she could have sworn the ground was moving beneath her feet, her stomach lurching with its rocking movements. She felt the earth tip slightly, as if it meant to push her toward him.

He was white, his skin tan from the sun, and he stood at roughly 5'10". He appeared to be around her age. His medium brown hair was just long enough that a few rebellious curls stuck out around his ears, framing his oval face. His dark brown, almond-shaped eyes held something Audrey wanted to name—something like mischief. There was something oddly familiar about them. She thought for a moment she recognized his smile, which was broad, and kind, and slightly crooked.

"I-I might," she managed to stammer, smiling at him.

"You should," he said matter-of-factly. He nodded toward Sam, who was holding out a paper application for Audrey to take.

She took it, watching him lean forward to grab the empty cup from the counter that had her drink order written on it, never taking his eyes off her.

Audrey noticed his name tag. *Zachary.* But you and I know him as Z.

"I'll take care of this for you," Zachary said, winking.

Audrey nodded, still smiling, and forced herself to turn away. A minute or so later when she went to retrieve her drink from the counter, Zachary was already taking someone else's order.

Audrey sat down again to study with her Cherry Bomb latte. Sam was right, it was very sweet. She loved it.

She tried to study for about twenty minutes, but she couldn't stop glancing over at the counter.

Maybe I should call Mom, she thought. She had been meaning to, anyway.

"Audrey dear," her mother said when she picked up the phone. "I didn't expect to hear from you. It's Saturday, aren't you usually with Paul?"

"Hi Mom," Audrey said. "No, not with Paul. He's still busy with midterms."

"Still?" Audrey's mother made a dissatisfied sound. Audrey and Paul had been good about seeing each other once a week since college started, but they were going on three weeks now, a fact her mother knew. "Well, that's okay dear. Men often need time to themselves."

Audrey nodded as if her mother could hear the gesture through the phone. "How are things at home?"

"They're fine, dear. Your father is at work, he's just hired Pam and Jackson's son as a cashier so he's keeping a close eye on things this week. You remember him, the boy with the freckles. Speaking of church, a few people were asking about you last Sunday. Angela wants to know when you and Paul are getting married. You know it gets harder and harder to maintain your purity the longer you wait, Audrey."

Audrey listened silently as her mother moved from one topic to the next, her weary mind finding comfort in the bits of news or gossip she shared about this person or that thing. It was all familiar, like an old blanket. As she listened, she found her eyes wandering to the counter again. Once, Zachary looked up just as her eyes landed on him, and she quickly averted them, feigning interest in a poster just above his head.

She felt silly. After all, he was a total stranger. They'd exchanged less than ten words between them, yet her heart pounded in her chest when she looked his way. Sure, she sort of wanted to cry every time his voice rang across the coffee shop, but she told herself it was simply because he looked so familiar. She was trying to place him.

Soon enough, she couldn't deny it.

I've been struck with some stupid, childish infatuation, she thought. *I must be* completely *starved for attention.*

Audrey tried not to worry about how little she'd seen Paul lately. Despite midterms being a decent excuse, she couldn't shake the nagging feeling he was mad at her for something. For what, she didn't know.

Between you and me, assuming someone, somewhere was mad at her had just kind of become Audrey's default after so many years in church.

You're just feeling lonely, she thought to herself. *You should probably call Paul after this.* Zachary's crooked smile flashed in her mind momentarily, making her stomach flutter. *And pray. You should probably pray, too.*

Paul's name on her mother's lips broke into Audrey's musings.

"It's not uncommon," she said. "Your father has had periods of distance, too. All men do. They just can't be troubled with matters of the heart when they're focused on something. It's how God made them. You understand that though, dear. It's why you're going to make such a good wife—you're compassionate. Paul knows that. He'll be back to his normal, doting self in no time."

"You're right, Mom," Audrey said. "Thanks... hey, I'd better go. I have some studying to do."

"Alright, dear." Audrey's mother made a kissing noise. "Talk soon."

"Talk soon."

Audrey gathered up her things and stood, preparing to put some distance between herself and the distraction behind the counter. On her way out, she glanced behind her. Zachary's back was to her as he readied a filter for the drip coffee machine. She forced herself through the door before she could call out an awkward, "Thank you!" and headed to her car.

Get a hold of yourself, Audrey, she thought. *This isn't a distraction you can afford.*

She filled out the paper application as soon as she got back to her dorm room.

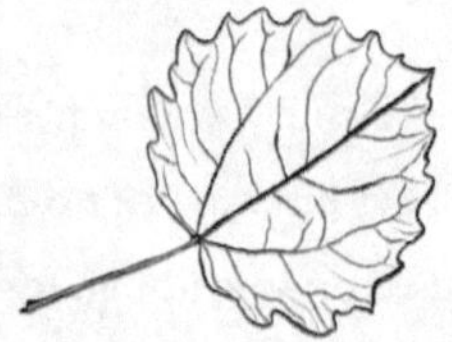

Once, she was a grove of Aspen trees. She sat nestled at the base of a mountain, just across the valley from a little boy who lived with his mom, dad, and younger sister in a small cabin. His name then was Zane, and he played among her branches his whole childhood.

Zane rested at the base of her trunks, played pirate with her fallen limbs as swords, and chased butterflies and bees along the perimeter of her body. She shook with delight, her leaves dancing in a soft symphony of gratitude as his fingers traced the dark scars that emerged on her pale skin each time a branch fell or an arrow missed its target. When the boy walked from his home to the grove, his feet wet from splashing in the stream that ran just beside her, she summoned a bit of wind to rush through her quaking leaves, whispering:

Hello, boy.

The boy grew into a young man, his stout form filling out as he grew upward. She grew with him, but did not age as quickly. The village near his cabin grew as well, encroaching on the valley a bit more each year.

Now he brought his lovers to the grove. During the day, a young woman with whom he shared poems and dreams and whose hand he tenderly held as he walked with her. In the night, a young man to whom he passionately, desperately, achingly made love—his heart filled with an equal mix of shame and desire. Above them her leaves quaked in celebration and anticipation of their love. Beneath them her roots stretched out like a lattice, cradling the boy as he wept in grief that his love could not exist beneath the sun.

Eventually, the boy became a man. That man knew he couldn't live forever in his parents' cabin, so he left. Before he did, he said goodbye to the grove of Aspen trees across the valley, with whom he had spent his life. He whispered that he would visit her if he ever came back.

Over the following years she could hear his voice occasionally carrying across the valley, mingled with the voices of his wife and their young children. Sometimes he came to see her, each year more weighed down with the preoccupations of his life than the last. The visits grew fewer and farther between as time went on. Eventually he stopped coming altogether.

Each year the village grew, and new souls came to visit her. Lovers, mothers, friends, and eventually, men with axes. They cut her faster than she could send up new shoots, and her energy slowly waned. She contracted, each year getting smaller until only a few trees remained.

It was then that he came, walking slowly and deliberately through the dark. His children, now nearly young men and women themselves, were asleep. He remained restless. He hadn't been home in many years and was saddened that his friend was barely visible across the cavernous mouth of the valley.

When he approached her, she was barely able to muster a hello. The night was still, and her leaves few.

He placed his hand on her skin. He could feel everything from that touch, just as he could when he was a boy. The density of the wood, the moisture running beneath the bark, the smell of her leaves when they were crushed underfoot. The barely perceptible quaking of the leaves above him brought a rush of memories. They mingled with new ones as he mentally shared his life with his friend—the laughs of his children, the comfort of his home, the sound of wind running through stalks of wheat.

Together they stood, a small boy named Zane and the silent guardian of his childhood's magic, sharing their life together once more.

After a while he bent down, examining her labyrinth of exposed roots. He pulled a knife from his pocket and took a cutting of one to bring back home.

And they lived happily ever after until (and after) their deaths.

3

Audrey was trying hard to focus on the task at hand, but a large portion of her attention was fixed on the warmth of Zachary Peters' breath as it brushed against her ear. Each word he said sent chills down her spine.

"There you go," he said. "Now raise it just a touch. There. Perfect foam."

Zachary was put in charge of Audrey's training on day one. The manager, Kelly, simply scheduled all of her shifts at the same time as his. When she came in on her first day he was already behind the counter, waiting.

"Cherry Bomb!" he exclaimed when he saw her. "You came back!"

She tried to ignore the way her heart fluttered when he spoke, but she soon realized there was no escaping the way he made her feel.

Audrey quickly understood why Zachary was put in charge of her training. She suspected he handled everyone's training. The way he spoke was calm, level, but firm enough to cut through the noise of the coffee shop. He was patient, making light of mistakes or joking about them, and always seemed to sense when he should step in and help rather than stand back and offer guidance. Audrey couldn't count the number of times he appeared suddenly behind her just as a customer ordered something unconventional, or asked a difficult question.

Audrey noticed with amusement that Zachary never seemed to stop moving. He was always doing something, his hands never still. Somehow, his energy still felt calm, steady. Over the week she'd been employed she found herself, against her better instincts, gravitating toward him because of it. And he, despite his busyness, gravitated toward her. She thought he was remarkably good at his job, juggling orders and cleaning messes, all the while with one eye and ear attentively on everything Audrey did.

Right now, he was extremely attentive to her hands as they cradled the metal pitcher of steaming milk. His fingers rested gently on hers, showing her how to tilt the pitcher correctly.

"Stop riiiight... there," he said. She turned off the steam as the red line on the thermometer approached 140 degrees, but it kept moving after she did, settling on the desired temperature of 160 degrees Fahrenheit. "Perfect. Good job."

Audrey smiled and nodded. He stepped away. It felt cold where his breath had been moments before.

She shook her head slightly. *Stop that*, she told herself. *Focus.*

She was risking enough simply being there. When she told Paul she applied for a job, he gave her the silent treatment for a solid five minutes before finally blurting out something about her ambition getting the better of her.

"What do you mean?" she'd said. "It's just a job, Paul. I want to buy Christmas presents with my own money, is that so bad?"

"I just worry it will distract you from what's important," Paul said. His body language was cold as he sat in the driver's seat of his parked car, his arms folded tightly against him like an angry toddler.

"Audrey, you already have a new school, new friends, a new city. You've barely had time to adjust, let alone attend to spiritual matters. I mean," Paul lowered his voice then, his eyes narrowed at Audrey, "When was the last time you witnessed to someone, Audrey?"

Audrey shrunk away from him, angry—ashamed.

A person who shared their particular brand of beliefs was expected to be a "light for Christ" *all the time*, no matter the consequences. Young people in her church relished the idea of *dying* in order to share their beliefs with others, despite having no real experience with such persecution. Failing to "witness," to metaphorically shout one's faith from the rooftops, amounted to nothing more than evidence of one's own fear—one's own failure as a Christian.

Audrey's lip curled up in disgust at Paul and his thinly veiled attempt to bully her. If she wouldn't show regret for getting a job, he would make her feel regret for something else, anything else.

Seeing he elicited the desired reaction, he quickly turned soft, his arms unfolding and his body turning toward her. Sweetly, he cupped her chin in his hand.

"I don't mean to make you feel bad," he said, in a way that clearly indicated he meant to make her feel bad. "I'm just looking out for your soul. It's my job, right?"

"Right," Audrey forced herself to say. As her future husband and therefore her spiritual leader, it *was* his job. Audrey swallowed her bitterness.

Paul kissed her, the smell of his cologne nearly overwhelming her. She kissed him back, reluctantly, and gathered her purse to leave.

"Who knows," she said as she put her bag over her shoulder. "Maybe this job will give me more opportunities to share my faith."

Paul straightened, nodding. He couldn't exactly argue with that now.

So that's how they'd left it. Audrey went ahead and took the job when it was offered to her, and showed up on her first day after breaking the news to Paul via text message. She included some nonsense about feeling strongly led in the Spirit to take the job, to avoid an argument. It worked, but she felt the tension despite the miles between them.

Audrey knew there was conflict brewing inside her, not only from Paul but from her studies. Even though she'd become good at pushing it down, there was no way to think about *any* of it without thinking about *all* of it. Paul, the job, her rapidly expanding worldview...

If she thought too much about any one of them, soon the rest emerged all tangled up as if in a web.

Then there was the vibration she felt in the air every time she was near Zachary. That came with a mountain of other anxieties she dared not consider.

She'd heard people say in Church that even *thinking* about other men besides your husband was cheating in the heart. Did this count? She wasn't married yet. And it wasn't as though she'd thought of *being* with Zachary. She just wanted to be *near* him. Even so, was God going to be mad at her? Was she failing some kind of test?

She hoped not. In any case, she didn't think too much about it. She couldn't. Instead, she found herself floating, in a not-unpleasant state of limbo, as she forged two separate worlds in which to exist.

A side of herself she hadn't yet encountered began to emerge in this new enclave, surrounded by new friends, strangers, and the smell of coffee beans. It was remarkably similar to the version of herself she'd been quietly mourning since she left Redding—comfortable in her own skin, confident, capable.

There was something else that felt new—something that had laid dormant, but was now roaming beneath the surface of her skin like electricity.

Passion. Curiosity. Perhaps a spark of rebellion.

Despite her thorough denial, that spark grew brighter when she was near Zachary.

She chalked it up to nerves, or excitement about the new job. This comforted her, but also justified the easy way in which she leaned into Zachary's warm and playful personality. She found herself enraptured by the sound of his laugh, which had a musical quality to it, always rising and falling in a predictable rhythm. She relished his ability to start and hold an engaging conversation.

What began as, she assumed, his polite efforts at including her in workplace conversations, quickly became private exchanges or inside jokes.

A small part of Audrey felt a sense of alarm at this rapidly emerging friendship. It was, however, quickly squashed by the part of her that felt totally at ease for the first time in her life, as if she was working alongside an old friend.

"Alright, it's official," Zachary said, breaking into her thoughts. "You've mastered the art of foam. Now on to espresso!" He posed dramatically with his finger pointed toward the sky like some sort of Superhero Barista, and Audrey laughed at his goofiness.

Oh boy, she thought. *I'm in trouble.*

4

Zachary was teaching Audrey how to clean out the espresso machine when the door chimed. Audrey looked up to see Paul. Her stomach did an awkward somersault when she saw him, several conflicting and surprising feelings emerging at once, including more than a little preemptive embarrassment. He smiled widely at Audrey when he saw her and approached the empty counter.

"Hey, beautiful!" he said loudly.

"Paul," she said, trying to sound excited but also not wanting to bring too much attention to herself. "I didn't expect you."

Paul's eyes darted toward Zachary as he leaned forward, putting his elbows on the counter.

"I thought I'd surprise you. You've worked here for what, two weeks? Three? And I still haven't seen the inside of the building." He turned his head to look directly at Zachary. "How's my girlfriend doing? She broken anything yet?"

He kept his charming smile plastered on his face as he said it, his voice emphasizing the word "girlfriend." Audrey wanted to sink into the floor.

"She's doing wonderfully," Zachary said curtly, meeting Paul's eyes. "And the only one who's broken anything today is Kelly."

He turned to smile playfully at Kelly as he said it, moving to help her stock cups and lids at the other end of the counter and leaving Audrey to speak with Paul alone.

Paul's eyes followed Zachary as he walked away, only turning his attention to Audrey again when he was at the other end of the counter.

"What time do you get off, baby girl?" he said, his voice still louder than it needed to be. "We can get dinner."

"Sure," Audrey answered. "I get off at five. There's a great little bookstore down the road if you want to kill some time."

"No thanks," Paul said. "I'll wait here."

Paul waited at Windmills for the full hour and fifteen minutes left in Audrey's shift. He ordered a hot chocolate and sat at the table nearest the counter, facing Audrey the entire time as he sat scrolling on his phone. Audrey felt his eyes on her every time she spoke to Zachary. She willed herself to speak to him as little and as formally as possible. Every chance she got, she asked Kelly for help instead, and at the end of her shift she rushed out the door with Paul without saying goodbye. Anything she could do to make Zachary seem like an afterthought, the better.

Thankfully, Zachary didn't attempt to say goodbye to her either. In fact, he largely ignored her for the rest of their shift except to quietly remind her about a step she was missing or an ingredient she forgot. He would say it under his breath conspiratorially, his hand sometimes brushing her elbow to silently get her attention.

When they left, Audrey felt an immediate shift in Paul's body language. She silently reprimanded herself.

First, she got the job when he didn't want her to, then she told him as much in a text. And on top of that, she had stupidly neglected to invite him to come and visit her at work right away. It was a misstep she should have recognized before now. It would have given her the opportunity to not only anticipate his arrival, but also to send a clear message: *I have nothing to hide.*

It was a message that was quite a bit harder to send now that his first impression was... well, judging from the rigidness of his spine and the set of his jaw, it was not a positive one.

No, he'd driven an hour in traffic to surprise her at a job she'd talked to him surprisingly little about despite having been there for nearly three and a half weeks. And what was the first thing he saw when he walked in? Zachary.

Zachary, standing just behind her, looking over her shoulder. Talking to her. Smiling. Laughing.

It was an objectively harmless image, yet in Audrey's mind, it was saturated with every possible insinuation one could make. Insinuations she instinctively knew were roiling within Paul's mind. Ones that would go through *any* man's mind. It was just how men were made, and every man she had ever been close to, including her own father, confirmed this belief to be true.

She suspected she was in for a rough night, and she was correct.

She spent the evening countering everything from subtle hints at Zachary's intentions to outright accusations of cheating. She used every tool in her arsenal, including insulting Zachary's looks and intelligence, to assuage Paul's anger. It was declaring him hell-bound and in need of salvation that seemed to be her strongest defense. That, combined with her doe-eyed request that Paul counsel her on how to maintain a pure heart in the midst of the evils of "the world"—the term Evangelical Christians used to talk about non-Christian people. Perhaps, she'd implied, with Paul's help, she could sway the sinful hearts of her coworkers.

That did it. Paul took immense pride in his ability to shove his beliefs down other people's throats, and wasted no time in giving her a thorough lesson.

If Audrey was being honest with herself however, she wouldn't change the fact that Zachary didn't share her beliefs. Not only because it meant temporary freedom from the expectations and restrictions she faced in her daily life, but also because it was the only thing that stopped her from feeling guilty about her infatuation with him.

Everyone knew what 2 Corinthians 6 said: *Do not be unequally yoked with unbelievers.* It was a line in the sand, one she knew she could never cross. So there really wasn't any harm in entertaining a few fleeting feelings.

The next morning, she had to fight to build up the nerve to go into work, afraid Zachary *had* only been interested in her romantically and would maintain his cold distance now that he knew she was taken. When he smiled warmly at her as she walked through the front door, she let out a deep sigh of relief.

A few hours into her shift Audrey was quietly wrapping baked goods in plastic wrap while Zachary cleaned out the pastry case next to her.

Business was slow, the few customers inside having settled comfortably while the rain fell outside.

"Your boyfriend seems nice," he said.

Audrey looked at him. He was smiling at her in a way that betrayed his subtle sarcasm.

"He means well," she said.

"I'm sure he does," Zachary replied.

Audrey chewed her lip for a few moments before replying. "I'm sorry if I acted weird before my shift ended. I was... nervous, I guess."

"You didn't act weird," Zachary said, turning to face her fully. "I could tell you were nervous and needed some space." Then, more softly, "I know his type. You don't have to explain."

Audrey just looked at him for a moment, not knowing how to process his words. She nodded, and they continued to work.

"Did you two meet at APU?"

"No," she said. "We met in church. We went to the same high school, too."

"I still haven't asked you where you're from."

"Redding, born and raised."

"Never been," Zachary said.

"It's nothing special. Where are you from?"

"Omaha, Nebraska."

"Omaha," she repeated. "What brought you all the way out here?"

"The weather," he said, chuckling. "And an apprenticeship." Audrey looked at him questioningly and he continued, "I'm learning to be a carpenter. One of my mom's distant cousins works as a carpenter in Covina, and agreed to take me on."

"That's pretty cool," Audrey said, nodding as she finished wrapping a blueberry muffin. "You work full time though, don't you?"

Zachary nodded. "Yep. 40 hours here, and 20 hours a week at my apprenticeship."

"Busy, busy," Audrey tutted.

Zachary chuckled. "I don't have much free time that isn't dedicated to sleeping or reading. I'm sure I'm no busier than you are though, between work and school. What are you studying, anyway?"

"Vocal performance."

"You're a singer?"

"I am," she said, smiling to herself.

Zachary nodded in solemn appreciation as he wiped circles on the glass in front of him with a coffee filter. "What is it you hope to do with your degree?"

Audrey smiled and shrugged, not looking at Zachary until she could feel his eyes on her. She glanced over at him and shrugged again, but decided to indulge in the idea.

"I've always wanted to sing on stage," she said. "Maybe as a backup singer, or maybe... well, I'd be happy singing anywhere, honestly."

"I can see it," Zachary said, nodding. "You're charismatic. You'd be great on stage."

"Thank you," Audrey said, not attempting to hide the surprise in her voice. No one had ever called her charismatic before. "What do you plan on... carpenting?" She wrinkled her nose, unsure of how to phrase it.

Zachary laughed. "I think you invented a word. I'll probably make and sell a few things to start. Eventually, I want to build installations for bars and restaurants. Counters, tables, wall art. Shit like that."

Audrey's eyes flitted to his hands, smooth with callouses. She'd stared at his hands many times, admiring their sinewy strength, but had never imagined them handling anything other than a portafilter or a steam wand.

"That sounds like a cool thing to do with your life," she said. "How long have you been woodworking?"

"A few years," he replied. "I first learned by fixing things around the house. My dad used to tinker all the time. I learned a little bit from him before he died, and taught myself the rest once I got older."

"Cool," Audrey said. Then, "I'm sorry about your dad."

"Thanks," Zachary said. In truth, his dad was a terrible piece of work. But he did miss him, sometimes. Especially as he got older, and his mother spent close to a decade trying to cure her loneliness with a long line of equally distasteful men.

He continued, "My mom is still around. Hanging out in the same old house in Omaha, making candles and incense to sell at the farmer's market." He smiled to himself. Some warm, happy memory danced behind his eyes. "What about your parents? Both around?"

"Yeah, they are," Audrey replied. She thought of her mother, who had texted her that morning to ask why Paul's mom had been the first to inform her that her daughter had a job. Her mother hadn't had a job since Audrey was born, instead keeping herself busy being the perfect Christian housewife. Smiling, docile, constantly swamped in household duties and church affairs. She was loving, attentive, and highly dependent on a careful cocktail of prescription drugs.

"My dad owns a hardware store," Audrey continued. "He's a workaholic. My mom has always stayed home with me and my younger brother, Isaac. They're alright," she said facetiously, shrugging.

Zachary chuckled, loading the pastries Audrey wrapped into the case thoughtfully.

"You're learning really fast," he said suddenly. "Soon you won't need me at all."

Something tight inside Audrey's chest loosened at the thought. Perhaps the buzzing, heavy sensation that hung between them would soon dissipate as well.

Once, she was a pirate. And she was running for her life.

Tree branches and dense foliage rushed past her, hitting her in the face and scratching her arms as she ran. She was out of breath, and the thick, humid air seemed to choke her, but she couldn't stop. Over the sound of her own harried breathing, she could hear them still, chasing her.

A part of her felt a wicked sense of gratification over the whole thing. If the shopkeeper hadn't called her sweet and slapped her ass, she wouldn't have had to cut his finger off. Of course, if she had known his entire extended family was out back playing cards, she may have chosen a less fitting punishment. In either case, he brought it on himself. A swift run through the trees of an unfamiliar island was a small price to pay for justice.

She stopped momentarily to glance at her compass, willing her breathing to slow so she could listen. Was that…? Yes, it was. *Dogs*.

"Shit," she muttered, and continued running.

Soon she came into a clearing and stopped short.

There before her stood a man, his mouth hanging open and a half-eaten chicken leg dangling from one hand. She couldn't venture to guess why she stopped so suddenly at the sight of him. He looked similar to many of the men she'd met at this particular stop in her travels, and by his appearance he was having a perfectly normal day before she emerged from the tree line, bleeding and out of breath. But something made her stop, and for a few moments the two of them simply stared at each other.

He, in fact, *was* having a rather normal day before she materialized before him. He had just been thinking about the particular blend of spices he'd need to recreate the flavor of that very chicken leg, when the most arrestingly beautiful woman he'd ever seen barreled out of the forest and stopped short in front of him.

She wore tan linen pants, and a weathered red vest that used to be a shirt. Its sleeves had been torn off, and scraps of them were tied around bits of her brown hair where the occasional bead or feather hung. Her hair was wild and tangled, bits of leaves and sticks accenting the more intentional decorations. Her eyes were a bright gold color that popped against her dark brown skin, and they were equally wild and wide with excitement. At her hip hung a long ivory blade, the image of a sun carved into it.

A slight smile played at the corners of her mouth as she took him in. He simply gaped at her.

Then, another figure emerged from the trees far to her right.

"It's *them*!" the man yelled.

Them? he thought. Before he could open his mouth to announce he was not, regrettably, a party to the beautiful woman before him, the man across the clearing was pointing him out to several other very large men who had just appeared. He dropped the chicken leg just as the woman grabbed his hand and pulled, hard. Panicking, he ran.

He trailed her through the jungle, running harder than he had in quite some time in an effort to keep up with the strange woman in front of him.

"Who are those guys?" he managed to yell to her as he ran.

"Assholes," she yelled back in between breaths.

Winded, he couldn't bring himself to say another thing. They ran in silence for several more minutes before she stopped, mercifully, and put up her hand for silence.

He did his best to remain quiet, save for his breathing. Suddenly, she was pulling him to the ground, her hand over his mouth. The two of them lay behind a giant fallen log, nestled in a deep depression in the earth just beside it. She took her hand from his mouth and quietly pointed in the direction beyond the log—toward the single member of the hunting party currently wandering by, listening for anything out of the ordinary.

He thanked his lucky stars it wasn't one of the men with a dog.

He turned his attention to the woman laying beside him. Her eyes were elsewhere as she focused on listening. He had to stifle an actual giggle as he lay there, watching her, the sheer tension of the situation overpowering his senses. This was the most exciting thing that had *ever* happened to him.

The woman, after remaining immobile for what seemed like a long time, looked at him.

"I think he's gone," she whispered. "But we should stay down for a little longer, just in case."

"Okay," he whispered back. There must have been a lingering smile on his face because she raised her eyebrows at him before saying,

"Are you okay?"

"Me? Yeah, yeah, I'm fine," he blurted quietly. "This is just exciting."

She stifled an incredulous laugh. "Are you crazy?" she whispered. "I almost got you killed just now."

"It's totally fine," he said, awkwardly attempting to wave away her comment as he lay prostrate on the ground. As if she had spilled curry on his shirt.

She had to cover her mouth to avoid laughing out loud.

"Who *are* you?" he whispered.

She smiled widely. "I'm nobody."

He smiled back. She did not look like nobody.

After a moment, she said, "Okay. You stay here for a few more minutes, just in case. I'm going to make a break for the beach just through those trees. You think you'll be okay getting home?"

"Wait, you're leaving me?" he said, suddenly feeling panicked. He didn't want her to go.

"Sorry, chicken leg," she said. "My ride out of here is just through those trees. So unless you're trying to run away—permanently—you aren't coming with me."

"But you can't..." He trailed off—he didn't know what to say, exactly.

She waited, her eyebrows raised, thinking he was going to ask for an escort home.

Instead, he said, "I don't know if this sounds dramatic. But I have a feeling this may be the last truly surprising thing that ever happens to me. Which means... it's all kind of downhill from here."

She was silent for a few moments, thoughtful.

"Well," she whispered finally, "if that's true then I hope you never forget it."

Then she leaned forward, put her hands on either side of his face, and kissed him.

Time slowed down. Nothing, not a single thing in his life, had ever felt like *this*.

When their lips parted, she stayed still for several moments, looking at him. It was just long enough for him to see a flicker of something in her eyes—something that echoed the burning he felt in his own heart.

And just like that, she was gone, rushing through the wall of trees that separated them from the ocean. He lay there, stunned and thinking, for several minutes.

As she broke through the tree-line, she found the yawl just where she left it, along with her other passengers. The two of them sat up at the sight of her.

"Running from someone again, are we?" said Yarrow as she approached.

"I may have over-worn my welcome," she answered, bending to push the small boat out onto the water. She hopped in as it began drifting from shore.

"Time to go then," Yarrow said. Her first mate handed her the bottle of brown liquid they'd been drinking so they could operate the oars. She took a long drink, savoring the burning in her throat and knowing it could just as well have been a knife.

From behind her she heard their other companion, Theo, echo, "Time to go!" as he also turned his attention from drinking to rowing.

Minutes later, they approached the ship. She climbed aboard ahead of her companions and yelled at her crew to prepare the ship for departure before heading to her quarters to deposit a few precious items she acquired on the island.

When she emerged, she approached the railing and looked out toward the hunk of land. A smile played at her lips. She had liked that man with the chicken leg.

"It's too bad," she muttered under her breath.

And then she saw it.

It was him. Swimming. Toward her.

"Oh my god," she said quietly. Then, "Oh my *god*!" She leaned forward as if it would give her a better view.

"WHAT ARE YOU DOING?" she yelled at him.

He yelled something back at her, but she couldn't hear it over his splashing. She ran, returning a moment later with a block of cork attached to a rope. She chucked it as far as she could toward him, releasing her pent-up breath when he reached it and clung on. She pulled, hauling him painstakingly toward the ship.

He finally reached the vessel and grabbed the rope that hung on its side for dear life before climbing up and slumping to the ground, a wet mess. The woman from the jungle knelt down in front of him.

"You *are* crazy," she said, not without a hint of admiration in her voice.

"I'm sorry. I tried to go home, but…" He panted a few times, shaking his head. "I just had this awful feeling about walking away from you. Like I was walking toward nothing… and away from everything."

Despite what she believed were her better instincts, this made her smile.

"You can call me Ace," she said. By this time, a few of her comrades had gathered behind her to learn who the sopping mess on board was. Yarrow and Theo were among them, their fingers casually intertwined.

"Ace," he said, his eyes momentarily darting around, taking in the small crowd that had gathered. "I'm with you. Where are we going?"

Her eyes glinted at him. "Everywhere," she said.

And they did.

5

Audrey was midway through her sophomore year. The chill in the air made her breath fog up as she walked from her car to Windmills for her first shift following Christmas break.

She'd spent two weeks at home in Redding, shuffling between family obligations, church functions, and Paul. She felt more rested after the one night she spent in her dorm than in the entire two weeks she spent at home. Classes didn't start for another week, and work... well, work wasn't one of the stressful parts of her life.

As soon as she entered, she was greeted by a familiar voice from behind the counter.

"Cherry Bomb!"

She smiled, peeling off her scarf.

"Zachary!" she said, then swept herself into a low, theatric bow. "I have returned," she said dramatically.

Zachary laughed, and Audrey noticed he had been growing out his facial hair over the break. It was not yet a beard, but was more than stubble.

When she got to the back of the counter and clocked in, Zachary wrapped her in a warm hug. She melted into it, grateful to be back home. With him.

"It's a damn good thing you're back, too," he said quietly into her ear. "If I have to work another shift alone with Tori, I'm going to stick my hand in the coffee grinder."

Audrey laughed, looking subtly at Tori, Sam's replacement after she left for another job. She was currently wiping down the tables in the cafe. Her favorite activity. Every time there was a long line at the counter, Tori could be counted on to be wiping tables. Or, her second favorite activity, stocking cups.

"Oh, goodness," Audrey said teasingly. "How ever did you survive?"

"Only the thought of my best work friend returning so soon," he said.

It was true, Audrey and Zachary had become extremely close in just over a year. When Audrey came into her shift and saw his name on the schedule later in the day, it never failed to make her smile—really, truly smile.

Zachary rarely failed to do a celebratory fist pump when he walked into work and saw her there. They were two peas in a pod.

Usually, they had a conversation ready to pick back up from the day or week before. They'd keep one going all shift, pausing to help customers or get through a rush, then immediately resuming where they'd left off. When one of them came in for a shift and the other was there, they'd only wait until they were clocked in before one of them said, "So, where were we?"

They cycled through a number of topics—music, movies, books, conspiracy theories, aliens, and on and on. They even talked amiably about religion, despite their differing views. Zachary was agnostic, and had a general disdain for any sort of organized religion, but he appreciated the more philosophical aspects of many traditions. Audrey… well, Audrey's views on religion were becoming harder and harder to define. Where there were once concrete, immovable dogmas, there were now general principles, and Audrey had a hard time rationalizing even those sometimes.

She enjoyed the release of talking to Zachary about it. There were few other people she could talk candidly to about religion, aside from the more academic discussions about religion inside the classroom.

"I mean, I've always been told the Bible is infallible," she'd say. "But if that's true, then *which version* is infallible? Which one of the thousands of copies and translations and combinations of what has at one point or another been called 'scripture' is the *perfect* version?"

"Good point," he'd reply. "And if it is infallible, are we to believe our interpretations of it are also infallible?"

"EXACTLY!"

Last Christmas break, she tried talking to her high school youth pastor and his wife about the possibility that hell wasn't real—that it didn't have any biblical support to defend it as an actual place—and they looked at her like she'd just announced a promising new career in sex work. If her parents had any inkling they were paying for a private Christian education just so she could question everything she knew, they'd pull the plug in a heartbeat.

Zachary, on the other hand, listened thoughtfully and patiently as she sifted through the muddled ideas in her head. He had no expectations of her when it came to religion—or anything else for that matter. She loved it.

Today, there was no conversation to pick up since they hadn't seen one another in weeks. So they talked about their holidays instead. Audrey had cataloged at least a dozen specific things she wanted to tell him about while she was gone. She dared not text him from home. She spent far too much time with Paul over the break, whose eyes still darted to her phone like a hawk every time it made a noise. Zachary, as if following some unspoken rule, never texted her when he knew it was likely she'd be with Paul.

On some level, she knew she should feel bad about changing his name in her phone to Samantha. She *should* feel guilty for the warm, comforting sensation she got in her stomach when she was around him—a feeling she'd never gotten with Paul. She ought to feel at least a little ashamed for thinking about him when she and Paul did things that weren't *technically* sex, but she didn't.

"Wait, wait, wait," Zachary said later between gasps of laughter. "She actually said *'subliminal gay messages'*?"

Audrey laughed. "I think her exact words were, 'God, please protect our children from the *demonic* subliminal gay messages in their cartoons.'"

Zachary shook his head, still chuckling.

"Your family cracks me up. Of all things I thought Christians were angry about, Spongebob was not on the list."

Audrey smiled to herself as she wiped the counter in front of her. "You know," she admitted, "there was a time when I would have been angry right along with them. About all that stuff. It seems so stupid now."

Zachary put his hand on her shoulder, causing her to look in his direction. She felt warmed by his touch.

"Anyone would believe those things if it was all they ever knew," he said gently. "But that's not who you are."

Audrey searched his eyes and found only sincerity, and she smiled. They stood there for several long moments, looking at one another. Audrey felt a familiar tug in her heart, begging her to lean forward and touch him. Then Zachary lifted his eyes to the front door and swiftly removed his hand, making for the other side of the counter without a word.

A moment later the door chimed, and Paul walked in.

Audrey forced herself to act casually surprised as she turned and took in her boyfriend. She realized, with a bit of shock, that her first reaction to seeing him was irritation. As if he'd snatched something away from her, something she was savoring. She sort of wanted to slap him.

On another level, she felt happy to see him. Flattered even, that he took the time to surprise her so soon after they'd left home. Yet despite that, she couldn't shake the annoyance she felt at his unexpected arrival.

"Surprise," he said flirtatiously.

"Hey, you," she said, smiling as widely as possible to conceal her irritation.

Paul strolled to the counter and leaned forward to plant a kiss on Audrey's lips. She told herself she only imagined Zachary's hands clenching into fists when he did.

"I was in the area," Paul said even though no one asked why he was there. "Pastor Eric is giving a lecture at some school in Claremont. He invited me to come, but I left thirty minutes early so I could stop and see you."

Audrey's brow furrowed. Paul told her about the lecture, but never said where it was.

"Oh," she said. "I didn't realize the lecture was out this way. Why didn't you tell me?"

Paul rolled his eyes dramatically, looking in Zachary's direction for a moment as if to say, *Women, right?* Zachary did not return the expression.

"I *did* tell you. Last week. Jeez, you have the worst memory, Audrey."

Paul's tone was severe, and his particular brand of judgment rarely failed to cow Audrey into silence. But there in the safe space she'd built over the past year, she felt uncharacteristically bold.

"Actually, I have an excellent memory. Maybe you just forgot to mention it." She tried hard to ignore the almost imperceptible warning on Paul's face as she untied her apron. "But as long as you're here, I'll take my ten-minute break."

She looked at Zachary to confirm that he was okay to cover for her, but she found him staring at Paul instead. There was a look on his face she'd never seen. All playfulness and mischief were gone from his eyes, replaced with something like thinly veiled rage. Audrey scrambled to distract everyone involved from the tension by opening the pastry case and grabbing a large apple strudel muffin.

"Do you want something, Paul?" she asked, holding up the muffin.

Paul shook his head, eyeing the muffin like it was poison. "Do *you* really need that, Audrey?" he said. His eyes looked pointedly toward her midriff. "It was just the holidays, after all. Maybe you should take it easy."

Before Audrey had time to register the insult, she heard a dull *thud* behind her. Zachary had managed to remove his apron and throw it to the ground in one swift motion. He then *leapt* over the counter, balancing himself with one hand as he did so and landing hard on the cafe floor.

"Zachary!" Audrey blurted out, shock overcoming her.

He turned to her, and for a split second she saw the rage there in his eyes, no longer veiled, but burning openly for her to see. Something about it was pleasing, but her body was frozen with the danger it invoked. He was close to ruining everything. Paul would never let her set foot in the building again if Zachary confronted him like this.

Zachary saw the desperation on her face, and just like that, the fire in his eyes was extinguished. His posture relaxed, and he donned a casual, reassuring smile. "I just remembered," he said, his voice cracking slightly. "I forgot something in my truck. Can you wait a few minutes to take that break, Audrey?"

Audrey's body relaxed somewhat as she nodded, and Zachary turned to walk through the front door, a few customers looking curiously on as he left.

Audrey was scared to look at Paul, but when she met his eyes, they weren't filled with the retribution she feared. He wore a puzzled look on his face instead, having missed every subtle cue that passed so rapidly from Audrey to Zachary in those moments.

"Zachary is a really weird guy," he said. "I don't know why you're so nice to him."

Audrey released the last bit of tension in her shoulders. "Yeah," she said. "Super weird."

6

"Okay, okay," Audrey said, chuckling. "Would you rather never hear music again, or eat nothing but pumpkin pie for the rest of your life?"

Zachary gave her a look of unbridled disgust that made her laugh.

"You have a twisted mind," Zachary said. "I'd have to take the pie though." He gagged dramatically on the last two words.

"I'd do the same," Audrey said, ringing out a clean rag.

It was just after closing time. Audrey and Zachary were finishing up the last-minute closing duties before they left. Zachary was wrapping barely thawed muffins from the freezer in saran wrap to be loaded into the pastry case for the morning shift, while Audrey cleaned and restocked the refrigerators.

"I have one," Zachary said. "Would you rather eat the same thing for the rest of your life, or stay in the same city for the rest of your life?"

"Pfft, easy," Audrey said, ripping open a new box of whipped cream canisters. "Stay in the same city."

"Really?" Zachary said, incredulous. "I mean, I know you're kind of a foodie. But wouldn't you go crazy, never getting to go anywhere?"

Audrey shrugged. "I mean… as long as I'm near people I love and I'm doing something I like, I wouldn't mind it. I've never really wanted to travel, anyway."

Zachary stopped what he was doing and glowered at her. "Liar."

"What!" Audrey did her best to look offended, but she wanted to laugh at Zachary's severely unamused expression. "How would you know, anyway?"

Zachary simply gestured to her. "Your entire demeanor changed when you said that. You looked down, you hunched your back, your voice dropped. You looked like you were talking about a cancer diagnosis."

Audrey snorted.

"You're a liar, that's all I'm saying," Zachary said.

"Okay," Audrey said, her guard coming down at his matter-of-factness. "You got me."

In fact, Audrey had always dreamed of traveling. It was Paul who didn't want to travel, but somehow over the years she'd simply absorbed some of his opinions. They would bleed out of her at random moments, taking her over like one of those parasitic spores that exert mind control over small insects, and she'd blurt them out as if they were her own.

"I've always wanted to go to Italy," she confessed.

"Mm," Zachary said in agreement. "Same."

"*But*," she went on. "If I couldn't eat pasta while I was there it wouldn't really be the full experience, would it?"

"Don't forget tiramisu," Zachary reminded her.

"Ah!" Audrey said, clutching her chest dramatically. "Tiramisu!"

Zachary laughed. "Okay, you can eat whatever you want. Where else would you travel?"

"Hmm… Greece. Turkey. Japan. New York City. Victoria Falls. Madagascar. Peru." She shook her head, the list stretching on and on in her mind. "There's a lot of places I'd be happy to see."

"Okay, Miss 'I've Never Wanted to Travel.'" Zachary leaned against the counter, his arms crossed. "Someday, I'm going to buy a boat and take it to lots of places. Live on it for a while, even."

"Really?" Audrey said, excited at the thought. She imagined her friend, the wind tangling his hair, at the helm of a boat. Headed to some far-off, exotic destination. It suited him. But her heart constricted at the thought of him sailing away.

"That's the plan," Zachary said, a sort of childlike giddiness in his smile. "I've already figured out about how much I'll need to save to make it work. It's going to take a long while, but I'll get there eventually."

Audrey nodded assuredly at him. "Of course you will," she said. "What's at the top of your list to visit when you do?"

Zachary considered this for a few moments. "Well, I don't know where I'll start exactly," he said. "But the place I'm most excited to see is Cambodia."

"Cambodia," Audrey said thoughtfully. "I don't think I know much about Cambodia."

"Oh, it's beautiful," Zachary said as if he'd just come from there. "Home of Angkor Wat, the largest religious structure in the world, among other wonders." His hand made broad strokes in the air as he spoke. "My brother went there once. He said the only thing he loved more than the scenery was the people.

"Once, he got lost on a rented bike trying to find some old ruins outside of Battambang. A local came out of their house, saw he was lost, and guided him the rest of the way on their motorbike. That same night, he lost one of his shoes when it started pouring rain and the street outside his hostel flooded. He said it was one of the most memorable days of his life."

Audrey smiled, enjoying Zachary's faraway look. "I didn't know you had a brother."

"I do," Zachary said. "I did," he corrected himself. "He died when I was a kid."

"I'm sorry," Audrey said. Then, gently, "How old was he?"

"Patrick was twenty-three. I was eleven." Zachary smirked at her. "I know, kind of a big age gap. I was an accident."

Audrey smirked back, playfully nudging him. They were quiet for a moment, then she said, "That must have been hard for you."

"It was extremely hard," Zachary said quietly, his eyes looking down at his hands. "I loved him."

When Zachary looked up, Audrey could see the pain in his eyes, as if he was experiencing the loss all over again. It was like he was cracking open the doors of his soul, so she could see just how it felt.

She was taken back by his open, honest expression of pain, and his willingness to share it with her. Never in her life had she seen a man display emotional vulnerability, except on television, and even then she laughed at the cheesiness of it because she thought it wasn't re-alistic.

In fact, she had been *explicitly taught* that such emotional vulner-ability in a man wasn't possible unless there was something deeply wrong with him. It simply wasn't in God's design. So she scorned it when it appeared in movies, and never allowed herself to expect it in relationships.

But now, on Zachary, she thought it was the most beautiful thing in the world.

Zachary spoke again, now carefully placing the muffins he'd wrapped into the pastry case. "Patrick—my brother—he was always sort of a buffer between my dad and the rest of the family. Things were never *good*, but they definitely got worse after he died. My dad turned from condescending to downright mean. So on top of losing my brother, I lost what semblance of a father I had. It was the hardest part of my life. When my dad finally died... well, it was a relief, to be honest."

Audrey was quiet, shocked into silence.

All she knew about Zachary's dad was that he'd died, and Zachary had inherited some of his talent for working with his hands. She just assumed their relationship was healthy. She'd never considered he had lost not a beloved father when he died, but an abuser.

"I suppose that makes me seem cold," he said after a pause.

"Not at all," Audrey said. The firmness in her voice made him look up again. She met his gaze with what she hoped was a look of radical acceptance. Zachary's answering smile told her he understood, and the two of them went on with their duties in comfortable silence.

"Did you know," Zachary said eventually. "That there's a huge field in Laos that's covered in giant stone jars, and no one knows where they came from or what they were for?"

Audrey raised her eyebrows and cocked her head in a way that said, *I'm listening.* Zachary loved that look. He had actually started learning new things on his days off, simply so he could see that look on her face from time to time.

"Some of the jars are taller than you," he went on. "Some people think they were used for ancient funerals, but they've never recovered any bones."

"Well, they were obviously the birthing pods the aliens arrived in," Audrey said matter-of-factly.

Zachary snorted. The two of them often joked at the expense of a particularly bad television show, a sort of documentary series whose entire premise was that every feat or accomplishment of "ancient" humans (especially those with dark skin) could only be explained by the intervention of alien beings.

"Clearly," Zachary said, slapping the palm of his hand to his forehead. "I can't believe I never thought of that before."

Audrey shrugged in a mock self-satisfied way. "That's why I'm around, Peters. That's why I'm around."

They both laughed, and that comfortable silence fell between them again.

Often, when she was with Zachary, Audrey would forget about the efforts she normally took to adjust her behavior. The many rules of propriety she normally obeyed—around strangers, peers, her family, even Paul—would go strangely quiet, as if she was all alone. But it was better than that. Zachary's presence calmed even the voice of God, who so often whispered to her about sin, and shame, and hell.

To be near Zachary was to be in a place of radical acceptance.

It was several minutes before Audrey said, "I hope you get your boat someday."

Zachary smiled at her as he closed the pastry case, reaching out to take the rag she was now tossing back and forth between her hands.

"I'll save you a seat," he said as he held out his hand.

Audrey smiled, blushing, and handed him the rag. He turned and walked to the back room. Audrey watched him go. When he disappeared behind the door she swept her eyes across the shop, looking for anything they missed.

It was dark outside, the street empty and quiet. Warm light from the lamp stands pooled on the sidewalk, spilling in through the window and onto the tables at the edge of the shop.

Audrey sighed, enjoying the stillness. She loved the closing shift and often wished she could stay after the doors were locked in order to soak in the silence of her favorite place, alone.

"You coming?" Zachary said behind her.

Well, almost alone. There was one other person she might allow into her silent fantasy.

"Yeah," she said, flipping off the light and following him to the back. She and Zachary left together, Zachary locking the doors behind them and walking her to her car like he did every time they closed.

"I'll see you tomorrow, Cherry Bomb," he said as they approached her green Chevy Spark. Zachary's own dark blue Tacoma was parked on the other side of the street.

"See you tomorrow," she said. Then, stopping before she unlocked her car, Audrey turned back toward her friend.

"Zachary," she said.

He turned, waiting expectantly.

"Thanks for telling me more about your family. I always want to know more about you."

Zachary's face broke into a slow, wide smile. He just stood there, in the middle of the empty street, looking at her. The light from the nearest streetlamp cast long shadows on his face, making him look older.

Audrey felt a sudden rush of emotion toward Zachary that she couldn't explain. Her heart swelled, and she felt as if she would fall apart completely if she didn't walk headlong into his arms and sob. Her soul, in a brief moment of clarity, recognized him.

Just as fast as it happened, the feeling was swept away by Audrey's self-consciousness at the too-tender moment. She recovered by shrugging, and saying, "You know, so I can more easily blackmail you someday."

Zachary chuckled, his tender smile turning to an amused one.

"What makes you think that wasn't a fake story?" he said, tapping his head with his pointer finger. "I'm way ahead of you, Anderson."

Audrey laughed and got into her car. The lines of Zachary's face beneath the streetlamp stayed etched in her mind all the way home.

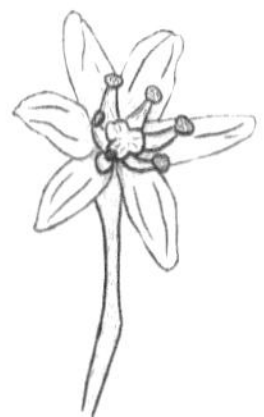

Once, she was a girl—and she was in love.

It began on a perfect spring day. She wandered through the mossy green forest near her home, her hands gently brushing every tree she walked past. She gradually became aware of a faraway sound. It began so softly she didn't notice at first, thinking it was just another layer in the cacophony of air, and water, and animals.

Soon however, she detected a clear melody in the sound, and as it drifted toward her, she drifted progressively toward it. As the sound grew louder, her footsteps grew quicker, chasing this unexpected new prey like a cat with a mouse. She ran, jumping over roots and branches until she was nearly right on top of it. She burst into a clearing suddenly, the music so loud she could almost feel the vibrations of the notes in her chest, and nearly shouted, certain she would find the source of the melody here, but the music suddenly stopped.

Disappointed, she stood there for several long moments, her hands slowly dropping to her sides. That was until she heard the tentative *pluck* of a string from behind her. She whirled around to find a boy standing there, his fingers stilled over his instrument as if her sudden arrival had frozen him in place. The gentle sway of his blonde curls and the slow smile forming on his face were the only signs of movement.

He looked at her with a mix of curiosity and surprise.

Aha! she thought, having finally found her quarry. She then sat down on the ground and gestured for him to continue as if it was the most natural thing in the world to do.

This was where it began.

For months after, she would go back to that clearing in the woods, always at the same time. And he would sing to her.

Sometimes he sang old songs, the ones all children learned from their mothers. Sometimes he sang new ones she'd never heard before. Eventually, he began to write songs just for her.

They engaged in more than the occasional concert there in the woods. They laughed with each other there, and they cried. It was there in the woods that they fell in love.

In the woods, she was not the youngest daughter of a wealthy merchant. And he was not the middle son of a poor family with too many children. They were just a boy and a girl—a boy and a girl who burned for one another with a passion neither of them thought possible before.

She soon found herself more at home in the woods than in her father's stately home, its empty rooms cold and silent. But every day that passed drew her closer to that "certain age" at which girls are meant to become women. She felt her freedom slipping away. Gone were the days when she could simply skip away to the woods and play, for there were certain obligations a lady had to meet as she got older.

So, their visits grew fewer and farther between.

Until one night as she lay fitfully in bed, and heard a rap upon her window.

When she looked out she found him standing there, his face stretched into a wide grin. Thrilled, she gestured for him to climb to her second-floor aperture, a feat he performed with surprising alacrity considering the age of the worn stones that made up her father's house, and the pale blue flower he held carefully between the fingers of one hand.

When he'd climbed high enough, she reached out her hand, pulling him inside and gesturing for him to be quiet. If her father caught them, he would surely toss her love straight out the window from whence he came.

He did not seem scared as he pulled her into a kiss. She stifled a laugh against his mouth as his hands trailed the curves of her body beneath her nightgown. He had never seen her like this, without the stifling layers of skirts and corsets she wore during the day, and his fingers took their liberties as eagerly as his lips. She was happily overcome by him, and allowed her hands to run through his tousled hair, to climb their way up his back.

The flower drifted to the floor along with their clothes, becoming quickly lost as the fervor of their lovemaking brought them to the bed.

That night they held each other tightly, the feeling of their skin against one another's an intoxicating drug that kept them awake until the sun began to rise.

Startled by the time, he quickly gathered his clothes from the pile on the floor and dressed, retrieving the blue flower as he did. He approached her and tucked it gently behind her ear, then went to find his shoes. He sat in a squat, ornate brass chair in the corner of her room as he pulled them on, his eyes scanning her bedroom in the pale light appreciatively. He was acutely aware that her bedspread likely cost more than anything he owned.

He was also aware of the consequences of a boy like him bedding a maiden like her. As much as he tried, he simply couldn't stay away. Nor did she want him to.

So he didn't. Each night he snuck away from home—not that anyone would have missed him—and scaled the wall beneath her window. Each time, he brought with him a pale blue flower to tuck behind her ear or braid into her hair.

Every day she could manage, she met him in the woods. She brought with her bread and cheese to stave their hunger, and he brought with him his instrument, and their days passed in effortless bliss.

Until one.

She walked into the clearing that day at a somber pace that stood in contrast to her normally exuberant gait. He could tell immediately she had been crying. He shot from the rock he sat upon, meaning to offer her comfort.

Before he could reach for her, she put out her hands.

"I'm engaged."

She said it briskly, as if she could hardly wait to unburden herself of the words.

She may as well have hit him with a carriage, despite his knowing this would happen someday. It felt wrong, the words being said there. As if they defiled the magical place in which they stood—their clearing in the woods, where they fell in love.

"It was not my choice," she said.

He knew that it wasn't.

"When?" he asked.

"In a fortnight."

He knew instantly he would never see her in those woods again. The rest of her days until her wedding would be consumed by activity, and then a stranger would come and take her far away from him.

He reached out to touch her, and she crumpled into his arms and cried.

This was where it ended.

But not really.

Years later, when she had children of her own, she often sat at the window of her bedroom and looked out upon the gently rolling hills. In the distance, a stretch of woods separated her husband's home from her father's by about a day's journey.

When her children asked her what she looked for from her window, a secret seemed to play at the corners of her lips. She would say she was listening to the birds or watching the clouds move idly by.

Occasionally, she held a pale blue flower in her hands, her fingers absently tracing its stem as she gazed at something no one else could see.

7

"Guess what tomorrow is?" Zachary whispered in her ear as he passed.

Audrey smiled to herself. She knew perfectly well what tomorrow was.

"Hmmm," she said, making a show of scratching the top of her head. "Isn't it... Tori's birthday, or something?"

Zachary's face fell so far Audrey had to laugh.

"I know what day it is tomorrow, birthday boy."

Zachary's mouth turned up into a self-satisfied smile. "And do you know what that means?"

"I suppose the world is going to stop turning?"

"How'd you know?"

Audrey chuckled and elbowed him in the ribs.

"It means," he said. "I can finally drink... well, legally. In public." He winked at her.

Audrey carefully composed her face. Then she swallowed the rogue butterflies she felt at that wink.

"Welcome to the club, *noob*," she said, rolling her eyes dramatically.

Zachary laughed. "Thanks, old-timer."

It was Audrey's junior year, and she turned 21 only eight days ago. She took the day off work, celebrating with her roommates over a nice breakfast, then dinner and a movie with Paul. When she got home that night, her roommates and a few other close friends were waiting with a cooler full of Smirnoff Ice, giggling wickedly over their contraband. APU was a dry campus, but the upperclassmen dorms were the figurative Wild West—that is, if the Wild West was student housing for a bunch of Christian kids.

The next morning she'd shown up to work with a terrible headache. Zachary was waiting with a small gift bag. He was already in the back when she came in, grasping it gingerly with both sets of fingers, bouncing on his feet as he waited for her to take off her jacket.

Inside the bag were several items. Audrey drew them out one by one.

First, a box of chocolates—cherry amaretto, a nod to her nickname and her near-constant sweet tooth.

Next, a tiny pin in the shape of an egg salad sandwich, a reminder of the time she brought egg salad sandwiches for her lunch for a week straight following Easter. She could barely finish eating them from laughing so hard at Zachary's melodramatic gags and whimpers from behind the counter.

Then, she drew out an amethyst necklace on a delicate gold chain. She once complimented a customer on a similar necklace, and upon finding out what kind of stone it was, she ran to the back to write it down in her phone before she forgot it. She never bought one, though.

Audrey's heart ached at the necklace. Partly because it was so beautiful; partly because she could never wear it in front of Paul.

Next, a pocket-sized leather journal with cascading music notes engraved on the front. "For your songs," he explained as she opened it. She was taking a songwriting class, and absolutely loved it. Zachary asked her about her songs almost every week.

And finally, a small bottle of ibuprofen.

"How did you know?" she laughed, shaking the bottle gently.

He chuckled. "A feeling."

Audrey looked at the gifts Zachary chose and felt a sudden heaviness in her chest. The thoughtfulness, the time it must have taken to find every little thing… it was a gift from someone who knew her—who noticed all the little, everyday things that made her who she was.

Then she thought about Paul, who gave her a silver cross-shaped necklace and a handmade coupon promising a reservation at a fancy restaurant in two weeks time. The heaviness only grew. She tried to push it down. It hurt.

"Thank you, Zachary," she said softly. "I love *all* of this."

He smiled widely in return.

Audrey thought of those gifts now, casually looking over at Zachary as he prepared a hazelnut latte. Since that day, she'd been racking her brain to find a gift that came anywhere close to the meticulous attention he'd shown in choosing hers. Something that reflected his personality, their friendship. But when she thought about it, so many possibilities came to mind she was overwhelmed, every idea shrinking into nothingness under her own critical self-doubt.

She felt a strange pressure to capture the very essence of Zachary in his gift, as if this was the only chance she'd ever have to tell him, however indirectly, how she really felt. Though she'd settled on a gift and was finished making it, she still felt anxious about the whole thing.

"Um," Zachary's voice cut into her thoughts. He stared at the milk canister in his hands as if it was the most interesting thing in the world as he spoke. "I'm having a little get together tomorrow. I know it's hard getting out, what with school, and friends, and... Paul. But I'd...I'd like it if you came."

Audrey's knees felt wobbly. For nearly three years, her relationship with Zachary had grown and blossomed around an invisible line—a barrier they both recognized, but neither of them talked about. And now he was tentatively—shyly, even—asking her to cross it.

She had never seen Zachary act *shy* before. It almost made her blush.

But that line... it was familiar. It was safe.

Audrey didn't know how Zachary seemed to know, without asking, the rules he needed to follow to be her friend. He saw the unspoken lines that had been drawn. Not by her, but by every other person in her life that mattered to her. He knew precisely when he could give her a spontaneous bear hug, and when he should pretend she didn't exist.

He knew that for her, work was like a second life. It was a world apart from her own world—the world of Paul, and mandatory chapel twice a week, and two extremely conservative parents who were waiting patiently for her to become a pastor's wife. He also seemed to understand what the consequences would be for Audrey if those two worlds rubbed together in the wrong way.

They could lead to a fracture in the foundation of all she knew, all she held dear, the very things she had been taught to find purpose in. And young Audrey was not yet ready for such a rupture, despite her growing discomfort with evangelical dogma.

Despite this, Audrey found herself saying, "Sure. I'll be there."

Any second thoughts about backing out were shattered when Zachary turned a beaming smile toward her in response, his shoulders dropping in relief.

From an outsider's perspective, Audrey's preparation for Zachary's birthday party might seem extreme. Yet Audrey didn't so much as consider the precautions to be anything more than commonplace. They were measures her own mother had taken hundreds of times, safeguards she and her girlfriends from church often gossiped about over afternoon tea.

First, she researched the location of the party. It was a bar on Azusa Ave., mercifully close to campus—and right across from a CVS Pharmacy.

The following morning she texted Paul as soon as she woke up. *I think I may be sick.* She stayed home all day, skipping her one class that afternoon, and occasionally sent Paul updates on her health. A puke-face emoji here, a selfie curled up in bed with the blankets high around her there. When he finally called and asked if he should bring over some soup, she reminded him of his upcoming Resident Advisor retreat and said she'd feel terrible if he got sick, too.

"Plus," she crooned sweetly. "I have soup already. Just hearing your voice makes me feel better."

She waited until just before she left to text him again.

I don't think I can sleep. I'm going to drive to CVS and buy up the whole medicine aisle. I'll probably fall asleep when I get home. Love you.

She wasn't sure how often Paul checked her location via the location-sharing app he insisted they have on their two phones, but he'd been known to bring it up on occasion. She could explain a slight blip on the map between CVS and the neighboring bar easily. As long as she didn't stay too long, this would work.

She arrived fashionably late and parked across the street. Leaving her phone in her car, she entered the bar and immediately laughed at the theme. Chairs like church pews, the windows all stained glass. The drinks—written in chalk on a large board above the bar to her right—were themed as well. She skimmed them, snorting at some of the better ones. Bourbon Baptism. The Last Supper. Old Fashioned Family Values.

Just ahead, his back to her, stood Zachary. When he saw her, he set down his drink and nearly skipped across the bar.

"You came," he said, smiling widely.

"I did," she said, returning his smile. They stood there for a moment, looking at each other. Audrey almost forgot to say, "I can't stay long."

She tried to arrange her face in a way that said, "I'm sorry" as clearly as possible.

Seeming to understand, he said, "That's fine. I'm just happy to see you, for however long."

"Some place you chose, Zachary," Audrey said, gesturing around her with an air of dissatisfaction.

Zachary laughed, his head tipping backward. "I hope you don't take it personally," he said. "I thought you might find it funny."

Dropping the offended facade, she laughed as well. "I do think it's funny."

Zachary's eyes drifted toward the card-shaped box in her hand. "Is that for me?"

She exhaled sharply, louder than she meant to, making Zachary laugh.

"It is," she admitted. "It's not much, but—"

"Staaaaap," Zachary said, smushing his finger to her mouth before she could say more. "Don't say it's not much. I don't give a shit. You brought me a gift. I'm going to appreciate it."

When she didn't look convinced, he continued.

"And if you're trying to top my birthday gift to you, you can just stop right there. I happen to be an exceptional gift giver. Everyone knows it. And I don't need you competing with me. You'll just need to accept that from this moment forward, I will always win at gift-giving. And that's how I like it."

She laughed, finally relaxing, and followed him to a table in the back corner of the bar. He told his friends, including a few of their coworkers, he'd be right back as they passed.

She sat down across from him and gently pushed the box across the table. Zachary lifted the lid excruciatingly slowly, then went still as he saw what was inside. Slowly, a smile spread across his face.

Unable to contain herself in the silence, Audrey burst out, "It's supposed to be a logo. You know, for your... carpenting." Zachary snorted at the word. "I designed it after—"

"The chair," he said, finally looking up. "It's the chair at the shop." His face beamed in affectionate recognition.

The chair was a squat, hideous monstrosity of leather and iron that sat in one of Windmill's many corners. Audrey's first impression was that it looked like a director's chair that doubled as a medieval torture device. At the ends of the leather armrests sat two bulbs that looked like antique doorknobs, matched by two bulbs behind the shoulders, and four at the bottom of each of the chair's legs. The legs came up from the floor a couple of inches before curving inward to meet one another, then outward again, then straight up to connect with the seat and armrests.

Zachary was obsessed with the chair and fiercely defended its merits to anyone who dared question its innate beauty.

"It looks like something out of a horror movie," a customer once remarked.

Zachary, who was not part of the conversation in question and was in fact nearly as far from the customer as he could possibly be, yelled across the shop, "*Actually*, it's an Italian Savonarola."

"It's not even comfortable," Kelly told him once.

"You just don't know how to sit in it," Zachary quipped back.

Indeed, very few people actually sat in the chair besides Zachary. Audrey had to admit, he did seem to know how to sit in it. He was the only person she'd ever seen in it who seemed to belong there, like it had been made exactly for his purposes. One leg crossed over a knee, an arm resting on one side while the other cradled his large Americano, he sat straight and proud in his ghastly little chair in the corner.

Audrey had managed to recreate the chair on paper, manipulating the writhing undulations of the front legs to make them look like a staggered "p" and "d." "Peters Design" was written beneath the chair in chunky capital letters whose curves mirrored the chair's own.

Zachary ran his fingers gently across the letters, then lifted the bulky card from the box it was in. On the front was her makeshift logo, printed, and inside...Zachary let out a short gasp as he opened it.

Inside, a 3D model of the interior of Windmills. Audrey had put her graphic design skills to use, as well as the expertise of the campus print shop, to make the pop-up card. She meticulously designed and arranged everything from the bar and furniture scattered around the shop, to the windmill pattern of the large rug that ran from the front door to the cash register.

"It's the shop," Zachary said quietly, still looking at it.

"With a few modifications," she said.

Zachary looked at her quizzically and she reached over, gently lifting the end of the cardstock counter to allow easy access from behind the bar to the sitting area. She couldn't count how many times Zachary had complained about having to walk all the way through the back to get behind the counter. "We could *easily* remove this part right here," he would say. "A few hinges is all we'd need, and we could have one of those cool swingy counter things to let us get in or out without going around through the back."

Zachary laughed, throwing his head back as he did. "You *fixed* it!"

"I did indeed," she said smugly.

Zachary looked at the card for several long moments, smiling to himself. When he was done, he closed it carefully and gently placed it back inside its box. His eyes lingered on the front once more before he replaced the lid and looked at Audrey, his expression suddenly serious.

"Damnit, Audrey," he said softly, his mouth a thin line. "I told you not to compete with me."

Audrey snorted with laughter, and his face broke into a reluctant smile.

"You win this one, Anderson," he said. "But never again. Mark my words." His face softened. "Seriously though, thank you. This is amazing. I can't believe you did this."

Audrey shrugged. "You're welcome."

Zachary just smiled for a moment longer before saying, "I'm *going* to use this logo, you know. And since this is a gift, I'm going to assume I don't have to pay a fee. I'm not going to get a call from your lawyer, am I?"

Audrey swatted at him before letting him come around to her side of the table and fold her into a long, warm hug.

She allowed herself those few moments to ground herself, her eyes closed, taking in every sound and smell and feeling that enveloped her. The steady thrum of his heartbeat. The smell of woodsy cologne on his neck. The scratch of the stubble on his cheek against her forehead. She allowed herself to feel those moments deeply, etching them into herself, appreciating them fully.

Then she detached. *Back to limbo you go.*

He seemed to know as he pulled away from her—at least some of the lines had to stay in place tonight.

"Do you want a drink?"

"Sure," she said. "Just a coke or something though. I have to drive back sooner than I'd like."

Audrey spent only ten more minutes at the bar before making her excuses to go. Zachary, knowing she would disappear like Cinderella from the ball any moment, spent the entire ten minutes by her side, making her feel included. He ignored his handful of other friends for those few minutes, as if he had planned the entire party in hopes she'd come.

He had.

When it was time for her to go, he walked her to her car. Audrey hesitated before saying goodnight. Zachary stood there, waiting, as if sensing she had something she wanted to say. But then she just said,

"Happy birthday, Zachary. I'll see you at work." And with that, the walls were firmly back up.

Zachary nodded, sticking his hands into his pockets. "See you at work, Cherry Bomb." He turned to go.

Suddenly, Audrey found herself saying his name. He turned and looked at her expectantly.

"I have a recital in two weeks," she blurted.

Zachary went still, waiting.

"It's only a junior recital, so it's not that big of a deal, but... Do you want to come?"

Zachary's mouth turned upward, slowly, before he nodded. "Yes, I do."

"Okay, then."

His smile widened as he recognized her reciprocation. She was reaching over the line again, asking him to cross it now, too. And he would gladly do so.

"Okay, then."

"Goodnight, Zachary," she said.

"Goodnight, Cherry Bomb."

Zachary stood outside the bar until Audrey drove away, taking his hand from his pocket to wave at her as she left. At the first red light she hit, Audrey heard her phone buzz from the center console. It was Paul.

Was it busy at CVS?

That night when Audrey got back to her apartment, she did so with a song on her lips. She imagined as she strung the words and melodies together in her head, that they were sung by a young man to his beloved. He sang, and danced around her, and knelt before her with his lively serenade as if it was all he had to offer.

She headed straight for the notebook Zachary gave her and turned to the first page to write the lyrics before they fled her mind:

If I had a, if I had a, if I had a ring

I would put it on your finger

I would give you everything

If I had a, if I had a, castle on a hill

I would give you all the keys

You could do with it what you will

If I had a, if I had a, if I had a kite

I would write your name upon it

Fly it in the fading light

If I had a, if I had a, if I had a dime

I would throw it in the wishing well

And wish that you were mine...

With the song bouncing in her ears and the image of Zachary's slow, hopeful smile filling her mind, Audrey drifted off to sleep.

8

Audrey stood just off stage, trying to focus on her breathing instead of the pounding of her heart. She'd sung in front of people hundreds of times before, usually at her church, but she still never failed to get nervous just before she began.

She peeked out at the tiny crowd—a few dozen friends, family members, and faculty, there to support the small group of students attempting to end their junior year on a good note (pun intended).

This recital was really to prepare for the more important senior recital next year. Instead of a sampling of different styles of music, they'd only be expected to really nail one song. It was essentially the final grade for a single class. Regardless, Audrey's nerves were on overdrive, and she wouldn't let herself think about why.

The truth was, she was nervous because she'd invited Zachary. Nervous—that he *wouldn't* be in that crowd when she walked out, and nervous about what that feeling meant.

Before she knew it, Elain Richards was finished with her spirited rendition of some classical German song, and her professor was at the mic, announcing her name. The pianist that accompanied Elain shuffled past her off stage. She would be singing *a capella*.

When she approached the microphone, the floor length skirt she wore brushing its stand, she took a moment to center herself before looking out into the crowd—and there he was.

Zachary sat near the center of the room, in line with her gaze. Audrey didn't know this, but Zachary arrived thirty minutes early to find such a seat. When she caught his eye, he smiled. It was a calm, reassuring smile. It held no expectations. No judgments. Just appreciation for her presence.

As Audrey opened her mouth to sing, she found she couldn't take her eyes off him.

Her voice started quietly, almost a whisper, then built dramatically as she continued. It rang with emotion—sadness, mostly. Confusion. Desperation. Love. She sang each word with feeling, allowing her face and her tone to shift with each new phrase so that it was almost like acting out a scene. She didn't need accompaniment for her voice; she *was* the accompaniment.

The song she chose was unconventional—a slower, shortened version of "Age of Reptiles" by Showbread. It stood in stark contrast to the classical pieces most of her classmates chose. But it made her feel something, and feeling something was the only reason she ever sang in the first place.

Zachary felt every one of those emotions with her as he sat in the audience, his eyes never leaving Audrey's face as she performed. He noted every expression, every carefully placed lull or waver in her voice.

Would it have changed Audrey's sense of calm resolve to know Zachary's serene demeanor masked a deep ache within his chest?

Would it have made a difference to know his eyes shone, not just from the lights in the room, but from barely contained tears? That it was her stare alone that kept him from weeping at the beauty and pain in her voice? I do not know.

At the end of the recital, Zachary stood casually at the edge of the crowd in the reception area. Audrey spotted him right away when she walked in, recognizing his nonchalant behavior for what it was—he was unsure if this was a safe place to be warm, to be close. He didn't know if Paul—or someone who knew Paul—was here, too.

She strode across the room to meet him, eager for her hug to be the answer he needed—Paul wasn't here, and neither was anyone else of note. She hadn't told a single soul about the performance besides her roommates, half of whom were in the recital with her, and who were now mingling among the small crowd.

Zachary visibly relaxed when she approached him with her arms out.

"Thank you for coming," she said as she hugged him.

"You were *amazing*," Zachary breathed in response. Audrey felt him squeeze a bit tighter around her waist. "I could listen to you sing that song at *least* a hundred more times."

In lieu of saying thank you and letting her voice crack, she squeezed him tighter, too.

The two of them then turned and surveyed the quiet, shuffling crowd before them.

They were silent for a few moments before Zachary said, "Do you want to take a walk?"

Only a tiny portion of Audrey's brain protested at the impropriety, the meaning of accepting such an invitation, the consequences—before she enthusiastically agreed.

The two of them walked down the street to 7/11 where Zachary purchased a single cigar, a bottle of water, and a Twix. Upon leaving the store, he handed the Twix to Audrey with a wink. She'd insisted she didn't want anything in the store, but she took it anyway, smiling at Zachary as she slid it into her jacket pocket.

They walked across the street then, entering a small empty lot adjacent to a grocery store. Zachary strode directly to a patch of concrete at the edge of the property and sat down, his back to the chainlink fence.

"A usual haunt of yours?" Audrey asked.

"You could say that," Zachary answered. He patted the ground beside him and she sat, pulling the Twix out of her pocket as she did so. When she looked up, Zachary was smiling at her.

"What?" she said, pausing her unwrapping.

Zachary just shook his head and continued to smile. After a few moments, he asked, "When did you start singing?"

"My parents said I was singing almost as soon as I could talk."

"Makes sense," Zachary said, now looking at his shoes. "I love to hear you talk. But I was not prepared to hear you sing." He let out a low whistle, and met her eyes. "Gorgeous."

He wasn't only talking about her voice.

Audrey swallowed, suddenly aware that they sat there with no wall between them. There were no lines, not here in this dark empty lot, not tonight.

She nearly jumped when Zachary put his hand on top of hers. Then she twisted her fingers so they gripped his own, her heart thundering as a ribbon of heat spread from his fingers and snaked up her arm.

For moments that felt like hours, they continued to stare at one another. She knew he wanted to kiss her. She *wanted* him to kiss her.

She was terrified.

And as if that terror shone through her eyes, Zachary let go of her hand, smiling gently as he did.

He didn't break eye contact as he said, "Weren't we in the middle of a discussion the other day at work?"

Audrey quietly let out a long breath, her fear dissipating along with the heat between them.

"We were," she said, somewhat shakily.

"I think..." Zachary said carefully, "we were arguing about something."

Audrey's face crinkled in frustration as she recalled the conversation. "Oh I remember. And if you think you're going to convince me that season finale wasn't a pile of sentimental garbage, you'd better think again, Zachary."

The next hours passed in effortless bliss. Audrey found herself forgetting about everything else in the world, honed in on the dance with Zachary that shifted constantly from rivalry to casual agreement to passionate consensus about this topic or that. No customers to interrupt them or listening ears to make them quiet their laughs or reign in their tongues.

The wall was down. Try as she might, Audrey couldn't find a reason in the world to use her energy resurrecting it. When was the last time she'd felt this relaxed? This comfortable in her own skin?

Why haven't we done this before? she found herself thinking.

She was so engaged in the moment, in their conversation, in the feeling of his leg against hers as they shifted closer and closer, that she forgot all notions of time as well. Eventually it dawned on her that she hadn't looked at her phone in... who knew how long? A brief wave of panic hit her, causing her to pull it quickly from her pocket.

Two missed text messages shone on the screen, mercifully only a few minutes old, and both from Paul. She released a breath and looked at Zachary, whose face had fallen slightly as he waited for her to speak.

When she finally did, she only said, "It's... late."

"Can I walk you home?"

"Yes."

They walked in amiable silence to Audrey's apartment, their fingers occasionally brushing against each other as they went.

Audrey quickly texted Paul back on their way: *Walking home from the grocery store.* She wondered if Zachary felt the same gnawing feeling in his gut that she did, as if she was forgetting something important.

He did.

"How's Paul?" Zachary asked, his chin jutting toward her phone as she put it away.

"He's fine," she said, tucking a loose strand of red hair behind her ear. Her building came into view. Their footsteps slowed.

"He couldn't make it to the recital," he said. It wasn't a question.

"He... actually, I didn't tell him about it," Audrey confessed. "You were the only person I invited."

Zachary's face twisted in shock. "But you worked so hard on that song. You were so... it was *so* beautiful."

Audrey struggled to find the words to explain. "It's just a junior recital. It's not as big of a deal as the senior recital, and, you know, gas is expensive..."

She sighed. Zachary's increasingly furrowed brow told her she wasn't convincing him.

"You're the only one that takes my dreams about singing seriously," she finally admitted. "Paul would have just criticized the song choice, or ask me why I didn't sing something by Hillsong United instead. I just wanted someone there who would be happy for me."

They approached the stairs that led to her apartment and stopped walking. Zachary opened his mouth to speak, then closed it, then opened it again. Finally, he decided what to say.

"I'll always support you. But I *won't* always be the only one. Once you get out of this school, you'll see. There's a whole world of people out there who will love you for who you are." Zachary's face darkened slightly then, and he took a step toward her. "Every fantastic, talented, breathtaking bit of you."

Zachary moved as if he would put his hand on her face, but Audrey wiped away the rogue tear on her cheek before he could, trying to use her smile to distract from the depth of her emotions. He didn't back off like she thought he would. Instead, he stepped closer, his hand indeed coming up to brush her face gently.

Unable to hide how she felt, Audrey closed her eyes and leaned into the feeling of his fingers.

When she opened them, Zachary's brown eyes were fixed firmly on her mouth. "Every single bit," he murmured absentmindedly.

Audrey shuddered at the look, at the heat spreading through her body. She imagined what it would be like to kiss him, to run her hands across his bare chest, to drag her teeth across his neck. Her thoughts showed on her face as plainly as Zachary's. Zachary, who was envisioning his hands running through her thick red hair, her face contorted with pleasure, nearly choked with desire as he took another step toward Audrey.

Their stomachs brushed against one another, and the warmth that filled her body made Audrey suddenly snap out of it. The awareness that she stood just in front of her apartment, surrounded by potentially prying eyes, brought her swiftly, painfully back to reality.

Zachary noticed the change the moment it happened and stepped back. His hands dropped to his sides, but his eyes held the same intensity as before.

"I'm sorry," he said.

Audrey shook her head forcefully. The last thing she wanted was for him to feel sorry. He grinned, understanding her meaning.

"Do you work tomorrow?" he said after a moment.

"No," Audrey said quietly, a piece of her still grieving the lost moment. "I, uh... I switched shifts with Jose. Tomorrow is *the dinner*. We're driving to Santa Monica, so we'll have to leave early to beat traffic."

"Ah," Zachary said, a hint of disappointment in his voice. "Your birthday present. Finally."

"Finally," she confirmed. "So I'll... see you Sunday."

"Sunday," he said, nodding.

She smiled. Then, as if to salvage what remained of the boundaries she'd set in place, she turned away, waving at him over her shoulder instead of offering a hug. He understood, waved back, and turned to go. Audrey was halfway up the stairs when he called her name. She turned to find him standing on the bottom step.

"You can leave him, you know," Zachary said. Her expression, which once would have cowed him into polite silence, only made his brows furrow, his chin rise slightly. "You *should* leave him. All this bullshit about God choosing your partner for you, all the nonsense about submission and loyalty and... all that. You don't *have* to believe it if you don't want to, Audrey. You can choose something different."

His eyes said what his mouth couldn't: *You could choose me.*

Audrey was stunned, her heart pounding in her ears. She couldn't speak even if she knew what to say.

He continued, "I just want you to know that. You can sing on stage. You can sing back up for Lady Gaga, or Avenged Sevenfold for that matter. Or you can make your own album, and sing whatever songs you feel like singing. And you can be with someone who sees you as an equal. If you want to." He nearly whispered the last part.

Then, as if the pained expression in her eyes was answer enough, he turned and walked away.

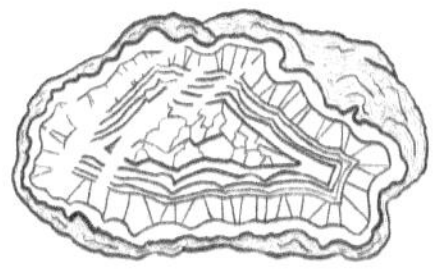

Once, she was a soldier.

As a young boy, she dreamed of marching off to war. Her father did before her, and his father before him. It was expected that she would do the same. For there was always another war to be fought.

In this world, there were many enemies.

She grew up tall and lanky, awkward and without much talent. She could not properly wield an axe, nor could she plant corn in straight rows. This did not bother her, since war was the business of her destiny. She would march off into the distance someday, and kill many men, and when she returned home her father would be proud. When she returned home, she would feel like the man she ought to have always been.

The day came when she was only sixteen. This new war just and righteous in cause, meant to exterminate a vile and disgusting plague that had washed onto their shores only months ago. People—if they could be called people, for it was said their eyes were as black as night, and their souls just as black—had invaded the lands to the South.

Our lands, she thought to herself. *Ours by right of birth, not simply there for the taking.*

They inhabited shores teeming with fish and fruit, pristine lands that had until now been uninhabited—desolate, really. They took the spoils of the land for themselves, building houses, giving birth, pissing in the great water. It was not right—this was the land of *her* ancestors. It was not fit for savages from beyond the edge of the world. It was not meant for monsters.

People all around her whispered of the coming threat.

"They've come to take our women."

"They've come to take our children."

"They'll want our houses next."

"Their false gods will bring famine and pestilence in their wake."

When she heard, she did not wait to enlist. The Army of Lynderia was the business of her family. It was her destiny.

She walked through town with an air of importance after that, her rifle resting on her shoulder as if she meant to end this war herself and deliver these simple, righteous people from the danger that loomed in the South. She meant to prove she was one of *them*, after all. All she'd need to do was kill a few monsters.

"Boy," her father said to her one day. "This is your chance to be a man. Do your duty, and come home. Marry a woman. Make her with child. And someday you, too, will know the honor of sending your only son off to war."

The marching lasted three weeks. Through valleys and marshlands, mountains and meadows, she and a troop of thirty other men made their way from their small highland village to the beach. The first foreign dwellings they found had already been emptied or burned, likely remnants of local hostility toward the invaders.

They were small, unassuming little villages, these foreign settlements. Family-sized huts made from fallen tree limbs and mud. Rudimentary nets for catching fish. Crude children's toys made from straw or stone or wood. No weapons, and no books.

Savages, she thought. *Uncivilized savages.*

They marched on in pursuit of the threat for days. On the sixth day, they stopped to camp at the top of a cliff overlooking a small bay. As she sat that evening looking out at the great water, she thought she had never seen anything as big or as grand as this. She was miles from her hometown, but she didn't feel afraid. Looking over the expanse, she felt a strange sense of familiarity with this place.

It was after sitting there for a while she had to make water. She could have pissed off the edge of the world right where she was, but she chose to walk past the tree line behind camp, hoping she would find some fruit.

The forest was serene, filled with a dim green light that shone all the way from the stars above through the large, translucent leaves on the trees. She relieved herself, then stood listening for a while to the sounds that surrounded her. The gentle sound of the wind moving the trees. The songs and sounds of insects and birds. The *crack* of a branch to her left.

She froze, then slowly reached down to retrieve her rifle from the ground near her feet. Another *crack*. She crept, slowly, in the direction of the sound, her gun raised. Perhaps it was only an animal.

Perhaps not.

A few steps brought her to a small clearing where the light of the stars lit up the ground like a giant spotlight, and there stood a man.

He was clothed in strange garb that fit snugly to his form. He was tall, much taller than she was. His hair was short and dark. His skin, pale. And his eyes, darker than any eyes she had ever seen, held in them the reflection of the blue starlight above. They looked like one of the precious stones her mother kept in the window, the ones whose dark shining surfaces were broken up with jagged lines of white and pale blue.

They were looking right at her.

The two of them stood staring at each other for a long moment—her with her rifle raised, him with those eyes. She looked into his eyes, and what she saw reflected back at her was not the gaze of a monster. It was the gaze of a man. It was *herself* she saw reflected in those eyes.

Then she pulled the trigger.

Drowned by the yells of her fellow soldiers in camp—wondering where the gunshot came from, preparing for attack—she wept. Her heart, inexplicably broken by the fulfillment of her destiny, seemed to bleed over the stranger before her. She had done it. She was a hero.

Soon she went home, and she married a woman, and she made her with child.

And for the rest of her days, she awaited her death.

9

Audrey felt like her body wasn't her own as she walked through the front door of her apartment.

It was the noise that hit her first, rattling her brain as her roommates screamed, shrieked with joy, and ran to embrace her. Then, she took in the decorations, barely remembering how to read as she spotted the giant banner above the dining table that read, *Congratulations!*

Her hands went limp, dropping her handbag just by the door, but Paul's fingers gripped her other hand tightly, preventing her from pulling away, reminding her to smile.

Just keep smiling. She bit her lip, hard. *Just keep smiling.*

Paul had picked her up that day at 4:00 pm for her belated birthday dinner. He wore a suit, and she wore her nicest dress per his instructions to "dress fancy," along with the cheap necklace he'd given her for her birthday two weeks prior. Audrey gazed out the window silently as they sat in traffic for two hours, Paul's road rage bubbling just beneath the surface, trying to keep her thoughts from her face.

She couldn't stop thinking about Zachary. About the defiance in his face as he stood at the bottom of the stairs and told her she had a choice—as if he knew no one else had ever given her one. The smell of his breath, the love in his eyes, it made her dizzy to think about it.

Then they arrived. And despite the fact that she didn't want a fancy dinner for her birthday, or to sit in weekend traffic to get one, the view of the coast from the window of the restaurant set Audrey's mind at ease.

She watched the waves roll in, out, in, out, as they waited for their food to arrive. She listened halfheartedly as Paul talked about the James Dobson book he was reading for a class, and barely heard him as he prattled on about his vision for a church that preached "Godly masculinity." She smiled and nodded, unable to remove herself from limbo, unable to think clearly.

Until he went down on one knee, and she was sucked violently back into reality.

Paul's smile as he knelt there was exactly the one she fell in love with—charming, brilliant, beautiful. His blue eyes, so vibrant against his ivory skin and dark brown hair, shone with expectation.

And the ring. It was... well, it was a ring. Pretty. Sparkly. Impersonal. Just like him.

She barely heard the words as he said them, but they registered.

"Will you marry me?"

Time stopped.

She knew a smile was plastered on her face, but she barely felt it. She knew everyone was looking at them. Yet, her brain couldn't seem to catch up with what was happening.

And there... oh my god, was that Paul's friend with a *camera* in the booth adjacent to them? Yes—everyone was watching, everyone was *waiting*. Her heart thundered. A few seconds passed in what felt like an eternity as Paul looked at her expectantly.

Then, just as she'd practiced so many times in her head, as she'd imagined from the time she was a little girl watching princess movies, she bleated with perfectly poised joy and surprise, "Yes!"

The ensuing applause, the occasional *Whoop!* from the gathered patrons, the way Paul scooped her up into his arms for a hug before he placed the ring gingerly on her finger—they were intoxicating. Her heart fluttered as they sat back down, and she smiled shyly and nodded at the other diners who looked her way, beaming in congratulations. She blushed and giggled as the waitress brought out a complimentary dessert, gushing over the ring and telling Audrey how lucky she was. Paul squeezed her hand across the table, his thumb gently stroking the diamond on her ring, and she met his gaze.

For a few perfect, sparkling moments, Audrey felt totally fulfilled. The love shining in Paul's eyes made her stomach twist. It reminded her of when they first started dating. She thought of her mother, who talked about Audrey getting married as if it were the paragon of her existence. Her father, who loved Paul like he was his own. She thought of every intimate moment she'd spent with Paul and the promise that lay beyond them. The promise of forever. The only promise she'd been taught to expect from life—from God.

Something deep inside Audrey sighed happily.

It wasn't until they left the restaurant that reality began to sink in again. As soon as the car door closed, Paul leaned over and grabbed her, pulling her in for a messy, eager kiss. She indulged him, giggling against his lips, but when he pulled away his eyes were still hungry.

Hungry. Triumphant. Possessive.

Suddenly, it was Zachary's face before her. It was like a bucket of cold ice was thrown over her head. Audrey remembered what there was to mourn.

The rhythmic sound of Paul's Nissan Altima as it sped down the highway seemed to mock her: *Forever,* it said. *Forever, forever, forever.*

She spent several minutes listening to it, detached, quiet. Then, in an effort to bring herself back into her body, she reached into her purse and found a bag of M&Ms there. As she went to open them, Paul looked over.

"Seriously, babe? Haven't you had enough sugar for tonight?"

Some slumbering piece of Audrey woke, and started screaming: *Run, you have a choice! Run!*

But then Paul's phone began to go off as text message after text message streamed in, and she realized he had already posted a photo on Instagram, had already texted his parents. That meant *her* parents knew, as well. She heard Paul telling her how all her roommates had known for weeks, that one of them even helped him pick out the ring.

She realized with horror she had no choice to begin with.

Her entire world, save for one small coffee shop, had conspired to make sure this night happened. The path was laid before her and she, never fully aware she had any choice in the matter, walked down it willingly. After all, this was God's plan. Paul's plan. Were they the same thing? It didn't matter—it was too late.

It was permanent.

Forever: it was beginning... *now.*

Then the rationalizing began. She ran through all the reasons why this was right, why this was the obvious next step for her. She brought to mind every sweet, romantic, and genuine thing Paul ever did that proved he really loved her. She reminded herself of every coincidence she'd told herself were signs from God that she was meant to marry Paul.

Deep down, she knew the role those "signs" played in preserving her from an overwhelming fear of going to hell after having premarital sex. She clung to them nonetheless. Layer upon layer of psychological armor went up, telling her she'd done things right. Telling her she wasn't making the biggest mistake of her life.

To someone who knew Audrey it may have seemed obvious that she was exaggerating every smile, forcing every loving touch and carefree laugh to compel her feelings into something more pragmatic. Paul only saw the excitement, the smiles, the caresses, and took them as confirmation of his own desires.

The drive soon lulled her back into silence. She noticed nothing but the sound of the radio as they drove. And by the time they reached her apartment, she was entirely detached.

Her roommates were hugging her and she was slowly taking in her surroundings. In addition to the banner above the table, various balloons decorated the space. A giant hand-drawn "Ring by Spring" poster hung above their little couch. Everything was gold and black, including the bottles of champagne Brienne carried triumphantly from the kitchen.

She clutched the hands of her friends, and cried, and laughed, and gushed with them over her beautiful ring. She wondered—marveled, even—at how all of them could keep this secret for so long.

Yet it made her angry, primarily at herself, because she'd actually dreamed of exactly *this* for so long. The idea of everyone being "in on it" except the bride always seemed like such a romantic notion. Asking a girl's dad for her hand, the best friend ring shopping with the boyfriend, the surprise public setting. She thought that was *it*—the dream. In reality, it made her feel completely powerless.

Finally, they shooed Paul off, teasing him about having Audrey all to himself for the rest of her life and letting them have some time alone with her. She kissed him pleasantly goodbye, wiping away a tear that for all appearances was a tear of utter joy. Then they opened the bottles of champagne, and she gladly drank.

The next day, she called off work. She told her roommates it was a hangover, and while they were at the beach she stayed in her bed watching all her favorite romance movies. When she sobbed, she told herself it was in joy that her own happy ending was finally coming to fruition.

Halfway through the day, Kelly texted her. *Are you okay?*

Audrey could practically feel Zachary through the phone. Kelly never texted her, so he must have asked her to do it, afraid of doing it himself, perhaps wondering if he was the cause of her absence after their moment two nights prior. She knew they didn't know yet. Zachary was somehow not on social media at all, and she wasn't friends with any of her other coworkers online.

I'm okay, she responded. *See you tomorrow.*

Tomorrow came too quickly.

Audrey's left hand felt like it weighed a thousand pounds as she walked through the door of Windmills, knowing everything would now change.

Zachary caught her eye as she walked in and smiled at her. Audrey smiled in return, her hands curled behind her as she went to the back. He was already waiting for her there, the start of a conversation on his lips. He stopped short though, his eyes on her hand, now in plain sight as she gripped her hands together in front of her nervously.

He stood there, frozen, looking at her. She looked back, meeting his gaze but not knowing what to say. He looked like he might cry. She felt like she might, too.

"Are you..." he began.

She thought he was going to say, "Are you okay?"

Before he could, Kelly shrieked from behind him, "Oh my GOD, is that an *engagement ring*?"

She ran to Audrey and grabbed her hand, her mouth agape as she looked at the ring, and pulled her in for a congratulatory hug. Over Kelly's shoulder, Audrey looked at Zachary, who now seemed utterly lost for words. He met her eyes again, smiled sadly, and turned to walk away.

Audrey forced herself to shut her eyes against the image of his back to her. Her entire life had been veering toward this moment. She was an animatronic character moving on a wire track. This was what she must do. What everyone expected of her. It would take nothing less than the dismantling of everything she knew in order to justify walking away now. It would risk the love of all—or, almost all—who knew her.

And Zachary… he was never meant to be permanent. At worst, he was a temptation from the devil himself. At best, he was a pleasant distraction—one she would think about for the rest of her life.

10

Marriage was not what Audrey thought it would be.

As a child, marriage was portrayed as the end-all-be-all of female existence. The paragon of feminine virtue. The door beyond which life really started, the passageway from girlhood to womanhood. Beyond it laid children, domesticity, and the bliss that had long been promised to her. The mythical quality of marriage was so powerful that it caused her to disregard every single red flag that led her to this place—this... hell.

You may call her silly, but Audrey always thought things would just sort of work out. She, and many like her, thought the married state was some sort of magical satiation for those most dangerous and insidious of male tendencies.

But she was wrong. Marriage did not satiate Paul. It *unleashed* him.

Paul's every instinct burgeoned under the power of his new spiritual ownership of his wife. What was once a loan was now bona fide property. His romantic streak got more pronounced, but his worst traits compounded even more. The flowers, the weekend trips—they were not spontaneous acts of devotion.

They were his apologies.

She thought about this now as she lay on their bed, staring at the ceiling. Next to Paul's side of the bed, there was a clock that projected the time onto the wall. She had taken to staring at it during times like this when Paul was in one of his... moods. The large red numbers always made some sort of face if she was looking at them sideways, the first number often a hat, or large bushy eyebrows; the colon, the eyes; and the last two numbers a mouth, or a mustache.

It was currently 8:20 pm, and the little man on the ceiling wore a fur cap and a surprised expression, his mouth wide open beneath his curly mustache. Audrey stared at him, the sounds in the room fading into background noise as she questioned her life choices.

Why had she never wondered why boys weren't taught to aspire to marriage? She had been preparing for it from the time she was a little girl, but had ended up with someone for whom marriage was little more than a legitimate reason to have sex—a minor rite of passage in the life of a Christian man. She was like a lamb led to the slaughter, but didn't see the cruelty of it until it was too late.

She had been bred for loneliness.

Paul swiped at her ankle with his hand, pulling Audrey out of her disassociated state.

"Are you listening to me?" he demanded.

"Yes, of course," she said flatly.

She didn't need to, though—not really. She could practically recite his favorite lines in her sleep.

Like the following, which he said to her now: "Where were you, really? Just fucking tell me, Audrey."

Audrey pushed herself up onto her elbows and looked at him, her anger plain on her face.

"I was at the bookstore," she said, her voice menacingly quiet. "Like I told you, three fucking times already. I went to the bookstore, I got gas, and I came home."

"Your car had a full tank of gas the other day, and you were gone for THREE HOURS!"

Paul screamed the last two words, the sudden crescendo causing Audrey to jump despite knowing it was coming.

"Paul, you saw my location on your phone," Audrey said, exasperated. "Do you think I'm Houdini or something?"

"How do I know you didn't leave your phone there and drive to someone's house?" he said. "Did you drop off your phone with one of your friends, Audrey?"

She wanted to scream, "*What fucking friends?*" Instead, she rolled her eyes at him.

Audrey no longer had time for friends. She and Paul moved into an apartment considerably closer to Paul's school than hers after the wedding. His reason being that he had responsibilities at his church—now *their* church—that he couldn't risk over a commute. It left her driving an hour to and from school, then coming home and shouldering all of the housework and errands. She took a part-time job at a gas station around the corner to help with bills, but they were once again forced to rely on the generosity of their parents as the two of them made school their "job" for one more year. She would graduate in a month, among peers she now felt were strangers.

As for her old coworkers at Windmills, they may as well be strangers, too. She hadn't the heart or the bravery to visit since she'd gotten married, especially now that she and Paul shared a phone plan, making him much more adept at tracking her every move. Not that it mattered. He tortured her with his paranoid distrust anyway.

Paul suddenly lurched forward, sticking his face in Audrey's chest and inhaling. Audrey's instinct was to recoil.

"Did you just *sniff* me?" she demanded.

"You smell like someone else," he said quietly, his face terrifyingly still.

"Paul, you're being ridiculous," she said. "Why would I go to all this trouble to cheat on you? I've never done *anything* to suggest I would. *You*, on the other hand…"

"FUCK, Audrey!" Paul screamed. "I am NOT having this conversation again."

"Well I'm pretty sick to death of this conversation too," Audrey spat at him. "But I'm not the one Googling local girls to chat with, Paul, that's *you*. Yet *I'm* the one who has to listen to you accuse me of cheating every week, who has to take pictures of my timecards at work so you won't call me at night, drunk off your ass, and ask me who I'm *fucking*!"

Paul's sneer turned into a near-growl as he pushed her onto the bed. She brought her knees up, as if to intercept his next movement with her feet.

"You really like to make me feel like shit, don't you, Audrey?"

Audrey sighed. She had better sit back and settle in.

This was just the beginning of the second phase of the night—the first phase being paranoid jealous ranting. Now it was time for gaslighting, which would then be followed by a tearful rendition of his abandonment issues from childhood, then a brief lament concerning Audrey's alleged horrible treatment of him, and finally a pathetic backhanded apology.

Her job was then to gently touch him on the shoulder, apologize for not understanding his perspective, and hold him against her chest while he finished crying. The whole show, including the incredibly brief make-up sex afterward, could last anywhere from one to three hours. Paul would then roll off her, make his way to the living room, and play video games for the next six hours while she slept.

Indeed, the night went just as she expected. Audrey was still staring at the little man on the ceiling as Paul's footsteps faded away down the hall.

It was in those moments after Paul left the room and she could expect to spend the rest of the night alone, that Audrey often found her thoughts drifting to Zachary. Each time they did, an ache pounded in her chest that she couldn't assuage. It drove her to replay every little moment she regretted, each time changing some key detail that would have perhaps fixed everything.

She sometimes imagined she was talking to him, explaining every-thing. Explaining that marriage to Paul wasn't so bad. That it was the right choice—the only choice she could make. It was really just a way of rationalizing her decisions to herself. She even wrote a snippet of song about it once:

If you really think about it, then it's not that bad

If you give it some thought, it really isn't so sad

It's just a little heartache, I don't mean to deflect,

But it's nothing more than what my mother said to expect.

It almost seemed like a dream now, that time between her engagement and the last time she saw Zachary. For she truly had no idea the extent to which her marriage had already been arranged until later, when her mother informed her that the best wedding venue in Redding had one open date that summer, and she'd already booked it—six *months* ago. That left Audrey with only a few weeks until her junior year was over, at which point her family firmly expected her to be at home to prepare for a wedding in two months' time.

Telling Zachary she was leaving in less than a month was even hard-er than telling him she was getting married. The time it took for it to sink in—that she was leaving for the entire summer (rather than working and visiting home every few weeks like she'd done last year), was torturous. Watching the realization settle into his face—that she may *never* come back to work at Windmills—was devastating.

On the day of her last shift, Zachary called in sick. Audrey's first response was shock, then rage, which she spent the better part of her shift trying to swallow. It was a bitter pill, and she was only partially successful. She was still trembling with anger, on the verge of tears, when she walked to her car after work, a leftover cupcake clutched in her hand from the small goodbye party Kelly threw for her. Staring at her feet as she walked, she contemplated throwing it to the ground.

When she looked up and saw Zachary standing by her car, she nearly threw it in his face.

Until she realized he'd been crying. In fact, he seemed at that moment to be struggling to hold back tears.

Audrey dropped the cupcake.

"Hey, Cherry Bomb," he said quietly. "I'm sorry I missed work today."

He really, truly was.

"Hey," Audrey said, taking a step toward him, her anger dissolving all at once. "It's okay... I missed you, though."

"I'm going to miss you," Zachary said, his voice wavering as he held back a sob. Audrey went to him without another word, her arms out. She suddenly understood why he called off work.

Zachary held her, tightly, for a long time. His breath slowed as he squeezed her tighter, as if he was pouring every ounce of emotion he felt into that hug. When he stepped back, Audrey's face shone with tears.

"I'll come visit," she promised.

Zachary looked at her for a long moment before saying, "No. You won't."

Silence filled the air between them as she realized she couldn't argue.

He was right. Audrey felt such sorrow she thought she could have died. It was the anger from before, finally settling into its true form. This may be the last time she'd ever see her friend, and it was utterly heartbreaking.

Zachary must have seen the realization in her expression, because he stepped closer, bringing his hand up to gently touch her face.

"You deserve everything you want," he said softly. "You deserve *everything*. And if there's a God out there somewhere judging me for encouraging you to be selfish, or proud... well, *fuck* him. It's true."

Audrey bit back a sob and put her forehead against his shoulder.

"Thank you for being my friend," she whispered.

Zachary pulled her closer, and whispered back, "Don't let him put out your fire."

Then he straightened, pulling her away to look her in the eyes, and kissed her.

Gently, passionately, he kissed her. And when their lips met, it felt to Audrey as if her soul leaned in, desperate to touch his, just as their lips touched. Indeed it did—it reached, longingly, knowingly, toward her soulmate, and Zachary's soul reached back, anchoring them together for several long moments before their lips parted. Zachary rested his forehead on Audrey's then, and between their nearly-touching lips sat a gasp of air, still and heavy with one another's energies, as if their spirits were savoring the lingering closeness.

Then Zachary pulled back, looked at Audrey once more with pain and longing in his eyes, and walked away.

That was the last time she saw Zachary. He didn't text her. She didn't text him either. One day, he was in her life. The next, he was not. It felt like a death.

But you and I both know even death can't interrupt this particular love story.

11

It was Audrey's baptism day. She was standing waist-deep in Jenny Creek, shivering from the cold bite of the water. Her pastor was standing beside her, a benevolent smile on his face as he announced to her gathered friends and family what this commitment signified. Audrey, at the tender age of eight, was committing her body and soul to Christ.

She wore a white dress that day. White was a color of purity, her mother told her. Symbolic of her sin being washed away by Christ's blood. That's why she also wore white on Easter. She would wear it again on her wedding day, as her body and soul were put under the charge of her husband.

Her pastor tucked his arm around her shoulders, dipping her backward into the frigid creek. She shut her eyes, fighting the urge to gasp as the freezing water soaked through that white dress.

But when she opened her eyes, it was Paul standing there, holding her head under the water. He smiled, that charming smile she thought she loved, and everything in her began to panic.

I'm going to die, she thought, her body beginning to thrash in protest at the lack of air. He held her there, his hands gripping her with force, her own unable to reach him somehow. She opened her mouth to sob, to scream, anything, but water rushed in instead, choking her.

Audrey woke, splayed on her back and gasping. Her heart began to slow as she recognized her bedroom.

It had been nine months since she graduated from APU and nearly two years since she'd seen Zachary. She was now 23 years old.

Audrey spent the first week of summer on a "late honeymoon" with Paul at Lake Tahoe, followed by several mind-numbing weeks at home, looking for full-time work. Once she found it, she settled into a routine that could only be described as toilsome. She worked, came home, did housework, put dinner on the table, cleaned it up, pleased her husband when he wanted it, and went to bed in order to do it all again the next day.

Occasionally, she also had responsibilities at church. Tedious things, like bringing cookies and lemonade to a Church Council meeting she was not allowed to sit in on, or volunteering in the nursery. None of it meant anything to her. It simply kept her busy enough to distract her from the rage that burned quietly beneath her skin.

She and Paul had their routine, as well. He would wake up an hour before her to drink coffee and read his Bible—his "quiet time," he liked to call it. When she woke up, she'd get both of them breakfast and sit down with him to eat in silence until he finished taking notes for some sermon, or newsletter, or something.

Then he would ask how she slept, and she'd say she slept fine, and would clean up breakfast, and they would both go about their day until they sat down again for dinner. They rarely had a full conversation unless it was a fight. Most of the talking was done by Paul, who was either talking about himself or subtly criticizing her.

He only asked about Audrey during their weekly "couples devotional," when he would ask her to share with him how she was doing spiritually. At least once a month she was expected to remark on some weakness she was struggling with, or some question she had, providing him the opportunity to exercise his husbandly duties and "minister to her." At the end of each session, they would pray. Paul always handled the talking while Audrey bowed her head, silently agreeing with everything he said.

This morning he had more papers than usual scattered across the table, his narrow handwriting etching every line with notes. He didn't look up at her as she entered the kitchen and said good morning, heading straight for the coffee pot.

"Eggs?" she asked.

"Mmm," Paul said, still not looking up.

Audrey took the pan down from the cupboard. The noise seemed to get Paul's attention, because he finally looked up at her.

"Fully cooked this time, if you can manage it." His voice held a touch of humor, but Audrey bristled. His eggs were "too shiny" once, *three months* ago, and he'd brought it up every time she'd made eggs since.

She considered spitting in his eggs, but it was just an image. One of many that would flash through her mind during the day. Spitting in his food, hitting him over the head with a brick. It was satisfying, but she would never do it.

Instead, she drew in a sharp breath, as she'd done many times before to help her swallow the small bits of poison he fed her. It was no longer just the jealousy. Now it was the criticism. The double standards. The small demonstrations of power here and there. Sometimes they felt like torture. Sometimes she barely noticed them, a small weight added to an already heavy load.

Her job at least gave her an escape from the crushing expectations of home and church. She was working as the hostess at a small diner. It kept her busy, but she avoided forming relationships with her coworkers beyond basic niceties. The thought of becoming close to anyone made her anxiety rise, her thoughts always returning to Windmills, and her life suddenly being pulled out from under her.

Audrey had gone her entire senior year without setting foot into Windmills. Paul's constant interest in her whereabouts was only part of the reason.

She also feared seeing Zachary. She anxiously imagined walking in and finding a stranger—he would not grin, or wave, or say "Cherry Bomb!", but would only smile politely and ask her what she'd like to drink. The thought, outrageous as it was, kept her frozen. She preferred to cling to her memories. They were warm, and comfortable, and unchanging.

After she graduated, the distance between her life and her memories began to feel like a void that would swallow her whole. One evening, staring at the numbers on the ceiling, she decided she would try to see him.

She pulled out all the stops in order to do it, planning a dinner with two of her old roommates, Kathryn and Brienne, at a restaurant two doors down from Windmills. She suggested the location over the phone, encouraging them to look up reviews as they spoke.

When they did, Audrey asked, "Hey, as long as you have it pulled up can you text me the address? It's been so long since I've been there."

The text ensured Paul didn't think the location was Audrey's idea.

She arrived twenty minutes early and stepped into Windmills, but Zachary wasn't there. Audrey swallowed the lump in her throat as Kelly climbed over the counter to wrap her in a hug. After they caught up for a few minutes Audrey asked about Zachary.

"He left a while ago," Kelly said sadly. "Moved back to Omaha."

Audrey bit back tears, trying with all her strength to appear casual as she said, "Are you in touch with him?"

"Not really. I can give you the most recent phone number I have for him, though."

"That would be great."

The two of them then chatted about this and that. Kelly demanded to see pictures from the wedding, and Audrey congratulated her on nearly finishing her Master's degree. They parted ways, Zachary's phone number clutched in Audrey's hand as she made her way outside.

She waited until she was seated at the restaurant to text the number. *It's Audrey,* was all she wrote. But the reply came back immediately: an error message. No such number.

And that was that.

Now, as Audrey scrubbed the pan clean in which she cooked her husband his eggs, she thought about those few years working at Windmills. She thought about Zachary, and she thought about the woman she almost became—the person she came so close to embracing. Strong. Fierce. Independent. Free.

All for nothing, she thought. The growth she endured, the mental stretching, the burgeoning rebellion against the authority of her childhood religion. She came so close to something like freedom, the shackles in her mind loosening if not coming undone entirely. Then she stepped over the threshold into marriage, and everything changed.

As soon as she put on that ring, her life became a whirlwind of premarital counseling, women-only prayer groups, and the culmination of thousands of expectations from every direction—the most pressing being those of her parents. She had never seen them so proud as when they talked about her marriage. Never. Not when she graduated college a year later. Not when she got an offer to sing backup for a popular local R&B group on their new album. Not even when she turned it down because it would interfere with Paul's pastoral training, taking a job as a hostess instead.

Ushered forward as she was by such expectations, she barely had time to grieve the death of the woman she was becoming. With marriage came the assumption of new responsibilities—those of a good, Christian wife. As if a sleeper protocol were activated, the instincts of docility and domesticity took over her body against her will. Those new responsibilities required her to stop questioning her religious and political beliefs, or risk being miserable every second of her marriage.

As it turned out, it didn't matter. She stopped questioning her beliefs, stopped entirely, and she ended up being miserable anyway.

It wasn't only the incessant, possessive jealousy. Or the near-nightly rants about her whereabouts, her loyalty, her intentions. It wasn't even the monotonous, robotic sex. Paul was a bully, but she seemed to be the only one who noticed. Paul was still the golden boy, just like in high school.

But there were some who knew, and just didn't care.

There was the Pastor of their church, for one. When she'd sought his counseling, tearfully begging for some way to get through to Paul, to make him stop his nightly screaming, his terrorizing, his accusations, he reprimanded her for coming to see him without her husband's knowledge. Then he lectured her about the weakness of men, and the responsibility of wives to quell their husband's rage-filled tendencies through compassion—and sex.

When she arrived home that day, Paul was waiting, just having gotten off the phone with Pastor Mike. It was not a good night.

Then there were Sharon and Samantha, two women from her church small group she'd become close with, in a way. They were at her apartment for tea just months ago when Paul woke up and texted her from the other room, demanding to know whose voices he heard drifting down the hall. She'd excused herself to go into the bedroom and remind him she was having tea with her friends, as she told him the day before. It was another twenty minutes before she emerged from that room, her face tear-stained and red.

There was no possible way the two of them didn't hear it. The screaming, the crying, the way he'd punched the wall inches from her face as he roared at her, "THIS IS MY ONLY DAY OFF THIS WEEK, YOU DUMB BITCH!"

When she approached her friends, the shame she felt was plain on her face. They'd only brushed off her apologies and politely made their excuses to leave. To escape. To leave her all alone with the monster in her home, who was still seething in the other room.

When she saw them next, they didn't bring it up. Nor the time after that. They pretended nothing had ever happened.

Eventually, so did she. She stopped pushing back against Paul and his many "weaknesses," and instead learned to accept the satisfaction of a tearful apology the next morning, or a bouquet of flowers sent to work, or his sudden acquiescence to a request he'd previously denied.

Sure, she didn't feel an ounce of companionship or support in her life, but she did get that ring light she wanted to make videos of herself singing. Perhaps, after his next outburst, she'd get permission to actually post them online.

Or perhaps that was one request he'd use God to deny in his stead. It was his favorite rhetorical weapon: portraying anything she did, said, or desired as a sin. Despite the fact that his own behavior was a far cry from saint-like, he was the only one able to wield the threat of God's judgment in this marriage. His cock gave him moral and spiritual authority over her no matter *what* kind of a savage he really was.

Audrey thought of all this as she stood at the sink, scrubbing the pan so thoroughly she nearly scraped off the Teflon coating.

She thought about Zachary, telling her she could do anything she wanted, pushing her to make a decision that wasn't predetermined by some greater force. She pictured him, sitting in the audience of a small concert hall and listening to her sing, his face lit up with something like awe.

She wondered if she would ever sing on stage again. Perhaps, she thought, she still had a shot at being a church worship leader, or at the very least, the worship leader's backup singer.

12

Audrey stared, unblinking, at the two tiny vertical lines. Two tiny lines, so small, but not too small to completely determine the direction of the rest of her life. In her 26 years of living, nothing so *permanent* had ever happened to her before.

She was pregnant.

Audrey willed herself to feel joyful. Willed herself to feel happy, fulfilled, blessed, relieved—*anything* but what she felt, which was pure, undiluted panic.

Her life loomed before her, every step already placed with exacting precision, stretching all the way to her own cold, meaningless death.

The drip, drip, drip of the bathtub seemed to echo her horror: *Forever,* it said. *Forever, forever.*

Forever singing backup vocals to cut-and-paste worship songs at her abusive husband's evangelical church, where he was now a full-time assistant pastor. Forever the mother to a child doomed to repeat her mistakes. Forever cemented in a belief system that now rang empty and hollow, nothing more than a pretense for control.

Forever submissive. Forever devoted. Forever trapped.

She shot up from where she was sitting on the edge of the tub, suddenly desperate to get rid of the test. Paul was coming home. He would be here any moment, and the idea of telling him she was pregnant right now made her feel ill. With shaking hands, she lifted some of the trash in the garbage bin and tucked the positive test and the box it came in underneath. She washed her hands and splashed water on her face.

Then she began to cry, her body shaking with sobs. The tears came uncontrollably, and soon she was sitting on the ground, utterly at the mercy of her emotions. She couldn't remember the last time she'd really cried. It must have been at least a year. Far more than a year's worth of tears poured out of her now.

She'd only started to calm down when Paul walked in. She hadn't heard him come in the front door. He looked down at her, his face filled with wary concern.

"What happened?" he asked, his voice flat.

"Nothing," she answered. "I'm just sad."

Paul let out a short huff of air, his features contorting into something like disgust.

This was why she didn't cry. Paul needed a tangible reason for tears—a single, clear, triggering event that he could control, or confront, or diagnose. In such cases he willingly offered his concern, sympathy, even the occasional shoulder to cry on. But any other display of emotion put him on edge.

Usually, he assumed it had something to do with him, and became irrationally defensive. Truth be told, it usually *was* his fault, but even when Audrey said it was nothing and claimed she was only sad, the lack of definition irritated him just as much. There was only one thing that usually worked to make him simply walk away and leave her be.

"I'm just on my period."

The disgust remained, but it softened into a particular brand of disgust reserved for "womanly things." Audrey felt relief at that look. It meant he would stay away from her for a few days. He may even sleep on the couch.

"Oh," he said and stalked away into the bedroom.

Audrey sat there for a while, staring at nothing. A growing curiosity about how and when she would go about telling Paul arose, and if he would know she lied to him about starting her cycle. She doubted it mattered, though. He thought periods turned women into sobbing, irrational messes. He may not even remember their biological function. He would be focused on the announcement itself—the ultimate significance of it.

She continued to think about that for the rest of the evening. She thought of it while she cooked dinner, and while she washed dishes, while she distractedly watched a movie, and finally while she lay down in bed.

It was a quiet train of thought, one that stood in stark contrast to the absolute terror she felt about the pregnancy, but it was persistent.

It was like a small part of her brain had gone on autopilot. Every other piece of her was saturated in dread and grief, rebelling against the thing growing in her body. But that one piece was already going ahead with what it knew she ought to be doing now. It had even begun throwing out clever ideas about how to tell Paul. She imagined how she'd get his reaction on video, and how many likes on Instagram it would get.

It was also projecting images of tiny onesies, extravagant baby showers, and her mother crying with joy over becoming a grandparent into her mind's eye. They were like tiny serotonin bombs, those images, slowly lifting her from the fog that had settled around her.

It was that same piece of her brain that kept romantic proposals and diamond rings and beautiful weddings in the forefront of her attention five years prior, never allowing her to dwell too long on the reality of what came after. It was a conditioned response, drilled into her by a lifetime of training, telling her that the *only* logical reaction of a woman in this situation was sheer, utter joy.

That piece of her was smaller now than it was before. It was starved nearly to death. That night as she lay in bed alone, Audrey angrily pushed it down, strangling it into silence before she fell into a fitful sleep.

The horror Audrey felt didn't go away. Not the next day, not the next week. She felt a sense of foreboding, like the walls were closing in on her. How soon would she start showing? How long could she keep this to herself?

The only other time she'd felt a similar emotion was at the rehearsal dinner for her wedding. Her little brother Isaac came looking for her when she disappeared and found her having a panic attack in the parking lot. He sat with her that night until she calmed down, and when her wedding day came he kept approaching her, as if to see if she was okay. But that day she felt... nothing. Only fatigue, and a shallow sort of happiness, and the growing sense of awareness that the most wonderful day of her life would soon be over, her greatest moments forever behind her.

This time, the fear ran deeper.

She found herself not only panicking for herself, but on behalf of the child she didn't want. To have Paul as a father… it was not a romantic notion to think about.

Two weeks after she found out she was pregnant, she found herself asking a coworker if she could borrow her phone, claiming hers was dead. It wasn't, but Paul occasionally checked her phone log, and if he looked up the number she was dialing and found out it was an abortion clinic, he would call in an exorcist.

Her voice shook as she spoke to the woman on the phone, who was professional, but kind. Never in a million years would she have guessed she'd be in this situation. A decade ago she would have reacted in horror at another woman in her shoes, called her damned, a monster even. But a decade ago, she had no notion of what it was *like* to be in this situation. In fact, she had no inkling of how the world worked at all. How cruel it could be.

She would not bring a baby into this mess.

"Audrey, are you okay?" Audrey's coworker, Katie, said as she tucked the phone back into the pocket of her apron. Katie was one of the waitresses at the diner Audrey worked at, and though Audrey had kept her distance emotionally, they were on friendly terms.

Audrey meant to say, "Yes, I'm fine." Instead, she burst into tears.

Katie, her eyes wide with concern, took her arm and ushered her toward the break room. She pulled out a chair for her and sat down, waiting patiently until the wave of tears subsided.

"Audrey," she said finally, carefully. "I know you don't know me that well. But I'm being honest when I say you can tell me anything in confidence. I'm here for you."

Audrey considered this before she spoke. It had been years since she talked openly with someone who wasn't part of her church, or her family. This might be the only safe space she had. It was one she'd walled herself off from for years, not wanting to form deep relationships with her coworkers that she couldn't continue outside of work. She didn't want to explain that her husband would only allow her to spend time with certain people. She was embarrassed. But now, she felt she had very little to lose.

"I'm pregnant," she said, her voice nearly a whisper. Then, before Katie could respond, "and I don't want to be. That was... that was the call I was making. I was scheduling an appointment to terminate the pregnancy." More tears ran down her face, and she forced herself to meet Katie's eyes, to see the judgment in them, the hatred.

But there was no trace of judgment on Katie's face—only compassion, as she laid her hand on top of Audrey's, her eyes never leaving hers.

"I understand," she said. "Your phone isn't dead, is it?"

"No," Audrey said, letting out another sob. "If my husband finds out..."

"Okay," Katie said, straightening. "He won't find out then. Tell me how I can help you."

Katie was a godsend. She offered to go with Audrey to the appointment, but she wanted to go alone. Instead, she asked Katie to keep her phone with her at work on the day of her appointment so she could go without Paul tracking her. She told him she was working an extra shift that day. She even gave Katie her passcode, in case Paul texted her.

When she arrived at the diner to drop off the phone, Katie wrapped her in a long hug before she could leave.

"You're doing the right thing, hun," she whispered. "You're making a choice only you can make."

Audrey squeezed Katie tightly, her whole body filling with a new-found sense of confidence.

Still, she sat in the car for several minutes when she arrived at the clinic, arguing internally with herself. She'd had to drive through a line of protestors to get to the parking lot in the back of the clinic, the gates of which were opened for her by two security guards, and closed just behind her. She kept her hood up as she drove. For all she knew, some of her acquaintances may have been in that crowd.

She made herself think about Paul as she worked up the courage to leave the car. Yesterday morning he'd been invited to give the sermon at church, an honor only occasionally reserved for one of the assistant pastors. He chose to speak on 1 Peter 3.

Likewise, wives, be subject to your own husbands, he'd read out loud. *And husbands, live with your wives in an understanding way, showing honor to the woman as the weaker vessel.* He'd then launched into a ten-minute rant about the evils of feminism, and women who claimed they could fill the role of men in their own lives, prompting a smattering of "Amen" from the other husbands in the crowd.

Men, if your wives are at the grocery store with their midriffs hanging out, that is your *moral failing as a leader. Your wife needs you to guide her in this life, as she guides your children. For just as Christ is the head of man, man is the head of his wife.* He smiled as he said it—radiant, charismatic, confident. Once, it would have made her toes curl.

She'd sat in that pulpit, dutifully listening to her abuser preach about godly masculinity, and she had to fight to keep her breakfast down.

It was a soft knock at her window that finally broke her reverie.

Audrey jumped, then rolled down the window to speak with the young woman standing there, smiling.

"Hello," she said sweetly. "Are you here to visit the clinic?"

She was holding a stack of papers Audrey couldn't see from her seat. She thought she must work there; but no, she was too young. Perhaps she was a volunteer, there to walk her in.

"I am," Audrey said, opening her door slowly so she didn't hit her and rolling up her window. She took the keys out of the ignition and stood, purse in hand.

"I wonder if I could talk to you for a few moments," the stranger said. She held out her hand. "I'm Sarah. And I want to tell you how deeply God loves you, *and* your baby."

Audrey looked up from her purse, where she had just dropped her keys, suddenly realizing what this was. Her eyes darted to the pamphlets, where she could now see a detailed image of a human embryo on the front and some sort of logo that was probably for a church. She must have climbed a fence to get in here.

"Did you know your baby already has a heartbeat?" Sarah said, interpreting her hesitation as a willingness to listen.

But Audrey wasn't listening. She was trying, unsuccessfully, to push down the sudden rage that kindled inside her. She curled her fingers around the handle of her purse, imagining how good it would feel to smack this girl right in the face. Sarah opened her mouth to continue talking, but Audrey spoke before she could.

"You poor fucking thing," she said, her voice surprisingly flat for all the emotion she felt.

Sarah blinked. "What?"

"You know, I used to be you," Audrey continued. "You're what, seventeen?"

Sarah stayed silent, but her expression told Audrey her guess was close.

"Kids your age are powerful," Audrey went on. "You have limitless energy and high expectations for yourself and others. You're smart. Opinionated. You feel invincible. The tragedy, Sarah, is that you're still very easy to manipulate." Audrey's rage was replaced with a sadness that settled in the pit of her stomach like a stone. "You have such good intentions. Such strong opinions. But you have no idea where they come from, or how they'll end up hurting you."

Sarah looked at her, her mouth open as if she was searching for something to say. But Audrey simply nodded behind her, toward the security guard now rushing over to escort her out, and walked away. Then she went inside and strode to the front counter, where she wrote her name on the patient list with a sense of calm determination and sat down.

Audrey looked casually at the faces of the handful of other women who sat in the waiting room. Some looked at their phones, a few read magazines. One simply looked at her hands clasped in her lap. They were all different ages, different races, and presumably different religious backgrounds. She wondered how many of them risked being ostracized from their families to be here, like her.

The receptionist called Audrey to fill out some paperwork. It was almost thirty minutes after she completed it that she was called back for a brief examination. The kind nurse who examined her explained it was only a preliminary exam, and that she could decline to see the ultrasound if she wanted to. She did.

Then they had a brief conversation about the nature of the procedure and what to expect. There may be some discomfort during and after. They would send her home with something for pain if she'd like. There may be some spotting. The nurse asked a few questions, including whether she'd like information about her other options before going ahead with the procedure. Again, she declined.

Then Audrey was sent into another waiting area, where she was given pills to soften her cervix.

"All that's left to do now is wait," the nurse said after she took them, and patted her hand.

So she waited, for almost an hour. Her eyes stayed glued to the game show on TV in the corner of the room, a stark contrast to the cold, clinical setting. Every time that nasty voice rose up in her head, telling her she was a murderer, that she was going to hell, she pushed her palm into her left arm—right on top of the bruise Paul's thumb left when he grabbed her last night and shoved her out of his way, grumbling about a pair of pants he wanted washed that she forgot to put in the laundry. He'd later apologized, blaming it on the exhaustion he felt from the pressure of conducting the morning service.

She thought of the little boy or girl who could someday be sitting in the family room, watching Paul push her, yell at her, criticize her, and think it normal. She thought of the overwhelming responsibility of caring for that child, of sacrificing everything for them. She thought of the choices she might have to make—to submit to Paul's every whim in order to maintain a safe home for her child, or incur his wrath by trying to teach her child to be different than him.

If she was being honest with herself (which she rarely was these days), she had never wanted a child *that* much. She just always assumed it would make her happy. Now, on the threshold of motherhood, the thought of such a life caused her agony. So, she thought, she may be making a decision that would ruin her life and damn her soul like so many people claimed, but she could not make any other decision.

When the time came for the actual procedure, Audrey took a few deep, steadying breaths and followed the nurse to another room. She gently talked her through everything that was happening. She was kind but not condescending. The doctor who entered the room a few minutes later was professional but not cold.

"Would you like to hold my hand?" the nurse asked before the doctor began. Audrey nodded, and took her offered hand.

Here we go.

It felt like a pap smear, but with more discomfort. Audrey closed her eyes and listened carefully to the voice of the doctor as she walked her through it, and to the nurse, who told her she was doing well.

It was almost over.

The entire thing couldn't have lasted more than ten minutes. Before she knew it, Audrey was headed back to her car with a prescription for an antibiotic and a printed sheet of aftercare advice. She read it thoroughly, then disposed of it at the nearest Walgreens, where she had her prescription filled.

She also bought the smallest box of maxi pads available and opened them in the bathroom, where she used one and stuffed three more in the inner pocket of her purse, disposing of the rest in the trash can and hiding her prescription beneath the remaining pads.

An hour later, she was pulling back into the parking lot of work. When she walked in, Katie spotted her immediately. She came over to give her back her phone.

"All quiet on the home front," she said cheerfully. Then, more carefully, "How are you feeling?"

Audrey thought about the question for a moment.

"I'm... fine," she said honestly, a note of surprise in her voice. "Thank you, Katie."

She was, fine that is, and it deeply surprised her. What she expected to feel was unrelenting guilt, grief, and shame. She had done the *big, bad, thing.*

The thing her entire church and family viewed as the violation of a holy commandment. The thing they hinged their entire political philosophy on. The thing she was forced to contemplate for hours on end as a child and a teenager, from the occasional sermon, to her church's annual pro-life rally in front of city hall.

She'd once tried to stage a *filibuster* at a mock Congress session during high school to talk about abortion. Everyone in her church thought she was some sort of folk hero when her father shared what she'd done during testimonies. They gave her an *actual* award for it at youth group. *She hung it on her wall.*

Now, she'd done it, and the only thing she felt was an overwhelming sense of relief.

As she drove home, that sense of relief grew, spreading out from her chest and filling her entire body. She hadn't realized how constantly tense she'd been for the past three weeks. In fact, she hadn't realized how tense she'd been for the past twenty years.

Of all the millions of things Audrey policed herself on throughout her life—all the desires, all the improprieties, all the potential sins—abortion was never one she worried she'd commit. It was so taboo, so reviled in her small bubble of Christianity that she had no doubt in her mind she'd never so much as consider it.

Yet there she was having *done* it. And there was very little doubt in her mind that she'd done the right thing.

The heavens hadn't split open. Her heart wasn't broken. She was tired and drained, and she wished she didn't have to do it, but it didn't feel like she was destined for hell.

Yesterday, it felt like she was destined for hell. This felt like the first authentic, free decision she had made in years. It sparked a simple yet powerful question in her mind.

What else could I do?

It was a question she pondered for the rest of the day, and the entire day after. With that one question, a new one was prompted. Then another and another. With each one came a new wave of relief. Like she was pulling needles out of her skin.

What else could I do?

Could I start a career?

Could I stop going to church?

Could I leave my husband?

And in answer to every question she asked, a small but hungry voice inside her said, *Yes.*

The next morning, Audrey got out of the shower just after Paul left for work and packed a bag. Then another and another.

With each moment that passed, she worked faster, almost frantically, as if he was going to walk in at any moment. She checked her phone every few minutes, her hands shaking as she pinpointed Paul's location on the map. She kept going, willing herself to calm down, so as to not forget anything vital in her rush.

When she was satisfied, she took her bags to her car and did a final sweep of the apartment.

She left behind many things. Clothes she never wore, decor picked by Paul and her together, absolutely anything related to housework or cooking aside from her favorite coffee mug and some disinfectant wipes. She took all her photo albums, the books she couldn't bear to part with, and the throw pillows her mother gave her when she left for college. Everything else felt fake, like carefully placed props in an IKEA showroom.

This wasn't her life. It never was.

Before she walked out the door, she looked back. She saw glimpses of the life she had chosen and lived for five years, and a piece of her grieved mightily. It cried out in protest, rage-filled at the promises it had been given that never came true. It clawed at her, desperate to find some way in which the life she dreamed of, the man she dreamed of, might be real.

But they were not. They were illusions, and she was done dreaming.

Audrey allowed the tears she'd held back all morning to flow freely now, and they built quickly into sobs that racked her whole body with sadness and regret. She cried more than she had in her whole life, expelling each tear like she was exorcizing a demon. When she was finished kneeling on the floor, her body weak and rubbery, Audrey calmly stood and removed her SIM card from her phone. She placed it on the counter, along with her key, and wrote a note:

I want a divorce. –A

Audrey felt strangely light as she drove to the bank and withdrew her entire savings. She still felt light as she got in her car and drove as far and as fast as she could, stopping only when her eyes cried out for sleep. For days she drove, texting her mother from a prepaid phone to let her know she was okay, using only cash, and never telling anyone where she was.

Paul's reputation depended on him being one of the "Godly men" he spent so much time talking about, and divorce was not part of that ideal. He would manage to spin her absence to favor him somehow, but not before he tried to track her down and drag her home. Her own parents would likely fund the whole expedition.

Audrey was determined to get very, very far away from Paul before she found a place to stay and a lawyer to send him divorce papers. She wouldn't let anyone drag her back.

And that was how the phoenix finally came to emerge from the chicken egg.

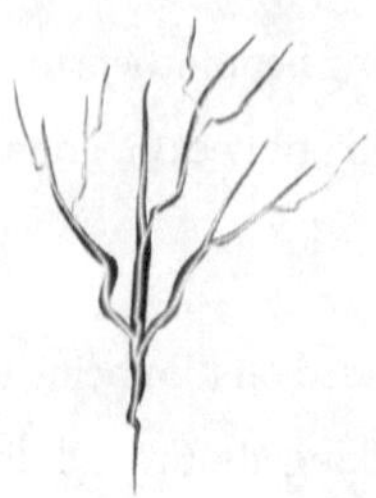

Once, she was asleep.

She had no awareness of how long she'd slept or even how long she had existed. In fact, the state of existence itself was wholly foreign, wholly new. One moment, she was not. The next, she was.

Sleeping, waking—to find herself in a cold, dark void.

She floated on invisible tides there for minutes, or days, or years. She knew not. She knew no time. Knew nothing but the dark, and the cold, and the will to survive.

Then, there was something... else.

It touched her, bumped up against her, and was gone. Beyond her own simple, primitive self-awareness, she experienced something other than herself for the first time. Its absence left her feeling something like loneliness, if such an emotion was possible for someone so small.

There it was again.

They touched, the slight friction between them becoming heat, the heat becoming energy.

And for each of them, a dark and lonely existence suddenly became something more.

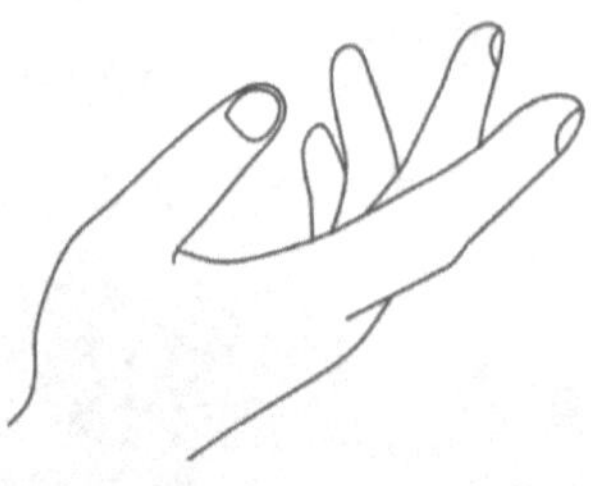

PART TWO

13

Audrey shifted on her three-legged stool, adjusting her hair using her phone's camera as a mirror. Her tall white bookshelf, arranged with careful aesthetic precision, served as her backdrop. When she was satisfied with her position, she turned on her camera's timer and took a deep breath.

Over the past several years, Audrey had developed a modest following on the social media app TikTok. She was 32 now, having fled her home and husband six years ago.

She started out singing covers and original songs, but now she split her content between music and what the men in her comments section usually called "angry feminazi rants." It was the latter content that finally caused her parents to stop speaking to her entirely.

"Until you've decided to stop this Godless nonsense online," her father had said.

"It's not only a sin, Audrey, it's an utter embarrassment," said her mother.

Her little brother Isaac, himself now a sophomore in college, was the only member of her family who still spoke to her.

The content began as a way to heal. She started reading voraciously after she left Paul, devouring authors like Gloria Steinem and bell hooks. She obsessively dissected the books she read as a teenager—books like *The Sacred Search*. When she started recording her journey of deconstruction, she began to understand she wasn't alone.

Sharing her voice, her songs, was joyful and empowering, but talking about her experiences in the church was like pulling off a bandaid. Wounds from her marriage, some scarred over, others still festering, were finally able to breathe.

Then, wounds from her childhood emerged. Soon she'd deconstructed almost every part of her life as an evangelical woman on-screen. The nasty comments and messages she received from Christians, more than a few of whom she used to attend church with, paled in comparison with the angry threats she got from Paul himself, always from a new dummy account.

Despite having re-married three years ago, Paul had never been willing to relinquish all vestiges of power over Audrey.

When her "godless nonsense" online turned into a huge following on multiple platforms and a small trickle of income on top of her job and her freelance graphic design work, that only made Paul angrier. Audrey tried for years to be the bigger person and ignore him, but when his harassment turned into live-streamed sermons where he projected their wedding photos and preached about adultery, she got angry enough to start naming names. That only made her following grow. Eventually, she quit her job to pursue content creation, music, and graphic design full time.

Audrey's parents had been deeply affected by her decision to leave Paul. For the first six months after she left they were in total denial, still sharing messages from Paul or calling her and trying to put him on the phone. She had to lie about where she was living for fear they'd put him in the backseat and deliver him to her themselves.

When the divorce papers arrived in the mail at Audrey's old home, her mother called her in absolute shock, demanding to know when exactly she'd lost her mind. It took another six months to finalize the divorce, at which time her mother reportedly stayed in bed for a week, grieving for the soul of her only daughter.

But it was her frank honesty about her life that hurt her parents the most. The years following her divorce were fraught with conflict between them, fluctuating from aggressive preaching, to outright hostility, and finally icy silence before the cycle started over again. It was only a year ago they gave up on her entirely, save for her mother's occasional emails filled with bible verses and photos of church events and the family cat.

After leaving Paul, Audrey ended up in New York City. She wasn't sure why she'd settled on going to New York, except to be as far away as possible from Paul. Once she started driving, it became almost a compulsion to keep going. She was, on some level, afraid that if she stopped for too long she'd simply turn around and go back. Perhaps driving to the other side of the country, stopping only when she stood dangerously close to broke, was a sort of defense mechanism. She stranded herself on an island of her own making.

Thankfully, she did not remain isolated there for long.

Just as Audrey finished recording her video, a knock sounded at her door.

"Come in," she said.

Ty opened the door and tossed a pile of mail onto Audrey's dresser.

"Hey," they said and leaned against the doorframe.

"Hey," Audrey replied, sliding off the stool to go look at her mail. "You just got home?"

"Yeah" Ty said, "But I have to go back in a few hours." They leaned their head against the wall in a sign of exhaustion.

Audrey whipped around to face her roommate.

"Are you serious? Again?"

"Third callout this week," Ty said, shrugging. "Oh, well. Let them get it out of their system before the construction starts. If I have to work a few doubles in the meantime that's fine."

Ty managed a popular restaurant in their Brooklyn neighborhood called Free Food that served food with only local or fair-trade ingredients—thus the name, and the prices. It was there that Audrey met Ty.

It was the second week of Audrey's life in New York City, and she was frantically looking for a job before she ran out of money. The dark colors and modern design of the building appealed to her, and Audrey walked in to find a gorgeous, sleek interior that immediately made her feel underdressed. Paper resume in hand, she approached the hostess to ask if they were hiring. They weren't, so Audrey walked back outside. She made it to the sidewalk before she slumped down against the side of the building, her feet aching.

She considered calling it quits to fill out applications online for a while, but typing her job history into her tiny phone screen over and over again was far worse than sore feet.

Besides, getting out and actually *doing* something made Audrey feel like she was in control, and allowed her to explore her new surroundings. It felt better than sitting in a dark hotel room staring at her phone.

"Excuse me," she heard from beside her.

Audrey looked up to find one of the most beautiful people she'd ever seen standing in front of her.

Ty wore a casual white suit with the sleeves rolled up. The pristine white contrasted with their dark brown skin and the blue shirt beneath the suit jacket. Their hair was buzzed short. They were tall and graceful, lithe but strong, built the way Audrey used to imagine angels were built. They were smiling at her, patiently awaiting her attention.

"Hi," she said.

"Hi. Were you just in there?" Ty asked politely, pointing to the restaurant.

"Yes," Audrey said. Then, "Oh, shoot, I can move if you need me to. I just needed to sit down for a minute."

When she moved to get up, Ty waved their hand, shaking their head as they said, "No, that's not it, you can sit here. I work here and I saw you inside. I thought for a moment I knew you. We haven't met though, have we?"

Audrey thought there *was* something familiar about them now that she really looked. She stood, trying to get a better view of the stranger's face, and realized they had two different colored eyes; one brown and one hazel. There was something in those eyes that put her at ease, as if she were looking into the eyes of a very old friend. But she was sure she'd remember meeting someone as striking as Ty.

"You are familiar," Audrey admitted. "But I don't remember ever meeting you."

"Do you live in the city?" Ty asked.

"I just moved here from California," Audrey answered. "Currently job hunting. Have you been to Redding before, by chance? That's where I grew up."

Ty tucked a hand under their chin, shaking their head. "Can't say I have. What brought you all the way here from California?"

Audrey hadn't been asked that yet. She didn't know if it was because she hadn't had a real conversation with anyone in two weeks, or because she immediately trusted the stranger before her, but she found herself telling the truth.

"I was running from my husband," she said simply.

Ty went still then, contemplating her, and put their hand out.

"I'm Ty Patel," they said.

"I'm Audrey," she responded, and took their hand.

"Where are you staying?"

"I have a hotel room paid up for the week," she said, her anxiety bubbling up at the thought of what she would do when her money ran out. "I'm... winging it, sort of."

Audrey thought she must have looked the part of a poor, desperate runaway when Ty then said, "Would you like some lunch? My treat."

Over the next several hours, Audrey and Ty got to know one another. Once she got past the sleek facade, Free Food's charming, friendly atmosphere relaxed Audrey. Its large windows opened to a view of the busy street outside, but the smell of bread and fresh roasted coffee made it feel simultaneously worlds away from the city.

Ty listened patiently as Audrey explained how she'd left, and why, and what she wanted to do now that she was gone.

"A little bit of everything," she'd said. "I feel like a dog let off its leash. I just want to *run*."

It seemed Ty had already done a little bit of everything. They grew up in a handful of different countries, including India, where their mother was from, and the U.S., where their father was from. Both were relatively well-to-do journalists who met while Ty's dad was working in Ahmedabad. Their work gave Ty the opportunity to live in places like Turkey, and Hungary, and Bangladesh all before the age of 18.

Ty had a Bachelor's degree in Hospitality Management and a Master's degree in Literature, but it was the former they had a career in because they loved "curating a space for people and watching them enjoy it."

The two of them continued trying to find out if they knew each other from somewhere, but to no avail. A few times, Audrey opened her mouth to speak, but realized she was about to say something like, "Remember that one time...?" But then she would stop, the fleeting thought suddenly gone, and she would shake her head, blaming it on her own exhaustion.

Of course, Audrey's soul was simply recognizing the souls of her friends from many lifetimes past, now happily united in a singular form.

"Amy was right," Ty said partway through their conversation when it turned to the subject of jobs. "There aren't any jobs here. But, I do know the owner of a bougie little cafe nearby who just lost a hostess." Ty took the last bite of their spinach feta quiche and wiped their mouth on a napkin. "I could probably get you an interview," they said through a mouthful of food.

Audrey nearly choked on her sandwich as she attempted to offer her immense gratitude.

"Ty, you don't have to do that," she said. "But oh my god, I would appreciate it."

Ty laughed, gesturing to one of the waitresses nearby to get a refill for Audrey's iced tea. "I'm happy to help. I feel strangely invested in your fresh start here in the big city. I feel like I've dropped square within the middle of a Lifetime movie." They paused to consider this, then clarified, "One of the sweet uplifting ones, not one of the murder ones."

Audrey snorted at that, covering her face to prevent tea from squirting out of her nose.

"Thank you, Ty," she said. "Seriously. I owe you lunch at the very least."

Ty waved the gratitude away as if this was just another Tuesday, and Audrey couldn't help but feel like she was watching a god grant a favor to a mortal. They had a striking energy—somehow grounded and serious, but buzzing with delightfully intense curiosity. Audrey felt drawn to them like they were a magnet. Ty, in turn, felt drawn to Audrey's bravery and enthusiasm.

A week later, Audrey landed the job, and she bought Ty lunch just like she said she would.

Ty was exceedingly happy for her, but also concerned about the hourly pay at which she was hired, and how it compared to her hotel rent. It surprised Audrey when Ty offered her the second bedroom in their apartment, causing tears to immediately fill her eyes. Ty insisted it simply made no sense to continue paying by the week for a hotel room, and that she would never get ahead that way. They weren't using the room after all, and Audrey could just stay until she got on her feet.

Ty had a certain penchant for strays. As a child they often brought home hurt or abandoned animals, much to their parents' chagrin. Once, when they were seven years old, they got off the school bus holding the hand of a small boy, then proudly announced to their parents that they had found a younger brother. It took the rest of the day for Ty's parents to figure out where the boy had come from and how to get him home.

It was natural, then, that Ty would want to help Audrey. Even without their cosmic bond, there was no better person Audrey could have come across.

What started out as a temporary situation quickly turned into an indispensable friendship for them both. Soon, Audrey was paying half the rent and spending every other holiday with Ty and their parents in Baltimore.

Audrey found herself surprised by how much she enjoyed domesticity when it was paired with mutual respect. Ty's apartment was warm, filled with eclectic art and fluffy pillows—a stark contrast from the cold, sanitized feeling of her home with Paul. She enjoyed caring for it and adding her own personal touches, which Ty welcomed. She even found herself enjoying housework. Rather than feeling like a burden, it felt like an act of love. She took on the tasks Ty had little patience for, like dishes and cooking, and in turn Ty handled the tasks Audrey hated, like cleaning the floors.

Audrey came to love Ty's warmth and hospitality, their love of art, and obscure music, and old books. Most of all, she loved their unflinching commitment to treating people with dignity. The two of them under-stood one another, accepted one another, and gently held each other accountable to be the best versions of themselves.

If Audrey still held on to the belief of an all-powerful God, she would have believed he sent her Ty.

"You found me yourself," Ty said when she told them this once. "Take the credit. You deserve it."

As the child of two kind and open-minded parents, Audrey found Ty an ally in her healing, never hesitating to point out when an expectation or idea she held about herself or the world was the product of her parents, or her husband, or their god. When Audrey found herself worrying about whether she was being too loud, too opinionated, too messy, or too vulgar, Ty would gently say, "That's the patriarchy talking, Audrey."

As much as Audrey owed Ty for the hand up at her most difficult point in life, the two friends saved each other. Ty had an anxiety disorder, and Audrey's presence was like medicine. She found her experience in the jaws of one monster or another (the church, her husband) to be useful in that regard. While she would never justify her abuse by saying it happened for a reason or served as part of some grand plan, she found her empathy and ability to work through difficult emotions heightened. When Ty was in the midst of an anxiety spiral, Audrey was skilled at reaching in and pulling them back out.

Audrey put a comforting hand on Ty's shoulder now, shaking her head. She could tell they hadn't been sleeping enough from the barely visible circles under their eyes. "I hope you know this means I'll be watching Westworld without you," she said with mock gentleness.

"You absolutely will not!" Ty said, shock plain on their face.

Audrey laughed and walked to the kitchen to make her friend a cup of tea.

"Of course not," she said. "It wouldn't be the same."

Once, she was an orphan. But she was not without family.

It was the four of them then, all children, feet dirty and hair tangled, surviving on the streets of an unforgiving city. She was called Ash in this life, a name given to her by her companions because of the soot that often coated her fingers.

Her parents died of an illness when she was barely old enough to walk on her own. Y—only a few years older and already orphaned themselves—heard her crying from inside her small, makeshift home. They peeked inside to find her alone, sitting beside the corpse of her mother. Without a second thought they picked her up and carried her home, to a dilapidated shack near the border of two adjacent worlds.

There, T was waiting.

T was called Tomas in this life, and was not an orphan but a runaway. He spent his mornings pickpocketing in New City Square, the only place where residents from both the old and new cities often congregated together. In the afternoons, he played lookout while Y doubled the coins he stole by playing games of skill or chance in Old City

Square. Y was called Ykara in this life, but Tomas called them *Yisul-uh*, a word roughly meaning "my other half" in the common language of their world.

Ash spent her days sifting through the incinerated remains of New City's trash, looking for gems or small bits of metal, or fishing. In their precious little free time, the three of them did things all children do—running, playing, and dreaming of a better life.

It wasn't until later that Z, in this life called Zaki after his father, joined their small family. It began with games, Ash and Zaki tossing a wooden ball to one another across the tracks that divided their two worlds. But the playmates longed to make other games—to run, and chase, and roll upon the ground. So he crossed the tracks, and soon he was spending hours each day playing and scheming with his friends, often arriving with food stolen from his household kitchen. When his mother scolded him for the dirt that covered his clothes and caked beneath his fingernails, he told her he'd been playing with the other boys—the other sons of policemen, noblemen, and dignitaries.

Once he arrived to find Ash sick, her body shaking with fever, and he ran home as quick as his feet could carry him to steal his mother's herbs and potions. He sat with her all day, and laid next to her all night, only falling asleep when he felt her fever break. When he returned home the next day, he received a lashing from his father for his absence, and several more when he refused to say where he was.

One day they strolled together through the Old City Square, Tomas and Ykara several paces ahead haggling with familiar vendors for cloth and other supplies. Ash and Zaki meandered slowly behind, their fingertips brushing against each other as they walked.

The noise began in the distance—bells, and trumpets, and incomprehensible shouting. Tomas ran ahead, weaving between bodies and disappearing into the crowd only to appear again several minutes later.

"*Yisul-uh*," he called as he approached, out of breath. "It's the army. They've surrounded New City Square. There's some kind of announcement."

Ykara took Ash's hand and held it tightly. "Come," they said, nodding to both Ash and Zaki. They made their way to the square, where crowds were now forming to hear the news. When it came, Ash felt the rift, reverberating through the crowd before it hit her, tearing her heart in two.

The King was dead.

He was killed by his army, who longed for an end to the fragile union between the two halves of the city. They longed to be separate, to thrive in peace away from the stench of the starving masses. They longed for the freedom to sentence Old City to a slow and painful death, cut off from luxuries like trade, travel, or arable land.

The noise of the crowd was deafening. Ash only barely heard the call from the men on stage to "Choose a side, choose a side *now*!" as men and women yelled, pushing, hitting, killing.

She felt Zaki's hand tighten around hers as Ykara gripped her shoulder, and she looked from side to side, panic setting in. The crowd was swaying, parting like the Red Sea, soldiers pushing and prodding with their weapons.

Before she knew it Zaki was being pulled away from her. She tore herself from Ykara to reach for him with both hands. His eyes wide, he held onto her, but the hands of one of his father's servants who recognized him in the crowd were stronger.

"No!" he yelled, and was gone, pulled away from her with the tide of the crowd.

"We must go," Ykara yelled. "We must run!"

So they did.

That night Ash snuck across the tracks, darting past soldiers who stood guard every few yards, her feet making a careful line toward the large cerulean home she knew was his.

Fire raged across the city, the plumes of smoke marking the boundary between rich and poor with eerie accuracy. She scaled the outer wall of his home, landing nimbly in a courtyard covered in climbing vines, flowers, and statues of men and animals alike. She paused for a moment, looking around her in awe at the grand adornments. She'd never seen anything like it.

Her admiration only lasted a few moments before a guard snatched her from behind, his burly arms wrapping around her in a vice grip that pushed the air from her body. He carried her, kicking and scratching, inside the house to a large room filled with men talking and yelling.

"I found this creature sneaking around the gardens," the guard said, and roughly threw her to the ground at the front of the room.

She looked up to find men, all richly dressed, all wearing looks of disgust or alarm—and Zaki, his face twisted in fear at the sight of her laying at his father's feet. He was dressed in fine clothes as well, clothes she didn't recognize.

"What are you doing here?" his father demanded. He was a large man, his voice deep and commanding. The look he gave her made a chill run down her back. "Are you here to take what is ours?"

Despite her fear, she stood and faced him. "I..." she stammered, her eyes darting to her friend and back to his father.

He caught the look.

"Zaki, do you know this... *child*?" He spat the word out like venom and turned on his son, a dangerous warning in his eyes.

Zaki looked back and forth between his father and Ash, his eyes wide and mouth hanging open. Ash realized with sudden clarity that he was terrified of his father, and an icy rage ran through her body.

"I came looking for bread," she said loudly. "This place looked like it might not miss a few bites of food." Then she stuck out her tongue, the rude gesture enraging Zaki's father enough that he disregarded the silent exchange.

As they dragged her away she caught sight of Zaki, his eyes filled with sorrow now instead of fear. Then they locked her in a dark, damp cage.

It felt like many hours before she heard a whisper.

"Ash? Are you there?" It was Ykara.

"I'm here," she whispered, her throat dry from weeping.

She heard Ykara's hands on the cage, then silence as they picked the lock. Finally, mercifully, a faint *click* and Ykara's hands were grasping at Ash's clothes. Ash fell into their embrace, relief flooding her body.

"You saved me."

"I will always save you, little sister." Ykara's hands stroked Ash's hair gently, then pulled away. "We must go."

Tomas was waiting outside the dark room in which she was kept, the lookout. He smiled when he saw her, then put his finger to his lips.

They snuck through dark passages and dimly lit rooms until they reached a kitchen. They left via the small door that led to the vegetable garden and scaled the wall. It wasn't until they were safe in their small home that Ash spoke.

"How did you find me?"

"Zaki found us and told us," Ykara said gently.

Ash smiled, filled with hope, but Tomas shook his head and put his hand on her shoulder. "He also told us you must never go back there, Ash. You must never see him again, or you'll be killed."

Ash, surprised she had any tears left, cried herself to sleep that night.

It would be nearly a decade before the two soulmates saw each other again. Ash was lithe and strong, no longer a girl but a woman—and a rebel.

Their small family quickly became part of something bigger when the King died. Mass starvation, rampant violence, and the stink of desperation touched everyone in Old City. For those it didn't tear apart, it brought them closer together—united by a deep, writhing fury.

Ash crept along the side of New City's capitol building, her fingers brushing the cool white stone until they found a divot large enough for a foothold. She wedged her foot in the dent, then found another, and another—imperfections put there days ago by their man on the inside, faintly illuminated by the light of the stars.

She reached the roof and located the chimney she knew would lead to the private quarters of the army's figurehead—once the private quarters of the King. She lowered herself carefully inside, inching slowly down toward a faint light, soot coating her arms and legs as she steadied herself against the narrow brick interior. Sweat coated her back, the summer heat amplified in the small space.

She landed softly behind the iron grates of the fireplace and pushed, slowly, her breath catching on every sound it made. When it was open enough for her to crawl through, she emerged to find a large bedroom decorated in rich reds and purples. A large, grand bed sat near its center, the curtains around it drawn.

Ash crept carefully across the room. She slid her knife from its sheath on her thigh and pulled the curtains back. The general slept soundly, drunk from the evening's festivities as she knew he would be. She took a deep breath, knowing the honor she was given by being assigned to this particular task, and plunged the knife deep into his eye.

"Sleep soundly," she whispered. "Murderer." Then she removed the keys from around his neck—keys that would unlock the prison cells of dozens of her comrades.

When she emerged into the hallway Tomas was waiting, the two guards stationed at the general's door slumped unceremoniously on the ground. She nodded to let him know the job was done. He nodded back, and they headed toward their exit.

"Are the charges all set?" Ash asked.

Tomas nodded. "The rest of the team is already out. Ykara is waiting to blow the lid off this place as soon as we leave." He stopped at an open window and peered outside. "*Yisul-uh,*" he called softly. They answered with a bird call. Tomas turned to look at Ash.

"After you," she said.

Tomas disappeared out the window, scaling the wall carefully as he descended. Ash watched, then froze as she heard the fall of footsteps behind her. When she turned and beheld the man who approached her, her heart stopped. Zaki's body had grown into a man's body, but his face was unmistakable, even partially obscured by his helmet. He was clothed in the colors of the New City Guard.

They remained frozen there for what felt like ages, just looking at each other. Her, covered in soot and the light spatter of blood, an empty sheath on her thigh—and him, the picture of propriety. More footsteps sounded, still far away, but approaching. Zaki's face twisted in something like anguish, his fingers twitching near his sword, and Ash prepared herself to die. Instead, he only whispered: "*Run!*" Then he turned and walked quickly down the hall.

Ash didn't waste time hauling herself onto the window ledge. Before he left her sight, she called to him softly. He turned.

"Leave the capitol," she said. "As fast as you can."

He nodded, and was gone.

Later that night, the rebels celebrated as flames spread from the broken capitol building to the surrounding areas of New City. Tomas and Ykara sat by the fire, holding one another tenderly in their exhaustion. The other rebels drank, ate, and staved off sleep a few hours longer.

Ash stood at the edge of the crowd, her eyes never leaving the flames, and prayed that one of her enemies survived.

14

"I don't like him," Ty said. "I know that's not what you want to hear, but I'm not here to make you feel comfortable. *I love you* and I will tell you the truth, Audrey. He's a piece of fucking work, and I can't believe you don't see it."

Audrey seethed.

Ty hadn't liked Lucas from the moment they met, and she knew it. They kept it mostly to themselves until this moment, aside from the occasional comment, seemingly because Audrey and Lucas were now starting to get semi-serious.

"I thought you'd be happy for me," Audrey bit out. "I thought you'd be glad to have your apartment back to yourself."

"You thought I'd be happy you're giving me back the *empty spare bedroom* so you can move in with a man who trades NFTs for a living?" Ty demanded, their face aghast. "The same man who asked you to make him a peanut butter and jelly sandwich last week so he could eat a snack on the walk back to his apartment from ours? NO, Audrey, I am not happy. You've worked too hard to get your confidence back after that shit-show husband of yours to just move in with another emotionally manipulative man-child."

"He's not emotionally manipulative," Audrey insisted.

She knew emotionally manipulative people. And they didn't look like Lucas, who was relaxed, and genuine, and didn't need everything to be perfect all of the time. They looked like Paul, and her father, and Alice from church who never gossiped, but always had very specific prayer requests for other people involving barely veiled details of their personal lives. They didn't look like Lucas.

"You know what I think," Ty said. "I think this is a reaction—an understandable one, sure—but a reaction nonetheless, to a certain someone having a baby."

Audrey pursed her lips in frustration.

It was true, Paul and his new wife announced their pregnancy a couple of months ago and it had rattled her. It shouldn't have mattered, she told herself, but it still felt like he was moving on to something new while she'd stayed firmly put in the same place for nearly seven years.

"That's not it," she said, her tone barely convincing. "I'm just...ready for something like this, Ty. I mean, I love you, and living with a roommate at 32 years old isn't necessarily a bad thing, but god..." She sighed, sitting down on the stool next to her. "Don't you ever get lonely?"

"I don't get lonely," Ty lied, crossing their arms. "I'm all the company I need."

"Well then you shouldn't miss me too much," Audrey blurted angrily.

Ty closed their eyes and pinched the bridge of their nose, releasing a short breath as they did.

"Audrey look, I know you're gonna do what you want to do," they said finally. "But I'm telling you, it's not a good choice. He's not *nearly* good enough for you, and I'd say that even if you weren't my best friend."

Audrey's eyes burned at that, but her hurt pride won out over sentimentality as she said, "Then you must not know me that well at all."

She stormed into her room and lay in her bed after that for what felt like a long time, silently thinking.

She stubbornly believed this was the logical next step. It was the one area of her life in which she'd made no measurable progress, in her view. She'd made some progress in her career—she had a decent-sized following online, a steady but not overwhelming stream of graphic design work, and she had even recorded a few original songs that were doing pretty well on Spotify. Ty was right, she had come a long way in terms of her self-esteem and mental health.

When Audrey first moved her belongings—nothing more than what fit in three suitcases and a duffel bag—into Ty's home, she was a mess. And the guilt—oh, the guilt ate her alive, even when she told herself she was doing the right thing. There was a voice in her head that wouldn't shut up, constantly reminding her how much she'd let her family down, how she'd ruined everything, that she'd given up on a relationship that could have been good again if only she'd tried harder.

As Audrey worked to shut that voice up, Ty accepted her at every step in her journey—the depressed phase, the angry phase, the "everything is exciting because I've never been free before" phase, the promiscuous phase, and the "men don't exist if I don't acknowledge them" phase. Ty was there to listen, to share, and to obsessively watch feminist documentaries with her. They encouraged her to deeply feel and embrace every single one of her desires and emotions—something she hadn't done since childhood.

Ty had not been as celebratory when a date with Lucas, the first man she'd really dated in almost two years, turned into several more dates. Then, a standing biweekly dinner at their place where she cooked. Soon she was sleeping at his place three nights a week. Finally, there was talk about moving in together.

Part of it was the fact that the two of them had only met four months ago. Mostly though, Ty just didn't like him.

But Audrey had never meant to stay in the same place for so long. In fact, she hadn't even meant to stay in New York for so long. Ending up there was the result of running as fast and far as she could from Paul, but it wasn't somewhere she imagined staying forever. She occasionally put herself out there for opportunities in other cities. Her dream was to work with an artist she respected, to be part of an album or some other project, but thus far she'd had no luck.

Moving in with Lucas may not have been a move across states for a dream gig, but it was *something*, and she was ready to scratch that itch. She started packing her bags that night, and was gone within the week.

Two months later, Audrey was finishing a bowl of Kraft macaroni and cheese on the couch next to Lucas. He had paused his video game just long enough to inhale his own dinner, and when Audrey stood to bring her bowl to the kitchen he passed his off to her as well and nearly tripped getting back to his gaming chair. She sighed and headed to clean the dishes before she retreated to the bedroom to continue watching Westworld on her laptop.

Audrey moved in with Lucas days after her argument with Ty, taking only the essentials with her in her rush. She told herself she would go back and gather what she left soon, but so far, she hadn't been able to bring herself to go. She'd barely spoken to Ty since then, but she couldn't stop replaying their parting words the day she left.

"Please don't go," they'd said.

But she went. Now, the guilt she felt for doing so ate at her. She could hardly think about Ty without crying, let alone call them up.

A nagging feeling pulled at her as she made her way to the kitchen. She should be making more videos. She was almost through her drafts folder and experiencing a serious creative slump that made the idea of writing a new song or crafting a clever feminist spiel feel like a gigantic burden. She just couldn't bring herself to do the things she normally did anymore.

Perhaps it was because it felt wrong to turn on her camera and talk to her followers about crafting their worth outside of the men in their lives when she was currently living with one who treated her more like a maid than a partner.

Singing was rather difficult when Lucas was always either sleeping or screaming into his Turtle Beach headset in the background. Asking him to be quiet for a minute was what she imagined asking the Pope to punch a baby would be like. Like she was asking the world of him. Singing while he slept only *woke* him, which was irritating all by itself.

She had to wait for him to leave the house to sing, and since he somehow didn't know how to shop for groceries without her holding his hand, that was a rare occasion indeed.

Tonight, Audrey felt a sense of quiet, resolved defeat that drove her to the bedroom and her waiting laptop with a large glass of wine in hand. Before she turned on her show, she opened TikTok and chose one of the few remaining videos from her drafts. It was a song she wrote on her way across the country after leaving Paul.

She'd spent two weeks traveling from California to New York. She would occasionally stop in a town or city that looked appealing so she could walk around, browse the classifieds, and imagine herself living there. She felt a sense of awe that a new path was opening up before her, one she never predicted or planned. She felt as if she was at the edge of a precipice, about to step out, not knowing where she'd land.

One night, in a small city in Nevada called Elko, she sat in her hotel room and turned all her roiling emotions into a song:

I'm on the edge of the precipice, I'm looking out

On the edge of a precipice, I'm looking all around

And I see all the things I miss, there on the ground

And the lips of people moving, but I can't make out the sound

On the precipice, I'm stepping out

And it's not what I thought it is, that's not what it's about

After all, it's not an abyss; it's just the clouds

And I know I can move through them if I make the leap right now.

She watched the video of herself singing the song, a lump in her throat forming as she thought about the feelings she had when she wrote it.

She willed herself not to think about how similar she felt right now to how she felt just months before writing that song. When she was still with Paul.

Thinking about it was just too hard. It made her so angry she couldn't see straight. Instead, she downed her glass of wine and hit Post.

The next morning, she woke up to the feeling of Lucas' body finally slumping into bed at 7 am. She lay there, listening to him snoring for a while before she was ready to move. As she did, she stared at the time projected on the ceiling, so eerily similar to the clock Paul owned.

She stared and stared, unable to move, as if she was literally stuck in the past.

It was after Ceiling Man went through at least twenty iterations that she finally got up and padded to the living room. She grabbed a bag of chips Lucas left out from the coffee table and absentmindedly ate them as she scrolled through her phone. She did that for a while, not really seeing anything on her screen, only keeping her eyes open out of habit.

Until she came across a picture of Ty. It was a selfie they took at Free Food's annual food drive fundraiser the night before. She had attended the event every year she lived in New York. It was one of her favorite nights of the year, actually, because Ty loved it. They loved the cause and loved an excuse to plan a party in their beloved restaurant. Audrey felt a pang of regret for not going. In fact, she hadn't even remembered it was last night until just now.

Spontaneously, Audrey opened her messages to text Ty.

Then she closed them.

Then opened them again.

Then closed them.

Then, finally, she sighed loudly and started typing. She said the only thing she could think of, the thing she hadn't allowed herself to think of for months, the thing that was eating away at her.

You were right. You're always right.

She hit send, then stood up to walk to the kitchen. She felt a bit lighter, as if sending the message had taken some sort of weight off her.

It had, in fact. Not physical weight, but something much more real. Much more important.

Using the additional energy she had from the slight reduction in grief, Audrey made herself a smoothie and sat down to watch re-runs of her favorite home improvement show.

She had only gotten through one and a half episodes when she heard a knock at the door. She stood and opened it, expecting to see a UPS employee or one of Lucas' friends, but instead there stood Ty, holding what looked like several black garbage bags and two bottles of kombucha.

Audrey froze, her mouth open, not even remotely ready to say all the things she needed to say. Then, before she could say anything at all, a sob escaped her lips, and she was suddenly in Ty's arms.

Audrey cried for a long time—so long Ty had to gently move her into the apartment and close the door. Her body shook with weeks of pent-up emotion, the most prominent being regret, anger, and a deep sense of frustration with herself. She was angry and embarrassed that she ended up right back in the arms of a man who didn't respect her, who saw her as a mother instead of his equal. She allowed her discomfort about Paul's life to drive her there, where she nearly forgot how to live her own.

"I'm sorry," she managed to finally choke out against Ty's chest.

Ty was stroking her head as they said, "It's okay. Everything is okay. Let's go home."

Audrey pulled away from their grip, taking a moment to look into her best friend's mismatched eyes. Her composure broke as she nearly gasped, "You came to *save* me."

Ty's composure broke as well, a tear escaping from their eye. "I will always come to save you, Audrey."

Audrey shook her head, continually in disbelief at Ty's consistency. "I should have listened to you, Ty."

"You were having a trauma reaction." Ty waved their hand, brushing it off.

"I know, but…" Audrey let out another sob. "You told me to leave, and you have no idea how much that means to me. When I was with Paul, no one *ever* told me to leave."

She thought of Zachary that night, standing at the bottom of her stairs with his heart in his hands, and closed her eyes to push out the thought.

"When we were married, I mean," she clarified. "Even the people who knew the real him, who knew how awful he was to me. They never told me I should leave. And that silence was powerful enough to keep me there, trapped, believing it was what I deserved. I waited and waited for someone to tell me otherwise. Someone like you."

Ty was crying now, too.

"You told me the truth, Ty, and I pushed you away for doing it because I wanted to feel like I was moving on with my life. But I don't want to move on if it means not having you as my best friend. I'll never not listen to you again."

Ty wiped at their tears and pulled Audrey in for another hug.

"I don't believe for one second you're going to never not listen to me again," they said gently, causing Audrey to shake with laughter. "But I will always be your best friend, through good and bad decisions alike. I know you'll do the same for me."

Audrey squeezed Ty tighter in confirmation, then pulled away to look at their face.

"How did you know, by the way?" she asked. "That I wanted to leave."

Ty gave her an incredulous look. "Audrey, 80% of your stuff is still at our place. I have two months' worth of your skincare products from Amazon still sitting in their boxes by the door. You didn't exactly paint a picture of radical commitment to this move."

Audrey snorted, every bit of tension falling away at Ty's honest assessment of her bad decision, and grabbed for the nearest garbage bag.

"Shall we?" she asked.

An hour later, Ty and Audrey walked out of Lucas' place. He slept deeply enough that she was able to pack up all her stuff without disturbing him. She wrote a quick goodbye note on the back of the grocery list. It said, simply:

Don't call me. -A.

Ty scribbled their own contribution, a rather brilliant sketch of a hand, flipping him the bird.

"Very mature," Audrey chuckled.

Ty grinned, offering a deep bow.

Audrey followed Ty's car out of the parking garage, feeling lighter than air. It was raining cats and dogs, but it might as well have been all rainbows and sunshine for how she felt. She stifled her laughter as she watched Ty pull out of the garage and directly into a large puddle, splashing a poor stranger who was walking with his back to them. She drove away, more carefully than Ty, before the stranger could turn around to face her.

Zachary, who thought walking in the rain on his way to work sounded like a rather romantic notion, was now soaking wet.

He shook his hands as if it would help, and muttered under his breath, "Fucking asshole drivers."

15

Audrey took a long drink of water, swishing it back and forth to cure her cottonmouth before beginning.

She was at a small recording studio in the back of Adriana Hernandez's apartment where she occasionally came to record her music. Adriana managed to convert her second bedroom into a recording studio two years ago, and Audrey was one of her first clients. Adriana was also her accompaniment, as she was brilliant on both the piano and the guitar. She could string together the perfect music to go with Audrey's melodies without making it look hard.

Today she was recording a song she wrote a week after she left Lucas and came back home to live with Ty. After a brief period of crushing disappointment and many attempts to make amends to Ty despite them saying she didn't have to, Audrey entered a period of deep self-reflection.

She knew precisely what had inspired her most recent bad dating decision. It wasn't Paul and his stupid adorable baby.

Okay, it wasn't *entirely* that. Yes, it bothered her, but not for the reasons Ty thought. It wasn't because she wanted to be married and settled down with a baby of her own, and it wasn't that she didn't want

Paul to be happy or moving on. In fact, she wished he'd move *entirely* on and stop talking about her.

No, she was bothered because she felt like she was running out of time. She came excruciatingly close to shutting the door on every one of her dreams before she left Paul. It wasn't just a life with Paul that made her leave; it was the image of every stage she'd never sing on, every person she'd never meet, every place she'd never travel.

When she finally left, her life seemed stretched out before her, inviting her to seize every moment for herself. Now Audrey felt like she could hear a clock ticking, accusing her of wasting the time she had. She had so many more dreams, so many more plans, and she feared she didn't have enough time to do them all.

The idea of anything permanent scared her. It made her feel trapped. New York was starting to feel a bit too permanent. So, she jumped headlong into the familiarity of another codependent relationship in an attempt to force change and convince herself she wasn't stuck.

That clearly hadn't worked but the fact remained, she felt a strong need to plan for the future. She had been casually putting herself out there for opportunities in other cities for a while, but she felt it was now time to take a more structured approach to her future. She started researching cities she might want to live in, connecting with other artists who lived in those places, and generally padding her resume.

Which included recording more songs.

So Audrey called Adriana and took out a chunk of her savings to pay for her services. She was recording two songs, affording her a whole day with Adriana sipping hot buttered rum and watching her at work. All she had to do was weigh in, and sing a couple songs.

The song she sang now was a product of her most recent reflections. She wrote it at her bedroom window, gazing at the leaves on the trees that were just starting to change color. She called it "Rhythms of Change."

Come wind, come wind, come wind

And carry me away

Carry me away

Come rain, come rain, come rain

And wash away my sin

Cleanse my aching skin

I need you to carry me to where I belong

I've let the winds of love and change

Carry me this way, that way, for too long...

After recording, Audrey and Adriana sat at her kitchen table, sharing a large cheese pizza. Adriana wore worn jeans and a New York Giants sweatshirt, its hood barely concealing her brown curls. There was a still, satisfied air between them, the kind that follows a hard day's work.

"We did good today," she said, reaching out to give Audrey a casual fist bump. "We make a good team."

"We do," Audrey said, returning the gesture with a grin. "I still don't know why you won't perform with me. It would be so funnnn."

Audrey had found a nice balance the past few years between making art and making money. Singing on TikTok and making singles had been a fun way to grow and build an audience. But the fact that she didn't have a band or someone to accompany her made it difficult to transition to performances on stage.

"I don't perform," Adriana said, putting her hands up. "I worked really hard so I could make money without leaving my house. I like it this way."

"Okay," Audrey said acquiescently. "I just thought I'd give it one more try."

Adriana gave her a smug expression. "I don't blame you."

Audrey laughed and ate the last bite of her pizza. "I have to go. Got a date with Ty."

"Tell them I said hi," Adriana said, standing to wrap Audrey in a hug.

"I will," she said. "Talk soon."

As she left Adriana's building, Audrey pulled out her phone to text Ty. *Leaving now. Be home in a half hour.*

It would only take twenty minutes to walk home, but Audrey needed to stop at a corner store on the way.

On their "date nights," Audrey and Ty binged their favorite shows or several movies, always with a drink in hand. The night would always end with reheated food Ty brought home from work, and then dessert.

They alternated each week who would be responsible for drinks and who would be responsible for dessert. It had become a sort of game, each of them occasionally opting for comfort fare, or trying to impress one another with something new.

Tonight was her dessert night. Last time she was on dessert duty, she ordered a small custom ice cream cake from a bakery in Queens. White cake, fudge frosting, and amaretto ice cream. Ty was obsessed with it. Tonight, she opted for something familiar and reliable: Oreos.

As she browsed the cookie section, debating between classic or mint, the bell at the front door chimed to signal someone else had come into the empty corner store. Audrey decided on both flavors, and headed toward the front counter at the same time the new customer headed toward the back in the adjacent aisle.

They passed one another, the wall of products looming high between them, and something stirred within both Audrey and Zachary. Neither of them knew their long lost love stood just beyond a 6-foot-high display of overpriced snacks, but their souls stirred nonetheless.

Zachary found himself thinking suddenly of Audrey.

This in itself was no surprise. He had thought about her often since the last time he saw her. It was the vividness with which her laugh rung in his ears that made him stop in his tracks. He nearly clutched his chest at the emotion it stirred in him to think about her laugh.

Audrey smelled a familiar mix of espresso and sawdust.

She paused momentarily, savoring the sudden memory of Zachary. As if he would be standing just behind her, she turned. There was no one. Zachary himself had already made it to the end of the aisle, and was deciding between chocolate milk or strawberry. He did in fact smell like espresso and sawdust, as he had considerable contact with both throughout the day.

Audrey paid for her cookies and was out the door before Zachary turned around.

I know, I know. Near encounters like this one are almost painful to watch. For if either had simply wandered to another part of the store, they might have seen each other, and I can say with confidence it would have been a wonderful reunion. But it simply wasn't yet their time. It was for the best. You'll have to trust me on this one.

When Audrey got home, Ty was sitting on the couch with two fancy-looking drinks ready. They were each garnished with a sprig of rosemary. Audrey wagged her eyebrows at Ty as she eyed the drinks, indicating her excitement. Then she held up the Oreos for them to see.

Ty sighed and put their hand on their chest. "You read my mind."

16

Audrey let out a shriek of excitement when she saw the newest Instagram post from her favorite indie band, Echo Roc.

The band, an alternative quartet with a bluesy, funky sound and a female lead whose voice made Audrey's toes curl, had just posted an announcement. Jenni Griffin, the aforementioned female lead, was stepping down from the band to devote more time to her education. The remaining three members—Cedric, Stan, and Ditya—were seeking a new lead vocalist. Open video auditions would be accepted for the next thirty days on their website.

This was Audrey's dream opportunity. She had admired Echo Roc for years. Jenni Griffin's rich, deep vocals combined with the band's unique sound and moving, cryptic lyrics were an intoxicating combination. Their latest album remained on repeat on Audrey's phone for four months straight after it was released.

In addition to having a great sound, Echo Roc had been moderately successful in the past few years. From what she could glean online, they performed locally at various locations in their hometown of Sedona, Arizona *at least* three nights a week, and traveled to larger cities like Phoenix and Tucson once or twice a month. One of their songs was recently featured in a box office movie, and a handful of their songs had gone viral. It was no wonder the members didn't want to let the band die with Jenni's departure; they were just getting started.

Having a near-full-time gig singing with a band was Audrey's dream. On top of that, Sedona seemed beautiful, trendy, and small. It was unlike anywhere she'd lived in her life. The desert's stark, desolate beauty lay in sharp contrast to Brooklyn's metropolitan streets, or Redding's suburban greenery. The idea of such a drastic change was tantalizing—it made her heart pound with excitement.

So she got to work.

Two days later, Audrey was in Adriana's studio wearing her favorite casual black dress with a brown leather belt. Her red hair was down, a carefully arranged curl popping against her dark clothes. She wore the amethyst necklace Zachary gave her so long ago. She tended to wear it for luck whenever something big came up, or when she was sad. She fidgeted with it anxiously now as she stood against the white backdrop Adriana constructed, waiting for her to count her in.

Adriana had arranged what she assured her were perfect conditions for capturing Audrey's voice on camera. Thankfully for her, she was a talented amateur videographer as well as a recording artist. Audrey thanked her lucky stars she knew her.

"Okay, you ready?" Adriana asked.

Audrey nodded and began breathing deeply. Adriana counted her in silently, and she began.

"Hi, my name is Audrey Anderson. I'm 33 years old, I live in Brooklyn, New York, and this is my audition for Echo Roc. I'll be singing one of Jenni Griffin's original songs, 'You've Got to Pay.'"

Audrey took another deep breath and began.

You've got to pay to be alive,

You've got to pay to be alive

I don't know what you've been told sister, but

This ain't no free ride

You work, and you work, and you work, and you work,

And someday, you'll have to pay to die

You've got to pay to be alive

You've got to pay to be alive

Not a single one of us was asked if we should be here,

But the toll man awaits when we arrive

Doesn't matter if you're bleeding, get to grieving, no more sleeping,

Got to please the boss if you want to survive...

After three takes, both Audrey and Adriana were satisfied with the finished product. After paying Adriana and hugging her fiercely, Audrey drove home, wanting to show Ty before they left for work.

But when Audrey got home, Ty had already left. She texted them.
Did you leave for work early?

Ty texted right back: *Remodel stuff.*

Free Food's long-planned remodel had begun a week ago after many unexpected delays, and it was keeping Ty busy. Not that they complained. In fact, Ty seemed to enjoy going to work more than ever. Audrey suspected a bit of change was good for both the restaurant *and* its manager. As good as Ty was at their job, they seemed restless lately—bored, even.

Audrey was tempted to wait until she saw Ty to submit the audition, but she couldn't. She stopped only long enough to pee and then headed to her room where her laptop was waiting on Echo Roc's website. She found the application, filled in the basic information about herself along with a brief bio she'd spent hours crafting the night before, and uploaded her video.

She didn't allow herself to second guess it before hitting submit.

Audrey sat, staring at the confirmation page, for several long moments before allowing herself to squeal in delight. She knew that hers would be one of many submissions, but she felt giddy optimism nonetheless. Many of the other opportunities she threw her hat in the ring for felt like they weren't right for her, but her voice was perfect for Echo Roc's style. She hoped the fact she submitted early on with a high-quality video would make her stand out among the competitors.

She sighed at the thought of singing on stage with a real band, and real people watching her without a screen separating them.

Her thoughts drifted to her junior recital, and Zachary's rapt attention on her as she sang "Age of Reptiles." Her heart ached slightly as she wished she could tell him what she was doing now. Ever since she'd left Paul, she'd gotten into the habit of typing Zachary's name into her

Instagram search bar every few months, but always to no avail. He still wasn't on any social media platforms.

She wished she could tell him sorry.

Audrey wandered around the apartment for a while, snacking on chocolate-covered almonds and staring out the window, pondering what she should do with the rest of her afternoon. Finally, she couldn't contain herself. She was proud, and excited, and she wanted to celebrate making a step in the right direction.

She was also exhausted. She felt like she'd been holding her breath all day long, and now that the deed was done, she wanted a drink. But she didn't want to drink alone.

She texted Ty.

Is it busy? I just submitted that application, and I can't celebrate properly without you. :(

It took a few minutes, but Ty texted back: *Come here!!*

Audrey put her coat back on and left.

Before she even walked into Free Food she could see the large white sheet that blocked off an entire half of the restaurant, concealing the mess behind it. Ty told her they would be in the work zone when she arrived, and to walk right in. She did, carefully moving the sheet and stepping around a large toolbox on the ground.

Beyond the sheet, half the restaurant had been laid bare. It felt surprisingly large inside without the tables, and even the bar near the window had been torn up. A few men stood where it used to be, hunched over a large paper with their backs to her. Audrey noticed Ty in the corner of her eye, and she turned to see them walking toward her with two glasses of champagne.

"It's been way too long since you came here to drink in the middle of the afternoon," Ty said, maneuvering around the debris to a folding table that had been set up near the center of the room. "Come show me that video."

Audrey opened her mouth to reply, but stopped short at the sight of Ty's shirt.

"What the fuck is that?" she said quietly.

Ty followed her eyes to the white t-shirt and scoffed. "What, you don't like it? It was a gift, so I could be in this dusty ass room without getting my suit covered in sawdust."

Audrey couldn't believe her eyes. There, on Ty's shirt, was an Italian Savonarola chair. Beneath it were the words "Peters Design."

Ty's face fell suddenly at her expression. "Audrey, you okay?"

Audrey realized she wasn't breathing. She let out a breath finally, tearing her eyes from Ty's shirt and forcing herself to speak.

"Peters Design," she said.

Ty looked at the shirt as if to confirm, then nodded. "Yes." They gestured toward the workers, who were still talking over what looked like blueprints. "That's the company we hired to do the remodel."

"Is there..." Audrey hesitated, a small part of her wanting to run out of the room. "Do you know someone named Zachary?"

Just then, one of the men standing across the room turned. The *thud* of a tape measurer hitting the ground caught Audrey's attention, and she turned her head.

"Cherry Bomb?"

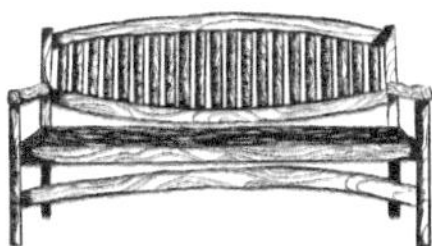

Once, she was walking in the park.

She often walked there on the way to work, but yesterday she lost her job. Even so, she found herself walking there, only an hour later than she normally would.

The flowers smelled sweeter that day than they had the day before. They seemed to turn their heads toward her as she walked by, and she winked at them. She felt a strange sort of giddiness at having the freedom to walk in the park past 10 am on a weekday.

She decided to pretend she was rich. After walking for some time, she had developed an entire backstory in her head.

She was a wealthy widow, her husband gone much too soon. Now she had nothing but wide open days to walk in the park, wondering what to do with all her money. The street cart bagel she carried in her pocket was nothing more than the occasional nostalgic indulgence in commoner life. She was, after all, just a little girl from the poor side of town at heart. Her enormous wealth had hardly changed her.

After entertaining her daydream for some time, she sat down on a bench and watched the birds. Occasionally, she threw bits of bagel to them, whistling softly as she did.

She was surprised when the dog approached her. He ran up from behind when she was distracted watching the birds. They skittered away when he appeared, panting and wagging his tail. He was a medium-sized dog, brown and black. A mutt. And very excited to see her.

"Well hello," she said, putting the bread back in her pocket. She scratched his head softly and he pressed his face into her hand, asking for more. "Where did you come from?"

She checked the tag on his collar, which had a number and an address as well as a name.

"Zig?" She laughed. "Your name is *Zig*? Well nice to meet you Zig, I'm Amanda."

Zig sat down and barked once at her. Amanda studied the dog as she pet him, wondering what it was about him that was so familiar.

"Have we met?" she asked.

Zig wagged his tail.

"Ah, I remember now. Tenth grade. Mrs. Baughman's class. You were the one covered in fur, weren't you?"

Zig licked her hand.

"Zig!" someone yelled from behind her. "Zig!"

Amanda turned around, pulling her long red hair out of her way as she did. The man yelling was jogging in her direction, a leash dangling from one hand.

She waved her hand at him. "He's over here!"

The man, relieved, slowed his pace as he approached her. He was tall, balding, but handsome with dark eyes and brown skin. When he got closer, he smiled. It was a nice smile.

"I'm so sorry," he said to her between heavy breaths. "He hasn't run from me like that in years. I don't know what got into him."

"Oh that's fine. We were getting along well." She reached her hand out to the stranger. "I'm Amanda."

"Amanda," the man repeated, taking her hand. "I'm Dominick. It's nice to meet you."

"You too," Amanda said, giving Zig another scratch behind the ears. "Zig and I were just agreeing we've definitely met somewhere before."

"Is that right?" Dominick seemed amused, and knelt down to re-attach his leash to the dog's collar. "Have you compared where you've lived and traveled yet? We could make a list."

Amanda laughed. "No, we tried that already. Perhaps it was in a past life, huh Zig?"

Zig stood up on his hind legs and barked at her, loudly.

Amanda's surprise showed on her face, and Dominick laughed.

"Well then, that's it," he said. "He just ran off to see an old friend."

Amanda chuckled and deftly placed her hands in her lap as Dominick and Zig prepared to leave. Before they left, Dominick hesitated, awkwardly turning toward her.

"Perhaps you two ought to catch up?" he said tentatively. "I'd love to buy you a cup of coffee—if you have the time?"

"Sure," Amanda said. "I have the time."

And the three of them lived happily ever after.

17

"Zachary?"

Audrey briefly considered the idea that she was in a dream. There before her stood the paradigm to which she had silently compared every man she'd ever dated, fucked, or flirted with. Her best friend. Her greatest regret.

There stood her soulmate.

He looked largely the same—his hair had the same defiant curl at the ends, his smile the same crooked slant. His short boxed beard was considerably more filled out, and she could see a few strands of silver standing out against his brown hair. His shoulders seemed broader under his denim Carhartt work shirt—he was less lanky, more muscled. And his eyes, Audrey could tell even from a distance they held the same gentleness and mischief they always had.

For a brief moment, Audrey felt a sense of panic. The last time she saw Zachary he kissed her and walked away, and she drove off into the metaphorical sunset with Paul. Never seeing him again was one of her greatest regrets.

What if he was angry with her?

Then Zachary let out a loud "HA!" and ran to her, enveloping her in a hug.

"Audrey," he breathed, saying her name like it was a prayer.

Instantly, Audrey's anxieties melted away. She pressed her cheek into his shoulder, his head resting atop hers in the most familiar way. He smelled like espresso, and sawdust, and some kind of musky cologne.

They held each other tightly and stood there for a long while in silence, simply holding on. Each of them felt a piece of their souls go quiet, as if they had been crying out for home and were now finally settled.

You'd be surprised to learn just how accurate such a metaphor can be.

Audrey realized after a while that tears were falling steadily from her eyes. She moved to wipe them and Zachary stood back, his hands on her shoulders as if to appraise her. His eyes darted around her face, shining with something like disbelief.

"Audrey," he said again. "It's really you."

"It's you," Audrey said, straining to keep her voice from breaking.

"What are you doing here?" Zachary asked, finally letting go of her shoulders.

"I live here," she said. "I mean, I live nearby. Ty," she gestured to Ty, who was still standing near the folding table about ten feet away watching the scene with rapt interest. "Ty is my best friend. We live together. I was here to see them. What are *you* doing here? I mean, not here in this room, I can see what you're doing in this room, obviously. But what are you doing in New York?"

Zachary chuckled at her nervous rambling and said, "I moved here about eight months ago. Needed a fresh start."

"Me too," Audrey said. She noticed Zachary's eyes dart subtly to her ring finger, and she clarified, "I left Paul. Almost eight years ago."

The declaration hung in the air between them. Audrey could have sworn she saw Zachary's shoulders relax a little, and his smile deepened with something like relief.

Before he could speak, Ty interrupted them.

"So," they said, walking toward them finally. "I take it you two know each other?"

Audrey turned her attention toward her friend. "Ty, this is Zachary."

Ty's expression said something like, *I know, I hired him.*

Audrey gave Ty a look. It was one she hoped said, *No, this is THAT Zachary. THE Zachary.*

Ty must have read the urgency in her eyes because their own eyebrows rose in response.

"Ohhh. *Zachary.* From Windmills." Ty let out a huff of laughter, looking at Zachary as if they were seeing him for the first time. "The same Zachary that's been ripping up my bar and making me laugh every day is *your* Zachary, Audrey?"

Audrey blushed at the way Zachary smiled when Ty said "*your* Zachary."

"Yep," she stammered. "M-my Zachary."

She felt like she was eighteen again, her heart fluttering nervously at his unexpected presence.

"Well then," Ty said, turning to retrieve the two glasses of Chardonnay and holding them out. "I'm just going to leave you two here and go check on a few things. You go ahead and toast without me."

With a subtle smirk in Audrey's direction, Ty was gone.

Audrey was left standing with Zachary then, awkwardly holding a glass of Chardonnay between them.

"What are we toasting?" Zachary asked.

"Oh." Audrey was suddenly brought back to reality. "Right. I just applied for a gig I'm really excited about, that's all. It's sort of a good luck toast."

Zachary's eyes brightened with interest. *God, how she'd missed that look on his face.*

"What kind of a gig?"

"A singing gig," she said, smiling at him. "New lead singer for a band I love. Kind of a long shot since I'm likely one of hundreds to apply, but it felt good to throw my name into the ring."

Zachary's grin twisted with pride, and he held out his glass to toast her. "Well, I'd say today seems like a good day for long shots."

Audrey and Zachary barely had time to toast before a "carpenting" emergency pulled his attention reluctantly away from her. He lingered, unable to walk away for several moments before he said,

"Can we have coffee? Soon?"

Audrey almost sighed at the slight plea in his voice. He looked and sounded as if he was afraid she'd disappear if he took his eyes off her for too long. It warmed her and crushed her all at once.

"Tomorrow?" she asked.

"Tomorrow."

They planned to meet after lunch at Audrey's favorite coffee shop, which apparently had become one of Zachary's favorites as well since he moved to Brooklyn. She wondered how she had never run into him, but remembered that her work-from-home lifestyle had her sleeping until ten or eleven o'clock most days, while Zachary probably arrived at a job site early in the morning.

The next morning, however, Audrey was wide awake at 8 a.m. She spent the entire morning in knots, bouncing between random yoga poses to calm her nerves, and organizing the kitchen drawers. At 10:30, having nearly gone crazy, she decided to go for a run. By the end of it her exhaustion and need for a shower lulled her into a calm focus that lasted until she had her makeup on and was standing in front of her full-length mirror, deciding what to wear.

That was when the nasty little thoughts began. Her hair seemed somehow duller than it had been when she was young. Not so fiery; more like red sand. She was also considerably heavier, her thighs thicker, her stomach large and soft instead of flat and muscled. And while she adored this body she'd been lovingly nourishing after a lifetime of self-deprivation, she wondered if Zachary would feel the same.

She shook her head, trying to knock the thoughts out of her brain. She had no clue if Zachary even thought of her that way anymore. She willed herself to go into the day with no expectations. For all she knew, today was the first day he'd even considered her since the kiss.

Nothing could have been further from the truth. Zachary, who had arrived at the coffee shop thirty minutes early to make sure they had a seat, was currently pondering just how much he'd thought about Audrey in the past twelve years. Daily, at first. Hourly, really. After what seemed like a very long time, only weekly. Eventually, her face popped into his head every month or so, and only occasionally he woke up crying when she came to him in a dream.

As Audrey was at home considering her love handles, Zachary was thinking she was far more beautiful than he remembered.

Everything he loved about her was still there—her green eyes that usually held a look of wonder or determination, her contagious smile, her warm, buzzy energy. She was the girl he remembered, to be sure, but she was a woman now.

The years since he saw her were etched into her face, clinging to her frame, and he thought they looked wonderful, intriguing. The only other consideration he gave to her body was how peaceful he felt with his arms wrapped around it.

Zachary stood when Audrey arrived so she could see him at his table in the corner. When their eyes met from across the room, a rushing feeling swept through his body, and suddenly he wasn't sure if he was actually standing or simply floating above the ground. As for Audrey, she had to bite down the impulse to actually run across the shop to him. Her feet felt awkward as she attempted to walk at a normal human speed to the back of the shop.

The two of them fell into an easy embrace when she reached him that calmed both of their nerves. When they let go, Zachary gestured for her to sit down.

"I'll go order," he said. "What are you having?"

"An iced white grasshopper," she answered. She had become addicted to the white chocolate mint lattes recently.

A few minutes later Zachary returned with her drink and an iced americano for himself.

"So," he said after a short pause. "Where were we?"

Audrey and Zachary caught up with one another's lives over the next two hours, each of them transitioning from coffee, to scones and tea, an hour into the date when they realized neither of them wanted to leave.

Audrey filled Zachary in on what she'd been doing for the past decade, carefully avoiding any mention of Paul. He listened with a concerned interest she realized she'd desperately missed. When she talked about her modestly burgeoning musical career he beamed at her, and asked thoughtful questions.

She blushed when he said, "I told you they'd love you."

Zachary loved listening to her talk about music. It lit her up from the inside. He thought about how beautiful she was when she talked, kicking himself for never being on social media, because apparently she was kind of a TikTok star now? He made a mental note to download the app when he got home. And though he was extremely curious about what happened with Paul, he noticed her avoidance of the topic and didn't ask any questions.

Then she asked him about his own career, and Zachary filled her in on the long string of temporary jobs he had after moving back to Omaha. They eventually led to him starting his own company with the money he'd saved. Peters Design started out as just him, designing and creating furniture and art for local businesses. Eventually, it grew enough for him to hire a small crew and start doing larger projects, like the one at Free Food.

"I can't believe you really used that logo," Audrey chuckled.

"I told you I would. And to be honest, it's been a serious good luck charm. People remember it." He took a thoughtful sip of his drink, then said, "I know we said no lawyers. But I'm willing to make a deal if you're looking for a cut of the profits."

He winked, and Audrey laughed.

She used the pause in conversation to bring up the question that had been nagging at her all morning. With an effort to conceal the warble in her voice, she asked,

"So... are you seeing anyone?"

"No," Zachary said. "Not since I moved. I was seeing someone in Omaha, but it didn't work out. You?"

"Nope," she said, biting her lip to keep a gigantic smile from forming on her lips. Zachary made no effort to hide his own wide grin.

The two of them sat in comfortable silence for several minutes, sipping their drinks. Audrey was thinking about how relaxed she felt. It seemed like she'd constantly had a headache of some kind for the past six months, but it was suddenly absent sitting here with Zachary.

"Did I ever tell you what I thought the first time I met you?" he asked.

Audrey put down her drink, her curiosity peaking.

"No, I don't think you did."

"As soon as I saw you, I almost laughed out loud."

"*Laughed*?" Audrey said incredulously.

"Not *at* you," he chuckled. "I almost laughed because I thought you were someone I knew. My immediate reaction was to jump over the counter and hug you like you were an old friend I hadn't seen in years. But then I realized I had no idea who you were."

He was silent for a moment, swirling his drink, his face pensive. "It was strange to have that feeling again. Yesterday, I mean. Except, this time, it was true."

His eyes met hers and a sort of heaviness formed in the air between them that made Audrey's breath come in short bursts. Almost everything between them felt the same, but this feeling—this was something altogether different. It felt like the beginning of something wonderful.

It was.

After they'd both had their fill of drinks and scones, Zachary offered to walk the few blocks to Audrey's apartment with her. She accepted, and they walked in amiable silence for a while. Audrey imagined what it would be like to reach out and grab his hand. She still wasn't sure if that invisible wall that once sat between them was truly gone.

They reached her complex and Audrey turned to look at Zachary. The image of his younger face, crumpled in devastation as they said goodbye, flashed in her mind. She sighed. She needed to get something off her chest.

"I'm sorry, Zachary," she said, partly to the man before her, and partly to the boy he once was.

Zachary's brows furrowed. "For what?"

Despite her best efforts, Audrey's lower lip trembled slightly.

"For leaving and never speaking to you again," she said. "I wanted to. But Paul pulled up to a Verizon Wireless one day after lunch, and the next thing I knew we were getting a joint phone plan. I just sat there while Paul handled everything, and when he told her not to port our old numbers *or* our contacts, I was so caught off guard I didn't know what to say. A week later when I finally worked up the courage to ask him where my old phone was so I could get my contacts, he just said it was gone, without any explanation."

The words were pouring out of Audrey, and she realized it was the first time she'd really talked about that process of isolation Paul put her through—slowly severing her old ties, separating her from her old friends, even from some of her family.

"And then I finally worked up the courage to go see you, but... you were gone." Tears were steadily streaming down her face now.

Zachary closed the distance between them, wiping the tears from her cheeks with his thumbs and cupping her face until her eyes were looking directly into his.

"No," he said softly, shaking his head. "You don't need to be sorry. I should have had the courage to remain your friend, no matter what. I should have found a way. I should have snuck in through your window every day so we could argue about movies and religion, and brought you seasonal lattes and egg salad sandwiches. I thought it would be too painful, so I didn't even try. I've always regretted it."

Something heavy in Audrey's chest suddenly melted away. Zachary had felt regret and loss all this time. She wasn't alone in that—wasn't alone in how badly she'd missed him. And he didn't blame her for pushing him away. It felt like a thick, black sludge fell from the walls of her heart.

She no longer had any reason to hold herself back from loving this man before her. She had no husband, she had no god, and she no longer had any fear. The wall was down, and with it, a heavy spiritual burden.

Suddenly lighter, Audrey practically floated onto the balls of her feet, and kissed him.

And for both of them, the world momentarily stopped turning. For in those rare moments when humans are aligned with their higher selves, time itself has no meaning.

18

Audrey woke slowly. Her body was deeply comfortable, her brain still foggy with sleep. She had just been in a delicious place, but the memory of it was already slipping away from her.

She longed to fall asleep again, to go back. But as she became aware of the arm draped around her waist, she happily accepted her return to the waking world.

She laced her fingers into Zachary's, pulling his hand toward her chest as she inched backward into his. He responded by making a happy, sleepy noise and tightening his embrace. They lay like that for several minutes, his face buried in the back of her neck, her legs intertwined with his.

Zachary began to kiss her neck then, slowly, moving to her ear and then upward to her temple. His hand traced soft lines from her stomach to her face, slowly drawing his fingers over her skin in a long, lazy pattern.

As Zachary's lips moved from her neck to her shoulder, his hands from her stomach to her thighs, Audrey was ushered slowly back into an awareness of her body. She began to respond to his touch, her back arching, her head twisting to grant him access to her lips. She reached her hand back, threading his hair through her fingers and gently pulling.

"Zachary," she whispered.

Zachary needed no more prompting than that. In one swift move he untangled himself from the bedsheets and hovered over her body, his lips moving swiftly from her neck, to her torso, and finally between her legs.

"Audrey," he breathed against her, making her shudder. He then proceeded to spend the morning worshiping her, like the goddess he knew her to be.

Afterward, the two lay tangled together for a long time. Audrey turned and laid her head on his shoulder. He ran his hands up and down her back tenderly. Every so often, he kissed the top of her head.

"Breakfast?" he whispered, breaking the period of silence.

Audrey squeezed his hand and mumbled her agreement. He unraveled himself from her, kissed her lips tenderly, and wordlessly left the room. Audrey didn't follow right away. Instead, she adjusted her pillow to more easily watch Zachary's bare, graceful body saunter from the room, and closed her eyes again.

It had been three months since Audrey kissed Zachary on the sidewalk by her apartment. Nearly every day since, the two of them had been together. The pieces of themselves that used to mesh so well fell into place almost immediately. The conversation, the laughter, the mutual support—it was all still there.

And they spent as much time as possible finding new ways in which they fit together.

In fact, about half of their time was spent searching one another inside and out, trying to unearth whatever was new, unknown, and unexpected. They devoured one another's stories and listened intently to new ideas or perspectives, each of them marveling at every new bump or scar they found.

When they were not reacquainting themselves, they were making up for lost time. They watched all the old movies they used to talk (or argue) about, ate each other's favorite foods, and reminisced about the good old days as much as possible.

It was the perfect balance of old and new, a bridge between two of Audrey's happiest periods of life. She felt it healing wounds she had long neglected—wounds of regret, loss, and things never said.

She woke again to the smell of something cooking. A glance at the time told her she'd only been asleep for ten minutes or so. The large cedar clock on the wall, which was carved into an intricate mandala by Zachary himself, showed it was almost 10 am.

The clock was just one of the many personal projects Zachary had around his home. Audrey felt giddy being there, enjoying him in his personal space instead of surrounded by coffee shop patrons. The wooden carvings, antiques, and old furniture all reflected his inquis-itive personality. And just above the fireplace was the original Peters Design logo in a simple black frame.

She sat up and stretched, then made for the bathroom to pee and throw on one of Zachary's t-shirts. When she emerged, she was pleased to see Zachary hadn't bothered to get dressed before he started cooking breakfast.

She enjoyed this leisurely version of Zachary. A few weeks ago, they were stealing moments together on his lunch break as he and his team pushed to finish the Free Food remodel before Christmas. They did, and now Zachary had plenty of time on his hands before the next job started. Free Food was already busier. The funky wooden accent walls and migrating bar brought in new customers for the Instagram photos alone. The restaurant's interior, in contrast with its former sleek, extravagant feel, was now warm and cozy while still retaining its class.

She wrapped her arms around him from behind as she approached, peeking past him at the stove.

"What's this?" she said.

"I'm making those crepes from that video you liked," he replied.

She smiled in surprise, straightening. "How did you know I liked it?"

Zachary laughed. "You practically climbed into my lap to watch it after you saw it over my shoulder, and you slapped my hand away when I tried to skip to the end."

Audrey snorted and kissed his cheek, then poured herself a cup of coffee. No sooner had she sat down than Zachary placed a plate of cranberry crepes in front of her.

"M'lady," he said as he set her plate down. "Your seasonal breakfast."

Audrey caught his hand before he pulled away, leaning forward to kiss his fingers.

"Thank you."

"Merry Christmas Eve, Audrey."

"Merry Christmas Eve," she said, biting her lip to tame her smile. Seeing him there, hair disheveled from sleep, bits of flour decorating his bare abdomen, made her stomach do flips, and she almost abandoned her crepes so she could drag him back to bed.

Audrey had been spending an inordinate amount of time at Zachary's apartment, a fact Ty didn't complain about only because they had been spending an increasing amount of time with their new girlfriend, Sofia. Sofia was a lawyer and a regular customer at Ty's restaurant. The two of them took up a casual flirtation shortly before Audrey and Zachary were reunited, which eventually turned into casual sex, and was now firmly in the relationship category.

Two weeks prior, Audrey and Ty ran into each other in the kitchen of their apartment. Audrey was just leaving, her duffel bag filled with fresh clothes, and Ty was just coming in after work. They fell dramatically into one another's arms, as if it had been years since they'd seen each other and not four days.

Ty happened to be on the edge of an anxiety attack when they came home. Apparently, the remodel was a pretense to sell Free Food to a new owner, now with a higher price tag. Ty, upon seeing Audrey, spilled over with fears about what it might mean, whether they would keep their job, and what else could possibly be changing.

"I thought the change was over, Audrey," they said. "I got through the remodel, I kicked ass, and somehow kept business steady through the whole thing. And then I felt this sense of accomplishment and relief when it was all over. But now I find out it's just the beginning. What if these new owners are assholes? We worked so hard on the new menu this summer, what if they change it again? I can't handle another menu change right now Audrey, it may sound simple but it was a fucking nightmare." Ty ran their hands over their head in frustration.

Audrey had set down her bags then, abandoning them to guide Ty to the couch.

"Let's talk it out," she said. "I'll get some tea."

She texted Zachary while the kettle heated, explaining that she needed to stay home that night and would see him the next day.

Okay, he'd responded. *See you tomorrow, Cherry Bomb. Tell Ty hi.*

While Ty and Audrey both felt happy for the other's joy in what was commonly (and pessimistically) referred to as the "Honeymoon Phase" of their relationships, they missed each other. Audrey knew these new relationships were just one more change Ty had to deal with.

For the first time in years, Audrey wouldn't be visiting Ty's parents with them for Christmas—Sofia would go instead. So that night, after talking through Ty's anxiety and helping them calm down, Audrey suggested they make a new tradition.

"How about a 'Friends Christmas Eve'?" she'd asked. "The four of us can stay here, drink, and be merry."

Ty's eyes lit up at that. "Ooh, let's do Secret Santa!"

"Done," Audrey said.

She was glad she'd be able to spend time with Ty celebrating Christmas. It was a tradition she'd grown to love. But she was also looking forward to spending this year with the man she was now truly beginning to believe was her soulmate.

Whether she understood the full extent of what this meant, or how it worked, was not important. What mattered is that Audrey's soul recognized its match, and Audrey was learning how to listen to her soul. From this dawning recognition sprouted parts of herself she had forgotten about, or never knew existed. Brave parts. Silly parts. Reckless, passionate, sensual parts.

Zachary felt much the same. The person he was years ago emerged from a cocoon as soon as Audrey came back into his life. The years since he saw her last had felt like the steady beating of a drum. He plodded forward, achieving his personal and career goals with a calm, methodical precision. He checked all the boxes—first, he finished his apprenticeship, then he got a new job, then a place close enough to his mom to help out now and then, and soon he started his own business.

He contributed to a retirement account every week, and to a boat fund, and he occasionally read a book from his to-be-read list. He lived a decent life, but beneath the surface was a sadness, trapped beneath layers of denial like thick ice.

Audrey, to him, felt like fire. Being near her made his skin tingle, and his mind come alive with wonder and curiosity. He felt high when he was with her, like he was looking at his life from somewhere up above. Life was decent before she came back into his life, but nothing else ever felt like fire.

After their Christmas Eve breakfast, Audrey and Zachary sat with their legs intertwined on the couch, each reading a book over their second cup of coffee. Audrey was engrossed in an epic fantasy romance, while Zachary was immersed in a dystopian sci-fi novel. Every now and then Audrey would giggle at something in her book, and Zachary would absentmindedly stroke her arm in response or ask her to read out loud what made her laugh.

They spent the afternoon in busy holiday bliss, baking, listening to Christmas music, and drinking buttered rum. By the time they got in their Uber to head to Ty and Audrey's apartment at 6:00, they were both happily tipsy.

Audrey could tell Ty and Sofia were well into the drink when they arrived as well. Audrey thought it may be for the best, since the only two of the group who didn't know each other well were Zachary and Sofia, and Audrey planned on monopolizing Ty's attention for a good part of the night.

Thankfully, Sofia was the type of person anyone could get along with whether she was buzzed or sober. She wore her long, dark hair in a braid, and the red and green eyeshadow she wore matched her delightfully ugly Stars Wars Christmas sweater. Zachary was deep into a conversation with her shortly after arriving about the merits of the old Star Wars movies versus the new. Audrey took the opportunity to pull Ty outside to their small deck.

"Hey, you," Ty said after she closed the sliding glass door behind them.

"Hey, you," Audrey said back, squeezing her friend's hand.

They stood there like that for a few moments, enjoying each other's company, the noise of the street playing in the background like their own personal serenade.

"You think they're okay in there?" Ty asked.

Audrey nodded. "They won't even notice we're gone."

Ty smiled, looking through the glass affectionately at the pair.

"How are things with Sofia?" Audrey asked.

"They're good," said Ty. When Audrey simply waited for more details, they sighed. "They're good, Audrey. I don't know what else to say. Sofia makes me happy. I think I make her happy, too."

"You deserve that."

"Yes. We all do." They paused, considering Audrey. "How are things with Zachary?"

"Same as always," Audrey said, sighing. "Fucking perfect. Part of me is still waiting for the other shoe to drop, honestly."

Ty smiled knowingly. "I get it, but that will pass."

The two of them stood together wordlessly a while longer, each with an arm around the other.

"Okay," Audrey finally said. "I can't stand it any longer. You have to open your gift."

"Weren't we supposed to open gifts all together?" Ty asked.

"It's not your Secret Santa gift, even though I did draw you."

"Well so much for the surprise," Ty said, chuckling.

Audrey smirked and reached inside her purse to retrieve Ty's present. "This one is special," she said, handing it to them. "I want you to open it out here."

Ty took the present from Audrey and weighed it in their hands.

"I bet I know what this is," they said.

"I bet you don't. Just open it!"

Ty obliged. Inside was an early edition of *As I Lay Dying*, one of Ty's favorite books. Ty's hand shot to their mouth.

"Oh Audrey, it's beautiful!"

"You like it?" Audrey asked. "I was watching it on Ebay for like centuries and finally got it."

Ty gently opened the cover and ran their fingers along the edges of the pages, handling it carefully, as if it were made of glass.

"I love it," they said. "Thank you."

Audrey watched Ty admire the gift for a few moments before she said what was on her mind.

"Remember when I told you I thought maybe God brought you to me?" Audrey said.

Ty nodded, still turning the book in their hands.

"Well, I know it wasn't God. But I do know I didn't meet you by accident. You and I are two parts of one whole, of something bigger than ourselves. And I think maybe, in the grand tapestry of existence, you and I are interwoven threads. Two pieces of a puzzle that just happen to be lucky enough to fit together."

Audrey paused, looking momentarily through the door at Zachary, who was watching Sofia dramatically reenact a story with rapt attention.

"It's funny. It's the same kind of thing I feel with Zachary. Like he and I—like all of us—are connected by something more than random circumstance."

Ty took her hand again and nodded. "I can see that."

Audrey continued. "I've come to see life as all of us just trying to find those familiar strands of the tapestry, the ones that keep crossing our path no matter how far we go away from them. And I'm just lucky enough to have found two of mine. What I'm trying to say is, I think you're one of my soulmates, Ty. And I am *deeply* grateful to have spent so much time in your presence."

Ty, their face wet with tears, pulled Audrey into a hug. In one another's embrace, both of them began to softly sob. Audrey was inexplicably overwhelmed with emotions, as was Ty. They both blamed it on alcohol, and the equally intoxicating effects of holiday nostalgia. The truth was, one can often feel it when an end is approaching, even if they don't yet recognize it as an end.

Thankfully, every end is soon followed by a new beginning—in this life, or in the next.

The four friends spent the rest of their Christmas Eve playing card games and drinking wine as planned. Audrey fell asleep in her own bed that night, her head resting on Zachary's shoulder. As she drifted off, she tried to put out of her mind the email she received a few hours earlier from Echo Roc, informing her she was one of five finalists chosen by the band to be their next lead singer.

19

Christmas morning, Audrey woke in the same position she'd fallen asleep in. Her cheek, nestled against Zachary's shoulder, felt numb from the prolonged contact. She rolled over and stretched, surprised by the lack of stiffness she felt in her arms and back.

Zachary woke, reflexively rolling in Audrey's direction at the sudden cold he felt in her absence and wrapping his arms around her, his face in her neck. He sleepily kissed her there as they cuddled.

"Merry Christmas," he said.

"Merry Christmas," Audrey mumbled back. Then, after a few moments of comfortable silence, "I'm starving."

Audrey's stomach growled as if on cue, responding to her sudden awareness of a heavenly smell coming from outside her room.

When Audrey and Zachary emerged they found Ty in the kitchen, fully dressed and sipping on their second cup of coffee, a worn copy of *A Christmas Carol* propped open on the counter.

"Good timing," they said to the pair. "Breakfast is almost ready to come out of the oven."

"What is it?" Audrey said longingly. "It smells like true love."

She heard Zachary quietly snort behind her.

"Thank you for your feedback, Audrey," Ty said in a mock-professional voice. "These are part of the sample sent over by our partner bakery. Potential additions to the breakfast menu at Free Food. Your comparison of their scent to *true love* is duly noted."

Audrey chuckled, jumping up to sit on the edge of the kitchen counter near Ty. "So we're the official focus group, is that it?"

"Precisely," Ty said. "Us, and the breakfast rush tomorrow morning."

A timer went off on Ty's phone and they reached for an oven mitt, opening the oven door to reveal an assortment of large, fluffy croissants. Audrey noticed several with bits of rosemary on top, and a few more that looked like they were filled with something sweet. Her mouth watered, and she looked at Ty in grateful adoration.

"Where's Sofia?" she asked, already reaching for a croissant from the pan.

Ty batted her hand away from the hot pastries with the oven mitt, then grabbed a spatula. "She's recovering over there," they said, gesturing toward the couch.

Audrey craned her neck and noticed Sofia laying on her back, her arm draped over her eyes as if the dim light was killing her.

Audrey stifled a laugh at the contrast between Sofia's anguish and Ty's clear-eyed domesticity. She'd kept a running list of what she called Ty's "superpowers" for years. Among them were the ability to make almost anyone feel at ease, a supernatural awareness of other people's bullshit and a propensity for avoiding it, and being absolutely hangover-proof.

Ty handed Audrey a plate of croissants and she hopped off the counter to kiss them on the cheek. Ty squeezed her arm in response. Audrey headed to where Zachary was sitting on the couch so they could share breakfast before going to his place.

Audrey felt a brief wave of anxiety about the email from Echo Roc as she sat down. When she read it, she was immediately joyful, but the anxiety she felt now came quickly behind it. As much as she wanted this—to sing on stage, to surround herself with music, to live somewhere new and different—she had never considered how difficult it would really be to leave. Especially now.

Zachary's groan beside her broke her from her reverie, and she looked over to see he had a mouthful of croissant.

"Mmm," he said. "Audrey, you were right. This *is* true love."

Audrey smiled and leaned back into the couch, choosing to put her worries away for now. Nothing was for sure after all; she had a one in five chance of being chosen. And one in five wasn't high enough to start thinking of goodbyes just yet.

She bit into the rosemary croissant and sighed. It *was* true love.

Shortly after breakfast, Audrey and Zachary bid their farewells to Ty and Sofia, who were driving to Ty's parents' house as soon as Sofia "felt human again." They headed to Zachary's apartment, where upon arriving Zachary insisted Audrey open her first present immediately.

"First? We agreed on *one* present!" she said, shocked at the betrayal.

"Forgive me," he said, pretending to be serious. "I couldn't help myself. But really, it's for both of us, so it doesn't count."

The present was a pair of green and black checkered pajamas. Audrey laughed at the Christmasy pjs and immediately put them to her face to feel how soft they were. Underneath them in the box were another, larger pair for Zachary in red.

"Are we having a family photo shoot in these?" she asked.

Zachary's eyebrows raised. "Are you interested?"

Audrey laughed and pushed him softly.

"Just kidding," he said. "I just thought we should be festive *and* comfortable today."

The two of them had agreed on a relaxing, low-key holiday. They baked their favorite pies and breads ahead of time (apple pie for Audrey, pecan for Zachary, and Zachary's grandmother's Swedish cardamom bread). They had all the makings of a giant charcuterie board in the fridge. They would spend the day eating, cuddling, and watching an obscene amount of Christmas movies.

Audrey rubbed the material of the pajamas in her hands appreciatively. "Crimson and clover."

Zachary furrowed his brows.

"The colors," she clarified, gesturing between the two sets of pjs. "Crimson and clover. Like that old song."

Zachary pulled her onto his lap and kissed her tenderly. "Never heard it. But I like the way it sounds on your lips." He kissed her again. "Sing it for me?"

She obliged, singing the words slowly, and planting soft kisses on his neck between each line. By the last chorus, Zachary had carried her to the bed, her legs wrapped around his waist, and the next several hours melted away in sweet holiday bliss.

It was only after they'd had their fill of each other, and enough meat, cheese, and bread to feed an army, that they settled down by the small potted fir tree in the corner of the living room to exchange presents.

Audrey excitedly pushed her present toward him, confident he would love it. "Me first! Open it!"

Zachary gingerly opened the wrapping paper on the flat, square box and opened the lid. His face lit up at what was inside.

"It's—" Audrey began.

"A planisphere!" Zachary finished for her. "And a *really* nice one."

He took the deep blue and gold disc from its box and examined it. Its outer rim was labeled with each day of the year, and an inner circle was marked with the 24 hours of the day. By spinning the inner circle, the planisphere revealed the position of the stars at any time of the year. At one point, these relatively simple objects were used to navigate on open waters. In fact, Audrey had relied on one herself, though of course, she could not remember it seeing as it was in another life.

Zachary turned the planisphere appreciatively in his hands, smiling. "Where did you find this?"

"An antique shop," Audrey said, shrugging. It was, in fact, the sixth antique shop she'd visited looking for the perfect gift for Zachary, who loved all things old, interesting, and tarnished. "It's so you don't get lost out there on the big, blue ocean." She placed her hand on his knee. "So you can always find your way back to me."

Zachary looked at her thoughtfully. "I hope I never have to find my way back to you, Audrey."

He leaned forward and kissed her, his fingers gently grazing her jaw as he did.

Audrey's heart pulled in opposite directions at his words. Her desire to stay a breath's distance from him forever, and the simultaneous desire to run off to a new place and sing on stage, threatened to break it completely. She squeezed his knee instead of voicing her feelings, hoping the tears in her eyes would say enough.

"I love this," Zachary said. "Thank you."

"You're welcome," she said, and kissed him again.

Zachary pulled away and wagged his eyebrows playfully. "Your turn."

He handed Audrey a black 4x4 box with a large red bow on top. She opened it to find a slip of paper with the Peters Design logo on it. It barely concealed an object wrapped in striped black and white tissue paper which she carefully lifted and unwrapped.

Inside lay a carving of a flower made from wood so pale it was nearly white. Its edges were painted with touches of blue and lavender. The flower had six outer petals and six smaller, inner petals that each ended in a protrusion about the size and shape of rice. In its center was a heart-shaped bulb that came up into a soft point.

Something inside Audrey stirred when she saw the flower, as if she had seen it before in a dream (or another life). She examined it, turning it carefully over in her hands.

Zachary had crafted it with utter care, his exactness showing in every line, from the sharp angles of the petals to the small protruding filaments. She lifted it, resisting the urge to hold the flower close to her heart like a child with a stuffed toy. She couldn't explain it, but it made her heart ache, as if it were a keepsake from her childhood, long lost and somehow forgotten.

"It's a Spring Squill," Zachary said, interrupting her awe. "When I first met you... I couldn't get you out of my head. I would find myself thinking about you at the oddest times, like when I was at the supermarket. I would see something and think, 'Audrey would love this,' even before I knew anything about you.

"Well, one day—it must have been a month or so after we met—I was walking past a little shop and I saw this flower in the window. It was made out of glass and attached to a long chain, and as soon as I saw it, I saw your face. I stopped, and I stared at it for at least ten minutes, trying to think of some reason to buy it for you. But I didn't buy it, because I barely knew you, and that would have been weird. Later on, I went back to look for it, but it was gone. I've thought of it ever since. Anyway, I thought I'd make you my own."

"Zachary. This is gorgeous. I might cry."

Zachary smiled broadly, taking the confession as a compliment of his work.

"There's more," he said, his voice giddy with excitement. "Inside."

Audrey furrowed her eyebrows, now inspecting the small wooden flower to find a seam or an opening. Zachary watched her eagerly, like someone with a delicious secret.

Audrey smirked, still marveling at the detail in the carving. "I didn't know you could make something like this."

At Free Food she watched him spend intermittent hours creating his wall murals. He installed six dark wood panels around the restaurant, each one carved with rough, geometric images of food that cascaded down the panels like a waterfall. The end result was beautiful and modern-looking, but nothing close to the detail of what she now held in her hands. Even the projects that decorated Zachary's house, like his clock, were less intricate.

"It's a skill I've been working on for a while," Zachary said. "You know, here and there."

Audrey smiled at him, shaking her head. "This is not a 'here and there' kind of skill, Zachary. How long did it take you to make this?"

Zachary frowned. "Don't distract from the matter at hand, Anderson. You have a puzzle to solve."

"Psh," she said. "I already figured it out."

Zachary gave her an incredulous look, calling her bluff. "Show me then."

"Fine," Audrey said and reached down to grab the circular center of the flower. To her surprise, it came loose when she pulled on it. She stifled her gasp and attempted to look unsurprised at her success, making Zachary laugh.

Where the removable center sat was now a small wooden tab. Audrey looked at the bottom of the piece she took off to find a small slot in which it once fit. She grabbed the tab and pulled gently. In response, the entire flower turned inside out. The tips of each petal turned down to become vertical, forming a small hexagon so one could place the inverted flower on a flat surface. Inside, once concealed by the petals, was a small, square piece of wood. Upon it, carved in tiny letters, were the words *I love you*.

Audrey's eyes filled with tears, and she looked up to find Zachary staring at her tenderly.

"I love you," he said out loud.

"I love you, too," Audrey said. "Truly."

They kissed, and the salty taste of their tears mingled between their lips.

When they parted, Audrey sighed audibly.

"What's wrong?" Zachary asked.

"I'm just realizing we're even now," Audrey replied, gesturing to the flower. "You definitely win this round."

Zachary smiled triumphantly and took the flower from her, standing to place it gently on the kitchen table. Then he stooped down and hooked his arms beneath Audrey's legs and back, lifting her up.

"Well then," he said, his voice dropping an octave. "As the victor, I request permission to revel in the glory of my triumph."

He wagged his eyebrows suggestively, making Audrey laugh.

"By all means," she said to him, her head dropping back as if she were helpless against his charms. "Revel away."

Zachary carried her into the bedroom, where they spent the rest of the afternoon confessing their love in new and interesting ways.

Later that evening as they shared the remains of the pecan pie in bed, Zachary pulled open the drawer of his bedside table to retrieve something.

"I have one more present for us," he said, and handed Audrey a small plastic bag that contained a handful of dried mushrooms.

Audrey gasped, her features widening in excitement. She had never done shrooms before, but was always curious about it—a fact Zachary knew well, since illicit drugs were one of their favorite weird topics of conversation. Zachary had tried them only twice—once when he was a teenager, and once just before he decided to move to New York.

"Zachary!" Audrey exclaimed. She lifted the bag to examine it more closely, the white linen sheet falling from her hands as she did and exposing her bare upper body.

He reached out and stroked her love handles appreciatively. "No pressure. Only if you want to."

"Of course I want to!" Audrey said. She took his hand in hers. "This has been the best Christmas of my life. I'm confident this can only make it better."

Zachary clapped in triumph and leaned forward to give Audrey a kiss.

"Let's do this then," he said, placing the remnants of the pie on the table next to him and sitting up straight. "And this has been my best Christmas, too. Just so you know."

Audrey smiled and opened the bag to shake the shriveled fungi onto her hand, separating the bunch into two even halves. Zachary took one half in his hand. Audrey picked one of the mushrooms up and brought it to her face, examining its golden cap.

What mysteries will you reveal to me, my little friend? she thought.

Zachary put his hand on her leg. "Let's stay together, okay?"

"Together." Audrey nodded. "Down the rabbit hole."

She was floating.

Or perhaps she was rooted to the ground.

No... she was both.

She was earth *and* she was air. She couldn't believe she didn't realize it before—that she was both. Both large and small. Solid, and also ethereal. Alive, and also dead.

She realized her eyes weren't open. The blue and yellow patterns she saw behind her eyelids, like paisley fish dancing in figure eights, were so vivid she had forgotten they were closed. She opened them, and Zachary's face took her breath away.

It was shrouded in golden luminescence. His eyes, which met hers with open fascination, glowed with an intensity she could *feel* in her chest. The edges of his body shimmered, surrounded by a subtle blue-green light that made him look like he wasn't solid. Audrey wanted to reach out and touch him, sure her fingers would simply pass through him like passing through mist. But when she tried, she realized her fingers were already intertwined with his, their hands resting between them on their laps. She felt suddenly awestruck, as if she were touching an angel.

He's a part of everything, she thought, filled with wonder.

"So are you," Zachary whispered.

Had she said that out loud? Had he? Audrey let the thought go, looking instead at her own body, which shimmered with a violet radiance that somehow felt like music. She had a sudden and overpowering urge to laugh.

So she did. She laughed and laughed, filled all at once with the closest thing to mirth she'd ever experienced. Zachary laughed with her and their laughter filled every corner of the room with dancing yellow light.

She was only vaguely aware of the passing of time. Their laughter could have lasted for only a few seconds, but it could also have been an eternity. Eventually they stopped laughing, the city noise replacing the ring of their joy with an overpowering presence. Audrey felt briefly overwhelmed by the noise until Zachary began to touch her, massaging her legs, then running his fingers through her hair.

This brought her awareness back to her own body, as well as his.

She ran her fingers up his arms, feeling every vein and follicle beneath her fingers like they were rivers or mountains. Then her hands found his chest, where there was a monstrous hammering just beneath the surface. It reverberated through her body, filling her with a sense of euphoria—as did the feeling of Zachary's fingertips tracing lines down her back. She leaned forward, giving in to the feeling of his caress as she buried her face in his neck.

She breathed in the scent of him, and it melded with the feeling of his fingertips on her skin, the roughness of his stubble on her face. She was consumed, every one of her senses hyper-focused on the feeling of him, until she lost awareness of where she was.

She was on the sea. She could feel the soft sting of water against her face and the tossing of the waves that rocked her back and forth. She heard the crash of water against wood. She smelled the salt in the air.

She looked up at Zachary. He was smiling, his eyes calm and reflective as they met hers. She reached up to gently touch his face.

"I don't think I knew you until now," she whispered.

Zachary leaned in to rest his head softly against hers.

"You've always known me."

Then he kissed her, and Audrey felt the force of his essence in a sudden rush as their spirits intermingled through their breath. She felt him fill her to the tips of her fingers and toes, his energy colliding with hers, dancing within and without their bodies. The kiss lasted only moments, but when they pulled apart, she knew somehow he was right.

She had always known him.

Exuberant with this knowledge, she wrapped her arms around his neck, pulling him closer. Their lips brushed against one another gently, each of them breathing the other in like they were air. She moved so she was sitting in his lap, her legs straddling him, and kissed him hungrily.

His hands, rough and roving on her back, were the plates of the earth, shifting and groaning against each other. His mouth was the center of the universe, pulling her in, devouring her and allowing itself to be devoured in turn. As he entered her, their bodies straining to move closer, closer, their joining was like the heat of the sun. Its light enveloped them, and as they moved in rhythm with one another, their pleasure went deeper than their bodies. For moments that felt like lifetimes they were nothing more than souls, and their ecstasy went soul-deep.

She still wasn't sure how much time had passed when Zachary whispered against her ear.

"How are you doing?" They were standing in the bedroom.

Audrey was looking intently into the mirror. She was marveling at the strength of her arms, the suppleness of her thighs. She saw not a frightened girl before her, as she sometimes did, but a dragon.

"Wonderful," she said, turning to kiss him. "How are you?"

"Hungry," he said.

"Ohhhh," Audrey said, suddenly remembering that food existed. "But the kitchen is so *far*."

Zachary laughed and leaned down to pick her up. Instead of carrying her to the kitchen however, he took her to the couch and planted a kiss on her forehead as he placed her there.

"Allow me," he said. "I shall deliver the food to you, my lady."

Audrey melted into the throw pillow behind her.

"You are my hero," she said.

Soon the two of them were sharing slices of fruit, cheese, olives, and a random assortment of desserts from a giant baking sheet Zachary called a "Charcutepan."

The two of them ate hunched over it, giggling and occasionally waxing poetic over some particular taste. Audrey felt like she was beginning to "come down," but the effects of the shrooms still left a magical lining around everything. It was all rose-colored.

"God, this is so good," Zachary said, his mouth full of food. "Here, try it."

He shoved the concoction, which was a tiny sandwich made from pears and cheese, toward her mouth. She took a bite and made a sound of deep appreciation. When her eyes were finished rolling back in her head, she looked at Zachary to find him staring at her intensely. She arched her eyebrows in a silent question.

"I'm just thinking," he said. "I'm so fucking lucky."

"And why is that?" Audrey asked.

"I just can't believe I found you... twice." He laughed on the last word, as if he was truly in disbelief. "It makes me wonder if some god somewhere owes me a favor."

Audrey laughed too, then felt suddenly sad. Zachary noticed her gaze drop and lowered his own, trying to meet her eyes.

"You okay?"

"Yes," she said honestly. "I'm great, actually. I just need to tell you something. I got an email from that band I auditioned for."

"Echo Roc?"

Audrey nodded. "I'm a finalist. They want to hear a live audition over Zoom in two weeks."

Zachary gasped, dropping the new tiny sandwich he'd just made back onto the Charcutepan in order to clap his hands together in excitement. "Holy shit, are you serious?" He took her hands in his and squeezed them. "Cherry Bomb, that's amazing!"

"Thank you," she said, allowing herself to show the pride and joy she felt. Then her face fell at what wasn't being said.

Zachary looked confused for a moment, then his face fell too as the realization that she might leave—again—sunk in. He took a deep breath, and his expression settled into a warm but sad smile.

"I'm so proud of you, Audrey," he said. "And no matter what happens, I'll still consider myself lucky."

That night they fell asleep holding each other tightly, so tightly.

20

"Just give me a hint," Audrey said, chewing her lip in anticipation as she sat in the passenger seat of Zachary's truck.

She woke up that morning to find Zachary fully dressed with a large duffel bag sitting by the door and breakfast already made.

"Good moooorning," he sang to her when she emerged from the bedroom, nearly skipping to pour her a cup of coffee.

"What is this?" she'd asked.

"A surprise," Zachary answered. "I'm taking you somewhere. Just until tomorrow."

Audrey immediately felt the need to prepare for this impending change in plans, but Zachary, sensing her tension immediately, closed the distance between them and took Audrey's hand.

"Everything is taken care of," he said. "I packed a bag for you, and everything else we need is in the truck. Ty already knows we're going. I just need you to eat and put on some comfy clothes for the drive."

Then he kissed her cheek and returned to the kitchen to fill two plates with bacon, scrambled eggs, and fried potatoes.

Starving and smitten with the man whose bed she'd spent the last three nights in, Audrey sat down and ate. A thrum of excitement ran under her skin, but she quietly squashed it, something small and scared inside of her not wanting to get her hopes up. But the longer she waited, the more her excitement got the better of her.

Now here she was, in Zachary's truck, headed... somewhere. It was nearly 11 and they'd been driving for around an hour.

"I told you, it's a *surprise*," Zachary said, taking his eyes off the road for a moment to emphasize the final word with a pointed look.

Audrey attempted to sulk, but she couldn't keep the hint of a smile from her lips. Zachary hadn't wiped the silly grin off his face all morning. He was loving every part of their spontaneous day trip, especially the parts that made Audrey squirm.

Once, Paul had done something similar. She woke up to him shaking her, telling her he had a surprise planned for the weekend. She was immediately excited, and jumped out of bed to pack both of their suitcases while Paul took the car to fill it with gas. An hour later they were on the road, eating breakfast burritos Audrey hurriedly put together while Paul did his devotions. Audrey's head had been filled with images of fancy hotel rooms and candlelit dinners.

What she got instead was two nights at a Motel 6 and the pleasure of sitting through a marathon-like seminar on "21st Century Evangelism" at a mega-church in San Diego. Paul took rapt notes on topics like "How to combat spiritual warfare on social media," and "Growing your flock on TikTok."

They spent their evenings at Paul's ex-roommates house for drinks and food, which both times was some variation of adult Lunchables. While Paul and his friend lingered at the table, drinking and reminiscing about college, Audrey was forced to make awkward small talk with his wife in the kitchen.

Some small part of Audrey felt anxious now at the possibility she was being ushered into an equally uncomfortable situation. But the idea of Zachary whisking her away only four days before her flight to Sedona just to abandon her to small talk and tiny pieces of yellow cheese was laughable. She took a deep breath, confident in Zachary's ability to make her feel at home wherever she was.

She gazed out the window as they drove, letting the hum of the truck usher her into a sort of calm reverie. Outside, snow stuck to the trees that flashed by. The sky was clear and blue, and the sun reflected brilliantly off the patches of snow on the ground.

Two weeks after Christmas, Audrey auditioned over Zoom to be the new lead singer for Echo Roc. This time she sang an original piece, "What if it's me?" To her absolute delight, Jenni Griffin told her she loved the song, and the rest of the band members seemed to agree that it fit Echo Roc's style.

Then the interview portion came, and Audrey was surprised by how comfortable the band made her feel.

Before asking any questions, they each shared a bit about themselves. Jenni spoke first. Audrey struggled to tame the temptation to giggle at how excited she was to be speaking to the frontrunner of her favorite band. Jenni was a Black woman whose hair hung in long dreads down her back and shoulders, highlighting her curvy frame.

Turquoise glasses framed her dark brown eyes. She shared her feelings about looking for her own replacement now that she was nearly finished with school and starting her career as an MD—both grateful and grief-stricken.

Ditya, who was not only the drummer for the band but also Jenni's long-time girlfriend, rubbed her thumb across the length of Jenni's hand as she spoke. Ditya was born and raised in Nepal and immigrated to the U.S. in high school. She worked at a local coffee shop when they weren't performing, and visited her extended family in Kathmandu every other year. She was tall and thin, and a pixie cut highlighted her sharp cheekbones and light brown eyes.

Cedric, a tall Black man with a charming Southern accent, was the band's guitarist. He wore a fedora on his clean-shaven head, and distinctive freckles patterned his face. He worked as an insurance salesman during the day, and he and his wife had three kids between the ages of six and twelve.

Stan, a White man with blonde hair that hung to his shoulders and bright blue eyes, was the bassist and backup singer. He was the only Arizona native of the group and part-owner of a local glass blowing studio and gallery. He wore a Hawaiian shirt and a pair of jean shorts with more holes than Audrey could count.

The four of them were intimate, happy being around each other. A certain sadness also hung over the group, all hyper-aware they were choosing to disrupt the harmony they'd achieved. Audrey found herself feeling envious of their friendship as they discussed their histories, every now and then one of them finishing another's sentence or adding details where they saw fit.

She wanted to be there, to be one of them.

Eleven excruciating days after the audition, Audrey got a call from Cedric offering her the gig. She broke down and cried on the spot, accepting the offer. Zachary, who was listening in on speakerphone as they lay together in bed, cried as well and showered her in kisses of congratulation.

Audrey had a single month after that to wrap up her life in New York. Logistically, that wasn't hard since Audrey had worked for herself for some time, and was never actually on Ty's lease to begin with. Emotionally however, Audrey had been a total wreck.

On top of the excitement and anxiousness she felt about starting fresh in a faraway city, Audrey felt an impending sense of dread at the prospect of saying goodbye. To Ty. To Zachary. To her first home after leaving Paul. Coming to New York was one of the first real choices she'd ever made for herself.

But now, she had made a new choice. As they drove, Audrey tried to focus on the possibilities that choice represented instead of the heartbreak it would bring.

21

"Almost there," Zachary said, reaching over to squeeze Audrey's thigh.

The trees were growing thicker, and Audrey spotted a sign that said "Fahnestock State Park."

Audrey rolled down the window of Zachary's truck and breathed in the smell of the air as the truck slowed. She smiled. One of her favorite things about road trips was that *first smell* of a new place. It was amazing to her that she could get in a car in one place, not even noticing the smells around her, and several hours later experience a new place wholly through this one sense.

They rolled into a campground and found their site: number 78. It was a small site, but one of the few that stood far apart enough from its neighbors to provide a decent amount of privacy.

Not that it mattered much. With snow still sticking, the campground wasn't exactly busy.

Zachary put the truck in park and Audrey reached for the handle, but it suddenly dawned on her that she had spent the last three days at Zachary's apartment, where she had only a pair of old sneakers and a handful of clean clothes. As if to answer her concern, Zachary reached into the backseat and retrieved her hiking boots, which to her knowledge had been in her closet at her own apartment since she'd bought them. Audrey took them gratefully, smiling at Zachary's thoughtfulness. He leaned forward to kiss her, then opened the door and climbed out of the truck.

"Explore a bit if you want," he said as he pulled on his coat. "I'm going to get lunch ready."

Audrey watched as Zachary winked and disappeared, smiling to himself. After she changed her shoes and slipped back on her coat and hat, she emerged from the truck into the cold, crisp air.

It was quiet outside, and the stillness made Audrey feel like she was standing in a giant snow globe. She looked over to find Zachary already had the picnic table wiped off. A small propane barbecue sat on top of it, and he was opening a package of bratwurst.

Audrey walked past him toward the line of trees at the back of their campsite. She entered the small grove and kept walking until the only sound was the soft crunch of snow beneath her boots. The frigid air pricked at her skin, making her feel awake and alert. She stopped to admire the way the soft light shone through the trees above her. She closed her eyes, enjoying the utter silence that surrounded her.

Eventually, the soft thud of a far-off truck door broke the silence, and she made the short trek back to Zachary.

"I'm going to find the bathroom," she told him when she got back.

"Okay. It's that way," Zachary said, pointing with the tongs he held in his hand.

When she got back, Zachary had a tarp spread out and was unrolling the tent she wasn't aware he owned until now. She joined him wordlessly to help set it up.

Part way through setting up the tent Zachary caught Audrey looking at him, a soft smile on her lips as she watched him focus intently on the task before him. He stopped what he was doing to look back at her.

"Are you happy?" he asked, his voice soft and genuine.

"I am," she said, tears pricking her eyes at the unexpected question.

Zachary smiled at that and continued assembling the tent rod he held in his hand, but he didn't take his eyes off Audrey.

"I love you, Audrey," he said.

"I love you, too, Zachary."

The two of them had lunch after the tent was set up. After he finished eating, Zachary hurriedly put out two comfy-looking camping chairs. Then he hauled a cooler from the back of the truck to near the picnic table and pulled out two beers, each of which he put in the mesh cupholders in the armrests of the chairs.

Audrey watched, her mouth still full of food as he once again disappeared, this time reappearing with a knit blanket and the book Audrey started reading two days ago. He placed them in the chair nearest to Audrey and then made a dramatic flourish toward them, as if to say, *Ta-da!*

She gave him an adoring look, clutching her hand to her heart for her own dramatic effect.

"The chair," she said. "The book. The beer. They *call* to me."

Zachary smiled and walked forward to kiss her on the cheek. "Your throne awaits, m'lady. Stay here and relax. I'm going to get a few things ready."

"Can I help?" Audrey asked.

Zachary immediately smushed his finger to her mouth and let out a low *Shhhh* sound, making Audrey laugh against his skin.

Audrey smiled to herself as she watched him walk away. He had a bounce in his step that appeared every time he had an opportunity to spoil someone. Usually, it was her, but sometimes it was a friend, or a neighbor.

For instance, during the remodel Zachary replaced Ty's desk with a custom standing desk Zachary made himself from leftover or repurposed materials. He snuck it into Ty's office on their day off. The next day Ty found Zachary standing at the front door of the restaurant before it opened, practically dancing in place with excitement to see their reaction. It was worth it, as Ty loved the desk and had been complaining for ages that their body "stopped allowing motionlessness as a rule" as soon as they passed thirty.

Audrey remembered watching Zachary with adoration as he related every detail of Ty's reaction to her later that day. That was when it hit her, how truly happy it made Zachary to take care of the people he loved. His friend had a problem and he was able to solve it. He didn't come down off of that emotional high for weeks.

Audrey knew better than to interrupt his process now as he took care of her, so she wiped her fingers on the nearest napkin and sank happily into her chair, spreading the blanket across her legs as she did.

She picked up her book, but stole a glance at Zachary before she opened it to find him popping his head out the door of the tent to peer in her direction. His satisfied smile at seeing her settled in her chair morphed into a laugh when he realized she caught him checking on her.

Audrey laughed, shaking her head as Zachary ducked back into the tent.

"Busybody," she said under her breath, and opened her book.

Soon Audrey was lost in the story. The heroine was just about to kick some serious ass in order to save her one true love when Zachary gently touched her shoulder, bringing her back to the present.

He sat next in his chair next to her and took her hand, interlacing their fingers as he looked into her eyes. Then he took his beer in the other hand and drank deeply. For several minutes he sat there in silence, his thumb gently rubbing Audrey's hand, his eyes staring out at the trees.

Audrey squeezed his hand after a while and he looked at her.

"This is one of those moments where I feel like I have everything I need," he said.

Audrey nodded, emotions swimming in her eyes— emotions Zachary understood without her having to say anything.

"When you leave," Zachary said, his voice breaking on the last word, "I'm going to feel like I'm missing an arm."

"You could come with me," Audrey said weakly, knowing already it wasn't possible. Zachary had jobs lined up for at least the next year since the Free Food remodel. Coming to Sedona would risk everything he worked so hard to build. It would be horribly unfair.

Still, Zachary smiled sadly and said, "Are you asking me?"

No, she thought. She was not. Just as he had never asked her to stay with him rather than go to Sedona.

Seeing the answer in her eyes, Zachary simply brought Audrey's hand to his lips for a kiss and returned to gazing at the trees.

The next few hours passed peacefully, the two of them reading, and drinking, and occasionally reading one another passages from their respective books. Eventually they became so engrossed in conversation, the books were forgotten.

Every now and then Audrey stopped and shut her eyes, focusing her attention on the way the sun felt on her face, and the sounds of birds, and the breeze moving through the trees.

What a way to say goodbye to New York.

When it started to get colder Zachary built a fire. He grilled dinner as well, a feast of marinated vegetables and steak that Audrey ate seconds of, and a batch of brownies cooked in a small dutch oven using hot coals.

Audrey shook her head as she ate her dessert, marveling openly at him. "You always do so much for me. You never let me do anything for you."

Zachary smiled, proud at the compliment. "You do plenty for me."

Audrey looked unconvinced, so Zachary turned toward her, his legs straddling each side of the picnic bench.

"You sing for me," he began. "You massage my back when it's sore. You buy me a book every time you go into a book store." Zachary chuckled, thinking about the ever-growing pile of books he planned to read, almost all of which were bought by Audrey in the past three months. "Oh, and then there's that thing you do with your tongue."

Audrey laughed and swatted at him. Zachary caught her hand and brought it to his lips to kiss her fingertips gently. She leaned in to kiss him then, and the conversation was settled.

The truth was, Zachary didn't like the idea of Audrey doing things for him. He knew what her marriage was like, and what was required of her to stay in Paul's good graces. Audrey spent years of her life cooking, cleaning, and nurturing—all for a man who saw her as nothing more than the services she provided.

Zachary would be damned if he was going to let her feel that way again, even for a second.

He gazed at Audrey, admiring the way the light of the campfire played against her red hair amidst the fading light. He became acutely aware in that moment of the deep sense of sadness he felt.

She would soon be out of his life once more. The way she felt about anything would be out of his hands, but just as much as he wanted to make her feel loved, he would also die before he asked her to walk away from her dreams—from her potential. It would be asking her to give up who she really was, and that was the last thing he wanted.

Audrey ran her hands down her legs to warm them and stood, aiming to get closer to the fire.

"Wait," Zachary said. "Come to the tent first."

He turned on the electric lantern hanging from the ceiling of the tent as they went in. Inside was a double sleeping bag that looked like it was lined in flannel, and two duffel bags. Zachary bent down to open one, taking out three pairs of Audrey's pajamas and lining them on the bed.

"I wasn't sure which ones you'd be most comfortable in, but I thought you may want to wear these baggy ones over the tighter ones, at least until we get in bed. They'll keep you warmer than what you're wearing now."

Audrey looked in the bag to find more of her clothes, along with most of her face and body products stuffed into gallon-size Ziploc bags. "You're the best," she sighed.

He smiled and opened the other bag to retrieve a pair of sweatpants. "Let's change," he said. "Then I have something set up in the back of the truck."

Zachary had another sleeping bag in the bed of the truck, this one unzipped and spread wide so they could lay on top of it. A giant fleece blanket was spread out on top, along with two pillows. Zachary moved the fleece and motioned for Audrey to join him underneath it. She did, and they curled up beneath the blanket, their arms around each other to watch the last few moments of the sunset.

When darkness finally settled, Audrey felt like she and Zachary and the stars were the only things in the entire world.

In the distance, she heard the sounds of other campers, and the crackle of the fire, but all she felt was Zachary, and he felt just like the millions of stars above their heads. They lay there for a long time, staring at the sky, the silence between them filling slowly with what neither of them had been able to speak about all day.

"So, this is... it," Audrey finally said, unable to hold it in any longer. "This is our goodbye."

She felt Zachary draw in a long breath beside her.

"I suppose it is," he said, wrapping her hand in his and squeezing tightly.

They had already decided. They would break up when Audrey left, so as to allow them both to focus on their dreams. Maintaining a long distance relationship would only distract them—hurt them.

So until they could each jump back in with *both* feet, this would be goodbye—their last night spent alone before she left for Sedona. When he brought her back to the city it would be to her apartment, so she could spend two nights alone with Ty followed by one night with the three of them all together. Then her life in New York City would come to an end.

When they'd decided to end things, Audrey cried. She was heartbroken, frustrated that she had to choose between her love and her dream. A part of her wanted to stay, to say no to Echo Roc, and to never leave Zachary's side again.

When she said as much, he pulled her gently into his arms and said, "You're a fire, Audrey. You need space to grow and right now, I'm tempted to put you inside a lantern and keep you all for myself. I can't do that to you. If that's what you want, I'll get down on my knees and beg you to stay right now. But I really don't think that's the case... is it?"

Audrey couldn't deny it. Her spirit yearned for the coming change, even as it grieved. So she said nothing, and continued to cry in his arms instead. He held her as he cried, too.

Now, laying in the back of Zachary's truck beneath the stars, the two of them held on to one another tightly, as if the contact would stave off more tears. When they could no longer keep their eyes open, they retreated inside the tent and fell asleep.

The next morning Audrey woke early, her face covered by the flannel sleeping bag and Zachary slowly stirring beside her. Immediately, she felt sad at the prospect of their short trip ending.

Zachary suggested they go on a hike before they left, his own way of extending their time together. So they dressed, but not before they stripped down to nothing and made love, their hands and mouths desperately trying to memorize one another.

Then they packed, and took down the tent, and ate muffins for breakfast that Zachary brought from Audrey's favorite bakery. Afterward, they found a trailhead and walked until it was time to turn back, the campground's checkout time weighing on each of them like an anvil.

The drive home was quiet, and Audrey felt a mixture of contentment and sadness as they drove that confused her.

For the following two days Audrey and Ty spent every waking moment together. They said goodbye, and I love you, in every possible way—through laughter and tears, over food, in heartfelt recollections about the good old days, and tearful musings over whether they would ever come again.

On her last night, Ty hosted a small goodbye party at their apartment. A handful of close friends came, including Adriana and her boyfriend Dave, a few employees from Free Food, and a couple of people Audrey worked with at her first job in New York.

After they all left around midnight, only Ty and Zachary remained, and the three of them laughed and cried with each other until they fell asleep on the sofa with the TV on.

The next morning Audrey felt like she was going to jump out of her skin. A ball of nerves rolled around in her gut, moving her back and forth from anxious excitement to sorrow and back again. Adventure called to her, a new home and a different life filling her with anticipation. She only wished it didn't mean leaving this one behind.

When Ty stood at the door to go to work the morning of Audrey's flight, they were both at a loss for words. They simply embraced one another, and just before Ty turned and walked through the door they whispered against Audrey's hair, "Go get 'em, Audrey."

Then it was just her and Zachary. Audrey didn't feel at a loss for words. She felt like there wasn't enough time in the world for all she wanted to say.

She could barely bring herself to move. She stood at the door, her bags by her side, and simply stared at her apartment. Zachary wanted to take her to the airport but she forbade it, hating the thought of saying goodbye to him in the midst of hundreds of other people, all bustling to get where they were going. She insisted on calling a cab and saying goodbye to Zachary somewhere safe, familiar—at home.

Zachary approached her slowly, looking at her as if she would turn to dust if he advanced too quickly.

As the gap closed between them, he held his hands out to touch her gently on each arm, running his fingers from her elbows to her shoulders, his eyes following his fingertips as if he was memorizing her shape. Finally, he pulled her slowly into his arms. As soon as her face touched his chest, she started crying. He held her there silently and let her.

When she pulled away, Audrey saw Zachary had been crying too. She reached up to brush a tear from his face and he held her hand against his cheek tenderly.

"Zachary," Audrey said, stepping back slightly and curling her hands together in front of her chest. She took a breath, thinking about how to begin. "Back when you and I first met. It took me years to admit to myself I was in love with you. That summer after I left... I *stumbled* through the following weeks in a fog until my wedding day. When I look back on it, I just remember feeling numb, punctuated by periods of crushing, desperate rage.

"I know now that it was heartbreak, but at the time I just told myself it was stress. Because, I couldn't call what I felt for you love. To me, love was something you had to make sacrifices for. Something painful, and bloody, and noble. It wasn't something effortless and happy, like what I had with you. That was... well, I didn't know something like that was something I was allowed to have."

Zachary moved closer to her, his body language gentle, protective, and he placed his hands on her shoulders as if to brace her.

Audrey continued. "But I look at you now and I know. I recognize every feeling I have now as love, the good and the bad. And when I feel my heart breaking in Sedona, I'll embrace it, knowing it carries with it a reminder of the most beautiful part of my life so far... you." Her voice broke on the last word, and new tears streamed down her face. Zachary leaned forward and kissed each one of them.

"Audrey Anderson, you are the most magical person I've ever met." He pulled away, and his eyes met hers with an intensity that caught her off guard. "I love you. I've always loved you. And this is *not* the end."

Zachary pulled her close, and he kissed her with such intensity that she believed him. When they parted, she stood there a moment to take him in once more, and then turned and left without a second thought.

Zachary watched her leave silently, etching the image into his memory as the door closed behind her.

Of course, he was right. This was not the end.

But you may think this a gruesome way to part. *Where is the grief, where is the anguish, the beating of fists upon one's chest in protest?*

Remember I told you earlier that Audrey's soul was beginning to recognize its mate? Well, there are a great many people who assume finding one's soulmate is an event that necessarily inspires feelings of jealousy, or possession—that one would want to hold on to such a kindred spirit at all costs.

This is not true at all. For when a soul truly recognizes its match, it must also recognize the nature of the relationship with this other soul. It is not something fleeting, or fragile. Nor is it something that must be hoarded, or consumed. It is a tether of stardust, stretched across thousands of lifetimes and the vastness of space. It is as strong as a chain of steel connecting two souls, but it doesn't place one soul in the possession of the other.

For in the span of eternity, a year or even a lifetime is but the blink of an eye, and *true* love doesn't break character for such unimportant things.

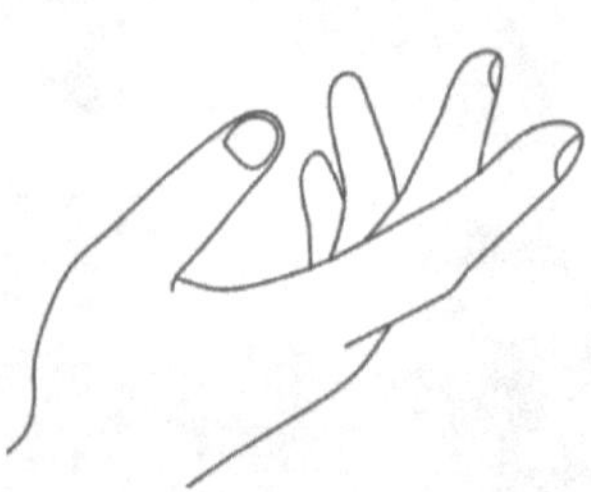

PART THREE

Once, she was flying.

Her powerful wings beat once, twice, and she let the wind carry her away from her mountain home. The world below was a smattering of muted color, trees and hills and villages barely perceptible even to her sharp eyes. The peaks of mountains rose above the clouds before her, a sight only her kind was privileged enough to see.

Her kind, who need not take a breath more than a few times in a minute, whose armored scales and silken fur shielded them from the cold. Her kind, who dwelt in the caves of the highest mountains, sleeping away over half of their long, solitary lives, waiting for winter to come to venture out again for food and adventure.

Her long, writhing body undulated against the frozen air as her wings stilled, its chill like fire against her skin, fueling her. The white of the clouds, the snow on the mountains, stood in subtle contrast to her deep blue and silver coloring.

Far below, small huts sat in chilled silence. The fields around them that were alight with color only weeks before now faded under layers of mud and frost.

She was rarely able to glimpse those vibrant colors herself. When she could, she woke up a few weeks early, giving her the opportunity to see the last of the fading blooms below. Sometimes, she braved the last of the summer heat to fly low, very low, to the villages below that teemed with tiny creatures that tended flowers, fruits, and trees whose leaves were varied shades of red and orange and yellow.

Once, she landed just outside the small village below her mountain. The heat down below in the early months was oppressive and she could not stay for long. But the colors in this particular garden were so beautiful, she couldn't help herself.

The plants were arranged in a large geometric pattern that looked like a snowflake. Snow and ice being her own particular brand of magic, she felt compelled to visit. When she landed, she found the scents of the flowers so intoxicating she climbed in, curling her body around itself and breathing in deeply.

When she opened her eyes again, they were met by the eyes of a small creature on two legs. It appeared to be a child. Mixed with the scents of the flowers she now smelled wonder, awe, and fear coming off the child in waves.

Slowly, she raised her head, and let out a soft *whoosh* of cold air. Her icy breath swirled in front of her, becoming a large, delicate snowflake that landed gently at the child's feet. When its face broke into a smile at the small bit of magic, she stood back on her feet and propelled herself into the air, out of the dwindling heat, and back toward her home in the mountains.

Each year, the garden grew larger and more beautiful, until she could smell the flowers from high in the air. In those years she woke up early enough to see it, she always flew as low as she could, until the tiny creature could see her from the ground, and she sent a flurry of delicate snowflakes to her in thanks.

It was too late this season, however, to visit her favorite garden. She slept late this year, a sign of her advancing age. Despite having a very long life, she was becoming almost imperceptibly slower. She mourned the youthful energy that allowed her to wake early and see color in her world.

Having just emerged from this year's hibernation, she was filled with energy. She let it propel her higher, higher, into the skies. She broke through the top of the clouds, tucking her wings in and twirling her body so that the sun bounced off her scales, creating a spectacular prism of light in every direction. Then she let herself drop, free-falling for several breathtaking seconds into the clouds.

When she opened her wings to stop, her breath came out in short huffs of laughter, causing tendrils of cloud to dance away from her in small spirals. All around her was white, grey, and fluid movement. She could see no more than a few feet through the mist, but she could *feel* how far the clouds stretched around her. She closed her eyes, feeling the weight of the minuscule droplets of water that stretched around her for miles, embracing the cold and the silence.

Then she breathed in deeply, touching that inner part of herself filled with ancient, elemental magic. It spread like a cold, writhing electricity. When she let go, it rippled out from her in blue waves, charging the very air around her and solidifying millions of tiny water droplets into intricate frozen designs.

The snow fell quickly, coating the land below until it looked like the world was covered in small white feathers. She didn't know this particular feat of weather was a symbolic event for the creatures below, who celebrated the year's first snowfall with raucous gatherings, and even made predictions for the future based on the position of the stars when it occurred. She only knew how wonderful it felt to fly through the snow after such a long sleep.

Soon she was breaking through the clouds again, eager to see the vibrant blue of the sky above them. The sun shone in her eyes, and in the distance, she could make out the shape of another one of her kind.

The same blue and silver coloring as her own was visible across the great distance to her keen eyes. A glimmer of recognition sparked within her, but no more. Her kind did not live in pairs, nor desire to. The winter could not sustain the appetite of more than one of them in the same place. Solitude was as natural as breathing.

She did not see another creature like herself until winter was almost over.

The air was still thick with moisture, but it was getting noticeably warmer. She found herself eating more often, her fur getting thinner and softer. She was preparing to sleep. She was also flying, as much as she could each day. She got lower and lower, her eyes straining to see the first signs of spring on the ground after so many months of white and grey, but to no avail.

So she started flying farther, heading in a new direction each day in search of something… something new.

It was on the day she chose to fly south that she found it.

She had been following the far-off reflection of something yellow for some time. Her eyes were fixed on the color. She wondered if she'd find flowers when she arrived, or trees, or something else entirely. The beads of sweat forming beneath her coat were sticky and uncomfortable, but she pushed herself forward nonetheless.

Just then, something flashed in her peripheral vision. She turned her head to find the sun reflecting off of something in the sky. Something beautiful.

Abandoning her yellow goal, she changed direction, flying closer to the flash of color she saw in the distance. For as long as she could remember, her world had been white, and brown, and grey, and blue. Glimpses of color—flowers, insects, birds—were the only novelty she knew. They were small bursts of wonder, punctuating a life of pre-dictability.

Though this creature flew, it was no bird. As she got closer, she realized it was a creature like her. But it was not like her.

While her body was large and strong, its own was more compact, and seemingly faster. In place of the thick white fur that lined her face and body, its own was accented by vibrant feathers that covered its wings and protruded in a dramatic arc around its face. They were every shade of green and blue and turquoise, with bright red and gold markings dotting their neck and chest.

As she got closer, the creature she now realized was a male began spinning, his body stretched vertically and his wings tucked tightly around him to allow for maximum speed. As he spun, a cloud formed around him, blocking him from view temporarily.

Suddenly, a crack of thunder rang through the air, shocking her, and it began to rain in the very spot he was once in. Then he emerged, and was flying right toward her.

A deep sense of foreboding coursed through her as he approached. Some ancient instinct whispered to her to run, warned her against the encroaching proximity of another predator of nearly her size and strength. But the sun was bouncing off the blue-green scales that ran the length of his body in the most beautiful way. She feared she may never again see something so beautiful.

So she stayed as still as possible, blending into the blinding white of the sun.

When he noticed her, he went still. She could smell his trepidation. She knew he must smell her own as well.

They stayed there, hovering, their fear mingled with open fascination for a few moments. Then, suddenly, he whipped his body in a tight circle. A puff of fog surrounded him, and when it dissipated, he was gone.

She went to sleep the next day, resolving as she did to fly south again at the end of next winter. But alas, there would be no next winter, and she slumbered in her cave for the last time.

But it would not be the last time she saw the dragon.

22

Audrey fiddled with her headband, her heart fluttering the way it always did just before she went on stage. She looked back to find Stan smiling at her. He raised his eyebrows as if to say, *Ready?* Audrey nodded and as if in response, the MC's voice blared over the microphone:

"Here they are, folks! Echo Roc!"

Audrey released one last steadying breath and walked out onto the stage. Stan, Cedric, and Ditya followed close behind. Their entrance was met with a steady wave of cheers and applause, the sound hitting her with the same force as the blindingly bright floodlights that lit the stage.

It filled Audrey with a thrill that made her vibrate from the tips of her fingers to the soles of her feet. She raised her hand and waved at the crowd as she approached her microphone.

Audrey loved coming to Tucson to play. The venues were better, the locals were younger, and the energy of the crowd buzzed so loudly it rattled Audrey's bones. Sedona was beautiful, and as much as she enjoyed the frequent tips they got from retired men and couples on vacation, sometimes Audrey wished Echo Roc was based somewhere else. Somewhere filled with *big* stages like this one.

"Hello, Tucson!" Another swell of cheers answered her. "I'm Audrey, this is Ditya, Cedric, and Stan, and we're Echo Roc!"

Ditya brought her drumsticks together above her head and brought them down in one swift motion, leading Stan and Cedric into the opening beat for their first song.

Audrey began to bounce to the rhythm, her eyes simultaneously scanning the crowd for Ty. She found them standing to the left of the stage wearing an Echo Roc t-shirt. They flew in that morning to see her perform, and would be coming back with her to Sedona to stay for a few days. It was the first chance they'd had to visit in the eight months since Audrey left.

What an eight months it had been.

Echo Roc was already building a large fan base before Audrey joined, and with the right social media marketing, the fans took to her as well. They only continued growing, with large shows like this one becoming more frequent. At the end of this year, the band was going on their second official tour—the first for Audrey. It would only be a short two-week stint, as that was as much time as the band could afford to take between day jobs, and in Cedric's case, kids.

Despite how brief it would be, Audrey was nothing short of thrilled.

There was a small part of her that wanted to continually marvel at the fact that it was finally all happening for her. But she kept shushing that voice, making more room for the part of herself that felt it was the most natural, normal thing in the world—as if she was the ideal candidate for her own dreams. This part of her craved the high she got on stage, relished the eyes and ears of hundreds of strangers listening to her sing. It kept looking forward, expecting more.

She let that part of herself be loud and obnoxious, drowning out the small piece of her wringing its hands in the corner, wondering if and when this dream would end.

Hand-wringing Audrey was not present as she bellowed the chorus to their first song, a piece her mother deemed in a recent email to Audrey as "shamelessly sacrilege." In fact, her mother had broken a months-long communication freeze with Audrey solely to tell her she would continue not talking to her due to this specific song, which asked the listener to consider who is to blame for the dreadful state of the world.

Maybe it's god, she sang. *Maybe it's the devil. Maybe it's me.*

But she didn't think about her mother as she sang. She didn't think at all. She simply felt the energy around her—the energy of the crowd, of each of her bandmates, and of the music itself. She felt like she was part of a giant wave of love and joy and excitement. It was like a drug.

Later that evening Audrey sat in a circular booth at a diner with Ty, Cedric, Ditya, Stan, and a local friend of Stan's named Ashley. They had just ordered and were now talking and laughing loudly, all of them still riding the high of a great show. Cedric had just finished telling a story when Audrey felt Ty squeeze her knee. She turned, taking the opportunity to escape into a private conversation with her friend as the rest of the group moved toward a different topic.

"God, it's so good to be with you Ty," Audrey said, placing her hand on top of theirs.

"You have no idea," Ty said. "I've missed you."

The look on their face betrayed a tiredness that Audrey hadn't noticed until now.

"Me too." Audrey rubbed her thumb across the back of Ty's hand. "I'm sorry I couldn't be there for you when you and Sofia split. It killed me not being able to hug you."

Ty waved a hand as if to dismiss Audrey's comment. "You were there for me, even if you weren't *there*."

Audrey planned two consecutive "date nights" for her and Ty from afar after the breakup. A combination of finances and Echo Roc obligations prevented her from flying to New York, so she relied on technology instead. She picked movies she knew Ty loved, they watched them together over FaceTime, and she even ordered delivery to Ty's apartment—food the first night, drinks the next.

"How are you feeling *now*?" Audrey asked.

Ty sighed. "I'm doing fine. I've accepted that it was for the best. Sofia and I want different things out of life. And I've been working a lot to keep myself busy but it's becoming kind of awful. I think I might actually be starting to hate my job."

Audrey gasped. Ty had always loved their job as the General Manager of Free Food. She had never heard them complain about it keeping them busy. She wondered if it had something to do with the new ownership.

"Wow," she said. "Do you think it's temporary? Or are you finally getting burnt out?"

"It's definitely the latter," said Ty. "The other day I imagined stabbing in the eye the next person who told me the ice machine was broken. Then at the end of the day when the machine *didn't* break for once, I was actually disappointed I didn't get to stab anyone in the eye."

Audrey snorted. "Okay. Time for a change then?"

Ty nodded, stirring their iced tea slowly with their straw as they did. "I'm thinking of getting my Ph.D., actually."

"No way!" Audrey gently shoved Ty's shoulder, and they smiled. "That's amazing! Tell me what you're thinking."

"I'm thinking literature," Ty said. "I don't know exactly where yet. But not in New York. I think I need a complete change of scenery."

"But what about poor Bryan?" Audrey said teasingly.

"Ugh, don't speak that name here!" Ty said dramatically. "I'd like to pretend for a few days that I *didn't* recruit a Craigslist roommate to live with me in a drunken state of loneliness and ruin my entire life."

"Come on, he can't be that bad," she said, despite the stories Ty told her suggesting otherwise.

"Audrey, the day before yesterday I found him cleaning his gym clothes in the *kitchen sink*. He looked at me like *I* was the crazy one when I stopped him just before he draped his sopping wet gym shorts *over* the clean dishes in the drying rack. I shrieked like a goddamn banshee when I realized what he was doing, and he just goes, 'Well where am I supposed to put them, *bro*?'"

Audrey was laughing so hard she was doubled over, one hand on her stomach and the other gripping Ty's knee. Ty, who was not as entertained, chuckled incredulously at their own story.

"I'm serious, Audrey," they said. "I am way too old to be living with a 23-year-old gym bro. His dietary supplements have eaten up all the counter space."

Audrey wiped a stray tear from her eye that escaped while she was laughing and shook her head, trying to transform her face into something resembling pity.

"I'm sorry," she said. "That's awful. I shouldn't be laughing."

"It is pretty funny, I guess," Ty said with a smile. They relaxed back into their seat.

"Well I have the solution you know," Audrey said. "Just move to Sedona. Get your Ph.D. there and be my roomie again."

Ty put a gentle hand on Audrey's shoulder and looked at her intensely. "Audrey, I love you, but I would rather let Bryan dry his skivvies on my nightstand than live anywhere in the state of Arizona."

"Yeah, I figured, but it was worth a try," Audrey said, chuckling. She took a long drink of her blackberry milkshake before she continued. "So," she said finally, twirling her straw in her hands and attempting to look casual.

Ty set down their iced tea and gave Audrey a pointed look, as if they knew precisely what she was going to say next.

"How's Zachary?"

Ty smiled. They were right.

"He's doing fine," they said. "Still busy. Just finished a remodel at some high-end clinic in Manhattan."

Audrey nodded, feeling unable to speak, her eyes glued to the table.

"He misses you," Ty said.

Audrey looked up, letting the sadness that had been lingering beneath the surface show on her face. Ty moved closer so that their shoulders were touching, a silent invitation. Audrey took it, laying her head on Ty's shoulder and breathing in their comforting scent.

They sat there for several minutes like that, watching the other members of their party and laughing along with their stories, but somehow still in their own world. Eventually, Ty spoke quietly so only Audrey could hear.

"We had dinner a few nights ago, him and I," they said. "He went all of five minutes before he asked how you were doing. Poor guy's hopelessly in love with you, Audrey."

Audrey let out a long sigh and leaned further into Ty for comfort.

"But," they said, "he's so happy for you as well. Watches your videos like they're a drug. Bought all your merch, too. He's the one who gave me this shirt, actually." Ty chuckled, and then continued, their hand squeezing Audrey's tightly to emphasize their words. "He's going to be fine, Audrey. He, and I, and everyone who matters knows you're doing the right thing out here. You both deserve the time and space to pursue your dreams."

Audrey and Zachary had kept in loose touch since she left, but every text message was like a dagger to the heart. The few times they'd tried to video chat, both of them became so depressed it made conversation difficult. Eventually, their communication slowed on its own, both of them recognizing the difficulty of focusing on their lives and missing each other simultaneously. After eight months, the messages had slowed to a trickle. It allowed Audrey to focus on why she moved to Arizona, for which she was thankful, but she hated it at the same time.

She missed Zachary. Terribly. It tore her up to be without him, especially after they'd been given a second chance. But she kept reminding herself to make the best of their time apart, however long it may be. She'd dived headfirst into her new life, committing to the band and their music wholeheartedly, and it was paying off. She felt like she was in the right place, using her gifts and doing what she was meant to do with her life.

Zachary gave her a gift by letting her go, and she would not waste it.

23

Just over a year after Ty's visit to Sedona, Audrey's dreams of playing for bigger crowds came true.

Transcend Music Festival was the newest of the many music festivals that lined the California coast. When Audrey submitted Echo Roc as a potential opening act, she wasn't certain they would make the cut. When they did, she nearly gave the rest of the band a heart attack as she burst through the door of Cedric's basement (where they practiced), screaming the news.

They were to open for a band called Fidget, a rap-rock group from Berkeley that had developed a cult following over the past ten years. Audrey looked out over at the group's fans, their bodies decorated in the signature black and blue colors of the band's logo, and nearly salivated at the chance she had before her.

This was the first festival they'd ever played together, and Fidget's fans (as well as Echo Roc's, she supposed) had turned out in droves. Though their musical style was distinct from each other, she sensed there was enough creative overlap to gain a healthy dose of new fans.

Not to mention this was by far the biggest stage she'd ever sung on.

She felt a squeeze on her shoulder and looked over to see Ditya, who looked just as excited as Audrey felt.

"Can you believe this?" she asked, her other hand spinning her drumsticks in rhythmic circles. She bounced on the balls of her feet, making her hair, which had grown out slightly, bounce as well. Bright blue tendrils stuck out amidst the brown.

"Yes," Audrey said, placing her hand on top of Ditya's. "I can believe it."

Ditya's eyes scanned the crowd, presumably looking for Jenni, who was using some of her vacation days to see them play.

Audrey often wondered how Jenni and Ditya did it. The two of them now lived over an hour away from each other, Ditya remaining in Sedona and Jenni residing in Flagstaff, where she was completing her residency program. The two of them stole as much time as they could to visit one another, but still often went weeks or months at a time without being in the same room. Nevertheless, their adoration of each other only continued to grow.

It made Audrey's heart swell as she considered what could have been, but no, she wouldn't allow herself to think that way. One hour and 27 hours were two very different things.

Audrey spotted Jenni as they walked out on stage. She was standing in the front row, her 5'3" frame obscured from view by several very tall men to her right. Once the band went on stage she was clearly visible, wearing head-to-toe Echo Roc gear and cheering loudly. She threw enthusiastic kisses to Ditya, who pretended to catch them and stuff them into her mouth, making Jenni laugh.

Audrey approached the microphone and faced the crowd, her heart thrumming in her chest with anticipation.

"Oceanside!" she yelled. "What a fucking pleasure to see you beautiful people!"

She was met with a steady thrum of cheers, its vibrations seeming to purr through her body. She took a moment to savor the energy that coursed over the crowd and danced toward the edge of the stage before shouting, "Let's go!"

Cedric, Ditya, and Stan broke into song expertly on cue, and the show began.

The swirling energy rose steadily in intensity as they performed, the vibrations of the band and the crowd mingling in a heady coalescence that made Audrey dizzy with joy. As she finished the bridge to their opening song, she realized with a rush of satisfaction that a sizable portion of the crowd was singing along with her.

Her words echoed across the open space, sounding gorgeous in the mouths of the spectators as she bellowed, "*Who is to blame?*"

The music intensified as the chorus began.

I said, Maybe it's god

Maybe it's the devil

Maybe it's me

Maybe it's me

Maybe it's you

You ain't been on the level

Or maybe it's me

Maybe it's me

After the show Audrey half bounced, half flew backstage, feeling carried on the current of the residual energy of the crowd.

"That was *fantastic*!" she exclaimed to her bandmates.

In response, Stan held up two hands, waiting eagerly for a double high five, his flowery Hawaiian t-shirt stained with sweat. Audrey and Cedric obliged, and with her free arm Audrey returned the hug Ditya wrapped her in.

"I won't lie, that felt really good," Cedric said.

"Hell yeah it did," Stan said, still slightly out of breath. "But I have to piss like a goddamn racehorse."

Ditya threw her head back and laughed, and Cedric said, "So that's why you were so jumpy during that last song."

Audrey let out a long breath and looked appreciatively at the group before saying, "Good job, you guys. I'm so proud of us."

Ditya nodded. "Me too. That was fucking awesome, and I love you guys. But—" She began to back away slowly, her hands out in front of her and her fingers opening and closing in a wave. "This is where I leave you. Jenni and I have plans to see some band she likes on the other side of the festival in like ten minutes."

"I'll follow you," Cedric said. "I want to ask Jenni what she thought of the show."

"Give her a hug for me," Audrey said. "I'm going to find something to eat and then wander around for a while. I'll see you all later?"

With that, the four of them parted. Audrey headed around the back of the stage and walked in the direction of some food carts she noticed earlier, her stomach growling so loudly she almost didn't notice the voice that addressed her from behind.

"Good show, Audrey."

Audrey stopped short. She knew that voice. She heard it in her nightmares.

She turned, and there before her stood the man she fled from almost a decade earlier, his arm casually draped over a lithe blonde woman Audrey recognized as his new wife.

Her thoughts raced, jumping from fear to anger to confusion, followed by a brief moment of amusement that she opened her show with a song about a woman poisoning her abusive husband—an allegory for the consequences of religious abuse, but inspired by Paul nonetheless.

"Paul," she finally said.

She looked him up and down. He was surprisingly similar to how she remembered him. His hair was several shades darker, as Audrey noted with some satisfaction, suggesting he dyed it to hide his age. The deep wrinkles on his forehead and around his mouth were also new, surely developed over many years of scowling at women and pretending to cry at church. Otherwise, he looked much the same.

Audrey saw a sudden flash of Paul's face over hers, his features twisted in rage as he interrogated her about some perceived slight, and a shock wave rushed through her body as if preparing her to flee.

"What are you doing here?" she bit out, feeling exposed.

Paul's face was smug as he crossed a foot over his opposite ankle. He placed his forearm atop his wife's shoulder and leaned heavily on her.

"What do you think?" he asked condescendingly, gesturing around him as if it was answer enough. "Andrea's parents have the kids for the weekend, so we're here on vacation." Paul's lip curled slightly as he considered Audrey. "I'm surprised at how many no-name bands are playing."

A small part of Audrey braced herself for the impact of the jab. For years she imagined a scenario like this—the unexpected run-in with her own personal monster. Even thinking about it made her palms sweat and her heart rate rise. But now that it was happening, she was surprised to find how little it actually affected her.

"What do you think, babe?" Paul asked his wife.

"I haven't been impressed," Andrea said, smiling sweetly up at her husband. Then she leveled her gaze at Audrey and it lost all semblance of its former sweetness.

Audrey was struck by the strangeness of the situation. The only memory she had of Paul attending or even talking about a music festival was the Christian music festival they went to with their youth group in 11th grade. Even then, he'd constantly complained about how hot it was. His presence seemed unnatural, like a raccoon trying to play it cool amidst a group of Dalmatians.

Despite her desire to be anywhere else in the world, a part of Audrey was curious what he would say to hurt her next, and was silently making bets on the possibilities. In her mind, there were three very likely topics: her weight, her singleness, or the fact that her soul was destined to burn in hell for all eternity.

Paul looked pointedly at each side of Audrey, as if someone would be hiding behind her. "No one came to see you play, huh?" His facial expression was a sickening parody of compassion, and he addressed his wife. "She was never really the relationship type anyway. Didn't matter if it was her husband, a steak dinner, or Jesus Christ himself, this one was never satisfied."

Triple whammy.

Audrey's first instinct was to strike out at him. She wanted to scream, to say horrible things, to hurt him in ways only she knew how.

She looked at Andrea. Her feet were firmly planted about a foot apart on the ground, and Audrey realized her left shoulder was slowly sinking as she struggled to hold Paul's weight, as if he was pushing down on her with all his strength. Her face was painted with disgust as she stared at Audrey, but Audrey realized she was actively working to maintain her composure.

They both were.

Suddenly, it hit her. Paul took his wife on vacation to the one place in the world he knew Audrey would be. He spent hundreds of dollars for a chance to insult her, his current wife nothing more than a convenient prop meant to somehow deepen the blow of whatever insults he still had planned. She wondered how long they casually meandered near the stage she was playing on so he could manufacture this moment. He had been waiting for this. She couldn't imagine the amount of hot air that swirled in his belly, begging to be let out, to lash out, to hurt her once again.

She wouldn't let him.

Audrey realized that Andrea would be the one to pay the price for anything that came from her mouth. She was vaguely aware that Paul was still talking, but all she could see was this woman, sinking slowly into the mud under the weight of her husband's personal vendettas.

"Wouldn't you agree?" she heard Paul say.

Broken out of her thoughts, she looked over to meet his expectant eyes.

"I'm sorry, what?" She said it with an air of irritation. He'd interrupted her musing.

Paul paused a moment, his chest rising slowly as he swallowed the insult of not being heard by her. "I *said* I almost didn't recognize you when you walked by. You're an entirely different person from the Audrey I used to know."

Audrey smiled slowly, understanding his insinuation—not only that she was fat, but that she had lost something. That by walking away from him, from the church—from manipulation, control, and abuse—she had left some special part of herself behind.

It was the part that made men like her.

"I *would* agree," she said finally. "You, however, Paul…" She gestured to him with a wave of her hand, willing her face to reflect a mix of disdain and apathy. "…aside from the hair dye, you seem exactly the same."

Audrey then looked from Paul to his wife immediately, not willing to give him the satisfaction of seeing his reaction to her words. She met the woman's eyes and simply stared, and her face filled with pity.

Andrea's former icy exterior seemed to crack just a bit under the weight of Audrey's pitiful stare, as if she was expecting to meet a monster and was surprised by what she found instead.

Then Audrey turned and walked away without saying another word.

Halfway to the food carts, she became aware of her heart beating wildly in her chest. Her hands were shaking, and the noises around her suddenly seemed louder than before. She realized she was coming down from the stress of her encounter, so she found a place to sit on the grass until she was calm.

It took several minutes to catch her breath. She held her head in her hands casually, as if she was looking at the phone sitting in her lap, but behind the hair falling in front of her face she had her eyes closed and was breathing deeply. After a few minutes, she found herself laughing, the stress now falling off of her like sheets of ice.

Finally, she opened her phone, feeling compelled to share her victory with someone she loved. Before she knew it, she was staring at her messages from Zachary.

It was a sparse conversation thread, but one she returned to often just to stare. Occasional check-ins, holiday or birthday wishes, or some-times a photo of something that made one of them think of the other.

The last message from Zachary was three months prior. It was a photo of a stunning amethyst table he helped create for a work project, and a message: *Do you still have that amethyst necklace?*

Audrey responded with a photo of herself wearing the necklace.

Still beautiful was his reply.

Audrey sighed, wanting to pour her heart out to Zachary like she used to, but well aware it was beyond the boundaries of their current relationship. Instead, she opened her messages to Ty.

You'll never guess who I ran into.

24

The wedding chapel looked like a small storefront on the outside, sandwiched between a bar and a tattoo parlor. It was advertised as the premier wedding chapel in Reno, "The Biggest Little City in the World."

Inside, the chapel had been thoughtfully decorated, making the small space feel bigger than it was. On either side of the center aisle about thirty white folding chairs were arranged facing a modest podium and enough space for the marrying couple to stand comfortably amidst their chosen decorations.

Isaac, Audrey's brother, and his groom-to-be, Ahmed, had chosen a modest arrangement of white roses. They were displayed on either side of the podium, which was draped in a rainbow flag with Isaac and Ahmed's initials embroidered on it—a gift from one of their mutual friends.

Audrey struggled to hold back tears as she took in her surroundings. She was one of the first guests there, but a few people were filing in behind her. They all looked to be about her brother's age, mid-twenties, and were most likely his and Ahmed's fellow graduate engineering students.

Now 38 years old, Audrey was beginning to feel like an alien when she found herself in groups of twenty-somethings unless she was on stage.

"*Audrey,*" someone whispered.

She looked over to see her brother peeking through a cracked door to the left of the podium. He waved her over to him and she quickly obliged, slipping through the door quietly and finding herself immediately enveloped in her brother's arms.

"Oh my god I'm so glad you're here," he breathed into the top of her head.

"I wouldn't miss this for the world," she replied, squeezing her little brother—who actually towered over her by 12 inches—as tightly as she could manage.

Isaac stood back from her, allowing her to take in his black suit, the white flower in his lapel, and the joy that radiated from his features. Audrey couldn't hold back her tears any longer.

"You make the most handsome groom," she said.

Isaac smiled, biting his lip nervously as he did. "Thanks, sis."

Audrey looked around at the small hallway they were in. "Where's Ahmed?"

"He's just in the other room," Isaac said, gesturing to a door behind him. "We haven't seen each other all dressed up yet. I was just going to see him but I wanted to find you first."

"Oh, I'm so honored," Audrey said playfully.

Isaac laughed. "Well I didn't *just* retrieve you so you could get the first glimpse of my suit. I also wanted to warn you."

"Warn me?"

In response, Isaac gestured toward the door and pried it barely open so Audrey could look out. She gasped. There, at the back of the chapel, was Audrey's mother, clutching her handbag and nervously looking around at the other guests.

Audrey pulled her face back and Isaac softly closed the door.

"She's *here*?" Audrey could hardly believe it.

Her mother had been devastated when Isaac came out of the closet. As if it wasn't enough having an unmarried, un-Christian daughter flaunting her bare arms and heathen lyrics on stage every week, now her only son was the very thing her congregation whispered about in disgust—the ultimate deviation from God's sacred plan.

According to Isaac, after their father exploded in rage at Isaac's confession and stormed from the house, Audrey's mother simply sat at the kitchen counter and stared, unspeaking. After several tries to get her to say something, she got up, walked to her room, and shut the door.

The last time Audrey saw Isaac, when he brought Ahmed to one of Echo Roc's shows to introduce him to her, he hadn't spoken to either of their parents in over six months.

Isaac's expression told her he was just as surprised as she was at their mother's appearance.

"That's why I stuck my head out and called to you," he said. "She called me from the cab a few minutes ago, wanting to know if she was in the right place. I figured I should prepare you before she walked in. When I sent Mom and Dad an invitation, I was just trying to warn them before the wedding hit social media. I honestly didn't think either of them would come."

Audrey shook her head, at a loss for words.

"Well," she said. "Thanks for warning me. Are you... okay?"

Isaac scrunched his face and shrugged. "I guess so? I mean, I guess I'm happy she's here. I just don't know whether to expect a family reunion, or a scene."

Audrey nodded, suddenly understanding the possibility that her mother could be there only in a desperate attempt at stopping Isaac from going through with the wedding. She took a deep breath and steadied herself.

"I'll go make sure," she said, turning.

Isaac grabbed her arm before she could leave.

"Hey," he said.

Audrey stopped and met his eyes. With a look, the two of them exchanged more than words. Audrey knew Isaac understood what a big ask this was. She had been estranged from both their parents for years, and though she rarely talked about it, Isaac knew how much pain it caused her.

She smiled reassuringly. "I'll be fine."

Isaac looked only slightly convinced, but he loosened his grip.

"You're right," he said. "And hey, maybe this will make her forget her issues with you. I think I've won worst child this year. It's my turn to take up the black sheep mantle."

Audrey didn't have the words for how that made her feel. Despite their age gap, Isaac had always been supportive of her. It wasn't until she left Paul that they really got to know one another, however.

She remembered thinking it was remarkable how easily he understood her need to make a new life for herself, to escape the expectations she felt had been forced on her. Now, Audrey knew Isaac felt like a black sheep wearing a white sheep's pelt long before she broke free of their family's mold. He understood her because he didn't fit the mold, either.

Audrey rose up on the tips of her toes to kiss her brother on the cheek and left him in the hallway.

Her mother still stood in the back of the room. Audrey was marginally aware of the other guests sitting down—about thirty people in total. Her mother stood just behind the last row, as if she might change her mind and take off running any moment. She stared straight ahead, her face impassive, the crease in her brow betraying her nervousness.

She didn't seem to notice as Audrey approached, her heart beating faster with every step she took.

"Hi, Mom."

Rebekah Anderson's breath caught in her throat as she turned her head. Upon first seeing Audrey, she seemed unable to speak—as if she were choking on the storm of emotions that shone in her eyes.

"Audrey," she finally choked out. Then, to Audrey's surprise, "my dear."

Audrey smiled tentatively at her mother, and was suddenly struck by how old she looked. Old, and tired.

"Hi," Audrey choked out. "I know Isaac will be happy to see you here."

She was testing the waters—why *was* she here?

Audrey's mother swallowed hard, and her eyes focused momentarily on the floor before they met Audrey's again.

"Of course I'm here," she said softly. "I... wanted to support Isaac."

Audrey's brow furrowed as she considered this. As surprising as it was, she believed her.

"That's great, Mom," she said. "I'm glad to hear that."

"I tried to get your father to come. But..." She trailed off, seemingly unsure of what to say.

Audrey was shocked her mother would even try to convince her dad to come. She smiled gently, trying to show her mother she understood.

"At least you're here," Audrey said, and her mother smiled nervously in response.

Audrey scanned the chapel. The officiant stood at the front near the podium, talking to a couple whom Audrey recognized from social media as Ahmed's parents. She checked the time. The ceremony would be starting any minute.

"Well," she said, weakly gesturing toward the second row where her purse was saving her seat. "I should probably..."

Audrey's mother nodded, but as Audrey turned away her mother's hand shot up.

"Audrey, wait," she said.

Audrey stopped.

"I just wanted to say... well, I know I've made mistakes. Everything..." Rebekah wrung her hands together nervously, her body tense and her voice shaking. "Everything is so different now from when I was young. And I'm learning. But it's hard trying to reconcile what I know with... well, what I'm trying to say is, I want to make up for the past. Maybe... maybe we can start talking on the phone again? Or... well, perhaps I could make it to one of your shows."

Audrey was overcome with a sudden sense of compassion for her mother, whose expression was now like a timid child asking for permission. Looking at her, her face filled with longing and trepidation, she saw a glimpse of the mother she knew as a child. Loving. Emotional. Attentive.

She imagined her mother during that time. She saw her sitting in church, listening to a sermon about sin and the dangers of hell. She wondered what that must have felt like—to believe her children might be separated from her in death, destined to suffer and burn for all eternity while she grieved for them in heaven, forever. She wondered how terrifying it might have been to then watch the very scenario she'd been warned about play out before her eyes.

"Okay," she said simply, trying to put as much feeling into the word as she could.

In response, her mother clasped Audrey's hand in hers and squeezed, her own eyes shining. When they each let go, Audrey felt moved to say, "We're going to be okay, Mom. Isaac and I will both be fine."

Rebekah's face filled with something like gratitude as Audrey walked away.

Isaac and Ahmed's ceremony was beautiful. The couple made their entrance together, holding hands as they walked down the aisle, and throwing flower petals from a basket that hung from their intertwined arms. Upon kissing, loud cheers erupted from the small group of guests, accompanied by the faint *click*s of the photographer as he strived to get the perfect shot.

Following the ceremony, the group moved to a beautifully decorated banquet hall at a nearby casino for the reception. Audrey sang "You Make My Dreams" by Hall and Oates, and ate two plates of appetizers while she watched Isaac and Ahmed's college friends drink enough chardonnay to kill an army.

Their mother left just after the ceremony, following what looked like an emotional reunion between her and Isaac. Apparently her flight there and her flight back were only a few hours apart, giving her just enough time to see the wedding and go back home. After considering it, Audrey realized her mother would have been able to leave and return home all within the span of her dad's normal work shift.

That night in her hotel room, Audrey wrote a song:

She said, 'This isn't what I remember, dear

Where did all the cowboys go? I swear they were just here.

I thought everything was rainbows,

But maybe it was just rain.

I guess I didn't want to feel the pain.'

She fell asleep feeling full from a day of love and celebration. She thought about her mother, tears streaming down her cheeks as she hugged Isaac after the ceremony, her hands shaking as she let him go. She thought about Isaac, who told Ahmed in his vows that he had "never felt more at home than right now."

And she thought about Zachary, as she did often. She pictured him living his life, saw him working, imagined his fingers tracing lines on a piece of wood the same way they used to on her thighs. She wondered what he was doing now, and if he still thought of her as often as she thought of him.

He did.

25

Audrey was sprawled comfortably on Ty's couch, her body relishing the horizontal position after her 4 a.m. flight to Los Angeles.

She was spending the morning with Ty before they needed to get ready for their party. Ty was celebrating their new status as a tenured professor at UCLA, as well as the recent release of their book about the oral literary traditions of pre-colonial India.

Seamus, Ty's husband of three years, was busy in the kitchen making something that made Audrey's mouth water every time he pried open the oven door. Audrey made a guttural sound at the smell of the newest batch of whatever Seamus was baking, prompting a *tsk, tsk* from Ty, who sat on the chair across from her holding a steaming cup of black tea.

"You'll have to wait until the party," Ty said. "Chef's rules. He's *very* strict."

"You're so lucky to have fallen in love with a chef," Audrey responded. "How you haven't gained a hundred pounds is a total mystery to me."

Ty's gaze drifted toward the kitchen, their eyes softening at Seamus as he worked. Seamus not only insisted upon throwing the congratulatory party for Ty, but planned the entire thing as well. Audrey's heart melted at the way he doted on her friend, and at the adoring look Ty had on their face anytime their husband was near.

"I am quite fortunate," Ty said, their voice so soft Audrey could barely hear them. They didn't tear their eyes from the kitchen for what seemed like a long time. Audrey watched them, still as a statue, the same calm intensity radiating from them as the day they met eighteen years ago.

Beneath her admiration, Audrey felt a sort of sadness. She was 43 years old now, and Ty was still her most steadfast friend. Over the years they took turns jaunting to various parts of the country to see one another, neither of them missing a major life event if they could help it. She wouldn't trade that kind of friendship for the world. But she also remembered what it felt like to share a home with Ty, and despite how genuinely happy she was for Ty and Seamus, she felt a twang of envy at the life they shared.

Ty finally looked at Audrey again, the intensity never leaving their eyes. "Speaking of successful men in our lives..."

Audrey sighed. She knew she couldn't put this topic off for long.

"Are you ready to see him?" Ty asked.

Audrey was silent for a moment. "I don't know," she finally said. "I know I *want* to see him. But whether I'm ready?" She let out a sharp breath. "I have no idea. I mean, after all this time, I still think about him... miss him. But nine years is a long time, Ty."

"Long by whose standards?" Ty asked. "Nine years is just how long it took, Audrey. You've both done more in those nine years than you ever dreamed. And besides, how long was it last time you were apart?"

"Twelve years," Audrey admitted.

"Twelve years," Ty echoed. "And it was like you'd never parted. Trust me, Audrey. Zachary is the same man you remember. Maybe even better."

Audrey thought of those words as she got ready that night in her hotel room, staring at the 43 years worth of sun on her face and wondering if she looked anything like the Audrey that Zachary once knew. She feebly attempted to smooth the wrinkles around her eyes, but they would not budge.

When she stepped out of her Uber at Ty's home that night, her nerves were on overdrive. She smoothed her black dress against her legs as she walked up the driveway to Ty's house, breathing deeply as she did. She could hear the steady hum of voices inside. Light spilled onto the concrete from the windows of the large modern home overlooking L.A. Audrey stood just outside the pools of light, taking a moment to steel herself before she approached the door, its black paint standing in contrast to the clean white lines of the house.

Taking in a final steadying breath, Audrey walked into the light and up the front steps.

Inside, Ty's formerly peaceful abode had transformed into a swirl of sound and color. The large living room, its high ceilings accented by built-in shelves displaying Seamus and Ty's collection of art from around the world, was filled with Ty's many adoring fans. Students, professors, personal friends, and everyone in between mingled and talked, drinks or hors d'oeuvres in their hands. Copies of Ty's book were strategically placed throughout the space.

Audrey spotted Ty immediately, wearing a deep purple suit and making their way throughout the room. Seamus may have planned the evening, but Ty was completely in their element. Despite leaving the hospitality industry years ago, they never stopped being an excellent host.

Audrey made her way toward Ty, her eyes scanning the room in what she hoped was a casual, and not frantically nervous, sort of way. It was when she rounded the corner between the living and dining room that she saw him.

Zachary wore a dark blue button-down shirt with the sleeves rolled up slightly, revealing his forearms, and a pair of jeans. His hair was a mix of dark brown and silver, and his salt and pepper beard was neatly trimmed. Audrey's heart nearly stopped when he laughed at something a woman nearby said. His laugh still had the same musical quality it always did—his smile the same subtle tilt. She could see the playfulness in his eyes from across the room.

Then, as if he felt her presence (he did), Zachary turned and looked directly at Audrey. The two of them locked eyes from across the room for a handful of moments that felt like eternity, and then Zachary walked straight toward her.

Her heart racing, Audrey started walking too, until they were face to face, both of them smiling deliriously and somehow out of breath. For several moments, they just stood there. Audrey's skin buzzed, aching to reach out and touch him, to grab him and pull herself into his embrace. Something in her chest tugged as if encouraging her—no, begging her—to give in to her desires.

She couldn't tell, but Zachary felt the same urge, as if a magnet laid dormant in his body that was only attracted to her.

Finally, Zachary said, "Hi."

"Hey," she replied.

Then, as if a single word was all it took to erode their self-control, they fell into one another's arms. They stood there, still and silent in the middle of the party, for several minutes. When they managed to pull away, Zachary's hands lingered at her shoulders. He flexed them as he brought them to his sides, as if to work out the urge to grab her again and never let go.

"Can I get you a drink?" he asked.

"Yes," Audrey responded—too quickly, she thought. Her eagerness relaxed Zachary, his shoulders dropping as he reached out and took her hand.

Several minutes later, the two of them sat at a small table on Seamus and Ty's sprawling back deck. Audrey was just remarking on what a perfect Old Fashioned Zachary still made, and Zachary was silently marveling at how she'd gotten more beautiful with time.

"You came a long way," he said. "Last I heard you were living in New Orleans?"

Audrey nodded, her eyes dreamy thinking about her raised center-hall cottage in Uptown New Orleans. She bought it after staying in the city for two weeks following a show. She became addicted to the buzzy energy of the city—its music, its food, its people—and it had quickly become her haven during her off months.

"Yes, but I was long overdue for a visit. My mom has been nagging me to come out West for months to see her, so this was a good opportunity to oblige."

"I see," said Zachary. "So you and your mom, you're...?"

Audrey nodded, knowing where he was going with his question. The last time she saw him, she and her mother weren't on speaking terms.

"We're better than ever," Audrey said. "My dad died a few years ago, though. Heart attack."

Zachary leaned forward and put his hand over hers. "I'm sorry, Audrey. That must have been hard."

Audrey smiled, hearing all the layers to his words in the tone of his voice. Zachary knew as well as anyone how complicated her love for her father was. His approval was once a primary focus of her life, but as an adult she'd spent decades healing from his rejection—a decades-long ploy to blackmail her into coming back to the church and saving face for her family. It never worked.

"Thank you," she said, focusing on the warmth of his hand over hers. "It was hard."

"How's your mom doing?" he asked, pulling his hand away to pick up his drink.

"She's great actually," Audrey said, chuckling. Her hand felt cold where his had just been. "A year after my dad passed she started dating a guy named Hank. They met online, and six months later she was moving into his place in San Jose. They spend all their time at the country club, golfing and drinking wine. She's never been happier."

Zachary's smile was genuine. He leaned back in his chair, casually spinning his drink in his hands and looking at Audrey like he was looking at a piece of art. She mimicked him, leaning back and observing him as well. She enjoyed the opportunity to simply stare, noticing every new line in his face, every silver hair, as if her eyes had been starved of him for all these years.

"You're the one who went out of your way," Audrey said. "New York to California is quite a journey."

Zachary nodded as she sipped his drink. "I owed it to Ty. For missing the wedding."

"Ah, yes," Audrey said, remembering Ty and Seamus' intimate beach ceremony and her utter angst that Zachary wasn't there. "Why did you miss it again?"

Zachary winced. "I fell off a ladder two days before my flight."

Audrey snorted, doubling over and covering her mouth to keep her drink from flying in every direction.

"Oh my goodness," she said, trying to recover.

"It's not funny," Zachary said, laughing incredulously. "I broke my arm in three places and tore a tendon. I had to have surgery! It took ages to heal."

Audrey stuck out her lower lip sympathetically and attempted to look at Zachary with a straight face. It didn't work, and the two of them both burst into laughter.

"Do you keep in touch with the Echo Roc folks?" Zachary asked when they both caught their breath.

Audrey nodded. Five years prior, Echo Roc broke up after Cedric announced he was accepting a job in Michigan that paid almost twice his previous salary. Following his announcement, both Ditya and Stan admitted they were nearing musical burnout, and needed a change.

But not Audrey. Audrey simply wanted *more*.

So she went solo, and within two years she was touring eight months out of the year and singing on stages 20-year-old-her would have never imagined. It was the life she always dreamed of—music, travel, excitement, and enough money to never have to rely on another person for the rest of her life. She missed the band and saw them as often as she could, but she was living her best life now—minus one thing.

"They're all doing great," Audrey said.

"And you?" Zachary asked, leaning forward. "Are you doing great? I mean, you seem to be. It looks like you're absolutely killing it."

Audrey did her best exaggeratedly smug expression. "I am killing it, aren't I?"

Zachary laughed but nodded appreciatively at what he perceived to be an accurate statement.

"In all seriousness though," Audrey continued. "I *am* doing great. The past few years have been mind-blowing. I've done more than I ever thought I would."

Zachary shook his head. "Not me. I always knew you'd end up here."

Audrey's eyes suddenly threatened to overflow. It was true, he never doubted her. If he had been more selfish, if he had only asked her to stay, she may have never achieved her dreams. But because he loved her, he let her fly.

Zachary's brows furrowed as he recognized the emotion swimming in Audrey's eyes. He sat up straight, and his hand moved as if to take hers, but she quickly downed her drink and changed the subject. The night was young. She wasn't ready to ruin it by sobbing.

"You must have hated being laid up with a broken arm," she said. "How did you manage with work?"

Zachary smiled slowly and sat back in his chair again. "I did not handle it well. I spent days obsessively micromanaging my crew until they basically forced me to go home and leave them be."

Audrey imagined Zachary anxiously barking orders at his crew, unable to use his hand, and clucked sympathetically.

"I got used to it," Zachary said, shrugging. "Actually, I haven't worked directly on any projects for at least a year. The show is kind of running itself at this point."

Audrey was surprised. She thought back to their last Christmas together and the pleasure it gave her to see him so at ease—so distinct from his baseline of constant movement and activity. She saw that ease radiate from him now. For some reason, it made her feel sad.

"What have you been doing with yourself?" she asked.

Zachary's smile widened. "Working on my boat, mostly."

Audrey gasped and swatted her hand at him, making him laugh. "Your boat! You finally got it?"

Zachary nodded emphatically. "I did. Been taking her out a little bit. Tinkering here and there. Turning it into something I could live in."

Audrey listened intently while Zachary told her all about his catamaran, like a kid talking about his favorite toy. She felt just like she was twenty again, making lattes and listening to Zachary muse about his future travels. Back then, she would imagine herself on that boat with a sense of shame, as if her thoughts were a betrayal. They were secret musings she never dared share with anyone. Just the fantasies of a foolish child.

There was a time, in New York, when those fantasies felt like promises. She not only saw herself on that boat, she knew it was where she belonged. The image of being with Zachary, alone, surrounded by the vastness of the sea and sharing a new adventure, filled her with a sense of deep longing she couldn't fully explain.

Now she felt like an outsider again, listening in. Zachary planned to set sail in just over a year. She wondered if she would ever see him again after that. Would they keep in touch? Do boat people have phones? She realized with a sense of dull panic how little she knew about him now.

When she pictured him, setting sail each morning with a sense of purpose, what would he be wearing? What would he eat for breakfast? She felt small thinking about it, as if she was relegated to some insignificant corner of his life where the view was obscured.

In reality, Audrey still occupied quite a central role in Zachary's life, despite the fact that they had fallen mostly out of touch over the past few years. That is not to say he sat around pining for nearly a decade. He lived well, just as Audrey did, working, and traveling, and achieving milestones along the way. He dated occasionally, some relationships lasting longer than others. But nothing ever measured up to Audrey.

And for Audrey, nothing ever measured up to him.

Before Audrey could spiral any further in her thoughts of missing out on Zachary's life, Ty and Seamus came outside and interrupted their conversation. The four of them spent the next few hours together, talking and drinking. Ty occasionally got up to make the rounds through the party, but usually Seamus kissed them on the cheek and went to do it himself.

"Keep talking with your friends," he'd say, gently squeezing Ty's arm as he did.

Audrey noticed with satisfaction how she and Zachary were drifting toward one another, inch by inch, as if they were being slowly pulled by some invisible force. Every movement either of them made seemed to bring them imperceptibly closer.

It was nearly midnight before the house was empty and Ty was half asleep, leaning on their husband's arm comfortably. Audrey knew it was time to make her excuses so she said something about an early flight and wrapped the two of them in a hug. Zachary did the same, and after an extended round of goodbyes, the two of them walked out together.

Upon the sidewalk, they lingered, their feet rooted to the spot and unwilling to move away from one another.

Seeing the same hesitation in Audrey's eyes he felt himself, Zachary blurted,

"You know I went to one of your concerts."

Audrey felt a rush of relief at the chance to talk more, followed by surprise as what he said sank in.

"You did?"

"In Chicago. About two years ago…" Zachary smiled at her. "You were amazing."

"Thank you. I wish you would have told me, though. I would have made time to see you."

"Then I was a fool not to tell you."

The two of them stayed there on the sidewalk in front of Ty's house for hours. First they stood, both still pretending they meant to leave soon, but eventually they sat on the curb, their shoulders touching. Audrey's dress pooled on the ground at her bare feet.

For those few hours, Audrey and Zachary felt an easiness they hadn't known in years. Just as it always had, the world outside their proximity quieted considerably. For how small her worries felt, Audrey thought they may as well be in the middle of the sea as they talked about books, and music, and all the newest conspiracy theories to emerge since they were young.

But the night had to come to an end and eventually, it did. The two of them stayed there on the curb until Audrey's Uber driver came, still close enough to touch. When a notification told her that her driver was about to arrive, Audrey bit her lip to stifle a sob. For nine years, she had been avoiding a situation exactly like this. Part of her thought after all this time it would be easier to say goodbye.

It wasn't.

Audrey stood, the strap of her heels dangling from her finger and her clutch held tightly in one hand. When she straightened, she was surprised to find Zachary standing close to her—very close. He raised his hand and ran his fingers gently across Audrey's cheek.

"Audrey," he said softly.

Then he leaned forward, his other hand rising to gently cup her cheek as he brought his mouth close to hers—almost close enough to touch. Audrey could feel him in her bones then, his breath filling her nose, his heart pounding just inches away from hers. When she didn't pull away, Zachary put his lips to hers and kissed her gently.

For the few seconds between that kiss and the chime of Audrey's phone alerting her to her driver's presence, time once again stood still for Audrey and Zachary. Or rather, the limitations of a linear experience of time were temporarily lifted.

As Audrey opened the door of her ride, she looked back at Zachary. "I'm still saving a seat for you," he told her.

Audrey smiled, her heart lifting, and ducked into the car.

Once, she was waiting.

Only a moment ago—or was it many years?—she was with him. But he left, and this time she did not follow.

She did visit him, however. And at times when his mind was receptive, she communed with him.

When he was deeply happy or deeply curious, she whispered things in his ear. When he pleaded with the universe for answers or comfort, she did her best to provide them. She was in the feeling of sudden awe that overcame him occasionally in prayer.

Sometimes, she talked to him just before he fell asleep. In those in-between places, she pressed herself up against the barrier that lay between them, and they were almost together once more.

Usually, he called her God. He called her God in the morning when he knelt with his family to pray. He called her God in the evening when he ate his final meal. He cried out to her when he made love to his wife.

He called her God at the temple, where he lit candles and prayed for forgiveness for sins he never committed.

Almost everyone he knew saw God as a vengeful, angry God. But in all his life, the only thing he ever experienced that felt like God, felt like love.

Indeed, she did love him, but she was not a god.

In fact, long ago she resolved never to involve herself so intimately in the affairs of any world that she would be considered a deity. She had several friends and acquaintances—even a few distant family members, if such a concept exists in the metaphysical world—who had gone down that road before.

Some beings were simply too curious. And they always paid for it in the end. When encased in flesh, souls were such fickle creatures. More often than not, they brought their deities nothing but heartache, using the lessons they gave them as no more than excuses to perform egregious violence.

In her opinion, incarnate beings were better left alone. For him, of course, she made an exception.

Sometimes, he called her inspiration.

When he became an old man, he found this inspiration to be more familiar than even God once was. He didn't realize it was the same thing—he had only found a new name for it.

His children grew and left his home, and had children of their own. His wife, a beautiful soul, passed on before her time. At least, that's what he thought.

In his old age, he became fixated on a single project. A cellar he built years ago lay dormant on his property. He no longer needed to store additional food, as he didn't have a large family to feed. His garden grew wild and provided enough food to feed himself and the animals who had come to call his home theirs. A portion of it he canned, and it filled a few small shelves in his home to get him through the dry season. The rest he allowed the dirt to reclaim.

Despite its disuse, the cellar provided a sense of solace and safe haven to him. The heat, present year-round on his small green planet, was nearly unbearable for an old man in the summer months. He often found himself sitting in his cellar then, staring at the earthen shelves he had shaped himself, now covered in webs and rodent droppings instead of preserved vegetables.

It was in this place he heard her. It was quiet and dark save for a lantern he sometimes carried, and its light cast shadows on the walls that twisted in fearsome and wonderful shapes. She spoke to him there, her presence magnified by the solace, the quiet, the smell of the dirt. He conversed with her, needing not words but only the ever-shifting impressions in his mind, the changing of his heart's inner tune.

He began to see shapes on the walls, and in his mind, he gave them stories. Over here there was a beast, and over there a monster, and far above, the wings of some great and fearsome bird flapped tirelessly along with the flickering of the lantern's flame.

Eventually, he began sketching. It was the height of summer, and descending into the cool of the cellar around midday soon became a daily habit. The relative darkness made it difficult to keep track of time. Often he would emerge from the ground to find the sun already beginning to rise above the distant horizon. Over time, his sleep patterns became so disturbed he started sleeping in the cellar, too.

Day after day, he sketched his visions on the wall with bits of charcoal and stone. He felt as if he were one with the light of the lantern, its movements, its impressions. After his eyes adapted to the darkness, the fire began to reveal small details he hadn't seen before. A subtle pattern in the scales of the beast, or the slight curl of the great bird's tail feathers, but it was the woman he spent the most time on.

She took up the larger part of the southern wall, bare of shelves to accommodate for a stack of wooden boxes that had long been absent. She was tall, taller than him. Her hair hung past her shoulders, a feather sketched hanging from one side. At her hip was a long knife, the shape of a sun drawn on the curved blade. Her hand was outstretched.

When he finished, he sat and stared at the sketch for hours. He wished he could reach out and take her hand.

Days later, the man finally laid down to sleep in his own bed. He drifted off easily, his aching joints beginning to remember the comfort of the mat beneath him.

That night she came to him in a dream, and he found himself finally able to reach out and touch her. As he did, his body took its last breath, and he joined her on the other side.

26

Audrey scanned the tables at the busy restaurant next to the concert venue, looking for Zachary's face. It was several moments before she spotted him. He stood up from a booth in the back corner and waved at her, smiling widely. She grinned, waved back, and headed his way.

As she got closer, she noticed the woman in the seat next to him. She had long white hair with thick streaks of black throughout. She looked to be a few inches shorter than Audrey, who stood at 5'3", and she had a kind, enthusiastic smile that reminded Audrey remarkably of Zachary's own.

"Audrey," Zachary said as she approached, his voice almost relieved, like he wasn't sure if she would make it. He held open his arms, and she eagerly embraced him.

"You look beautiful," he said immediately as they parted, his hands still on her arms. He looked up and down at her admiringly, his eyes catching on the delicate chain around her neck.

Audrey smiled, knowing he was right.

She wore a floor length emerald gown that shimmered when she walked. It was cut low, accentuating her breasts and the purple amethyst that hovered just above them. Her hair and makeup were still perfect, having been finished just ten minutes earlier in her dressing room next door. She looked beautiful, ready to go out on stage in just an hour and a half, but all she wanted to do was curl up in the booth across from Zachary and eat pancakes for hours.

"Audrey, I want to introduce you to my mom," Zachary finally said. "This is Linda. Mom, this is Audrey."

Linda stood and took both of Audrey's hands in hers, her smile widening.

"I've heard *so* much about you, Audrey. I mean, for years. *Years and years.*" She looked accusingly at Zachary for a second, making Audrey laugh. "You have no idea how long I've wanted to meet you."

"I feel exactly the same," Audrey said. "It's been a long time coming."

Linda nodded, satisfied, then leaned in toward Audrey conspiratorially and whispered, "I also happen to be a big fan!"

Audrey put her hand to her heart in thanks. "Well then I'm doubly happy to meet you."

She looked at Zachary, whose eyes were glued to her face with an expression she couldn't quite place. He gestured to the booth for her to sit, so she did. Zachary took his mother's hand as she lowered herself painstakingly onto the seat, then sat directly across from Audrey to his mother's left.

The waiter arrived a moment later and Audrey ordered a hot tea, waving away Linda's concerns that she must need at least *something* to eat before she went on stage.

"I can't eat too soon before a show," she said. "Some warm tea and good company are all I need."

"Well thank you for taking a few minutes to see us before your big show," Linda said. "Zachary said it's the last one in your tour, is that right? I tried to tell him you wouldn't have time for us."

"Of course I have time. It's not like they can start without me," Audrey said, making Linda chuckle. "Actually, I was hoping to see Zachary when I was in New York a few days ago, but he texted me before I could ask and told me he would be here instead. Lucky me."

She looked at Zachary and winked, and could have sworn he blushed in response.

"How long have the two of you been traveling?" Audrey directed the question at Linda.

Linda looked at Zachary before she spoke, beaming at him as if he were a prince. "Three wonderful weeks. Zachary has been taking me all over." She looked again at Audrey. "I've hardly been out of Nebraska my whole life. Zachary thought it was time for that to change, and with him all packed up to leave on his own adventure, it was a chance to spend some time together before he goes."

"Goes?" Audrey managed to choke out, the air suddenly gone from her lungs.

Zachary looked flustered as he met her eyes, but his hand was steady as he placed it over hers. One look at his face told Audrey all she needed to know. He was leaving, and soon.

Linda continued on as if she hadn't noticed the exchange.

"Zachary has been working so hard on getting his boat ready since the business sold. We've been all up and down the East coast seeing the sights. I can't believe what a good sailor Zachary is, considering he grew up landlocked. I can't fathom where he even learned it!"

Audrey attempted to avoid Zachary's gaze as Linda continued to brag about her son and all the places he'd taken her. She could feel him looking at her, but she thought she might cry if she met his eyes again. Instead, she focused on the solidness of his hand over hers, his fingers slowly curling around her own, and continued laughing and commenting on Linda's stories.

Audrey knew Zachary had sold the business a few months prior. They had kept in relatively steady touch since she last saw him. Ty's party was less than six months ago, and in the time since, the two of them had been approaching what felt like a rekindling of sorts. At the very least, a rekindling of their friendship. Since she'd started touring again, their communication had been thin—even so, she thought he would have at least mentioned the culmination of his lifelong dream approaching so soon.

She felt blindsided. Her mind was racing. She suddenly felt vulnerable, as if her anxieties were painted on her face. And what were those anxieties from? The fear that she was being left out of his major life decisions? She had forfeited the right to that knowledge nine years ago, but somehow it still stung.

Audrey was pulled from her preoccupations by an alarm on her phone.

"Oh, shit." She looked at Linda apologetically. "I'm afraid that's my cue to go."

"Oh sweetheart, I'm so happy to have met you," Linda said. "I'll see you at the show. I'll be the one in the front row with bells on."

Audrey expressed her thanks and stood. Then she turned and stepped away, knowing Zachary would follow her to the door.

"Audrey," Zachary said when they were several steps away, just loud enough for her to hear. She turned and was suddenly a breath's distance from him, the hem of her gown pooling over his dark brown loafers.

"I'm sorry," he said. "I meant to tell you later, after the show."

Audrey sighed, still unsure how she felt.

"We're still meeting later?" Zachary asked, his eyes anxiously searching her face.

"Yes," Audrey softened. "Of course."

"I know I should have told you before. But I promise I'll explain everything later." He took her hands in his and stared at her intently. "You are still the most important person in the world to me, Audrey."

Audrey's heart constricted at his words, which were so perfectly aimed at her fears she wondered if he could read her thoughts. She squeezed his hands, allowing her eyes to speak for her before she turned and walked toward the door of the restaurant.

"Good luck, Cherry Bomb," he called as she left.

A short while later Audrey stood at the microphone, smiling out at the cheering crowd. The sprawling auditorium was a far cry from the open halls she played with Echo Roc. The crowd was older and more refined. Quite often she missed the feeling of dancing across the stage in her tennis shoes, feeding off the energy of Echo Roc's fans. Her solo music was less funk, more soul. Now she stood at the microphone, her arms out, and sang to the crowd as if they were all her lovers, and each song was written just for them.

Tonight, she looked for the man her songs were truly written for. She found him front and center. Linda was next to him waving her arms, her cheers enveloped by the crowd's. Zachary was smiling and clapping his hands. He was close enough that Audrey could see the pride reflected on his face.

Suddenly she was transported to another time, another auditorium, where she once sang to Zachary as if he were the only person in the room.

She didn't take her eyes off him now as she began to sing.

I fell upon a fairy tale

When I was just a girl

My heart believed it was a trick

This couldn't be my world

And so I traded love for comfort,

Diamonds for a pearl

And the villain, not the hero, got the girl

He never wanted all of me,

Only just my name

He never loved the wild me,

He strove to see me tamed

And desperate though I was for love

I never screamed your name

'Cause I didn't know that love could feel so sane

But if you could hear that young girl's heart,

I know that it would say...

Zachary's eyes bore into her with an intensity she could feel in her bones. His hands were clasped in front of him, and he leaned forward in his seat as if every inch between them was more painful than the last. She could feel his soul reaching for hers, and hers reaching out in return, pulling at her chest like a string connecting them had gone taut. As she sang the chorus, the feeling grew.

I'm on my way, I'm on my way

I'm running toward you

I'm on my way, I'm on my way

How I adore you

You took my hand, I pulled away

But I'm reaching for you...

As she sang the last line she reached toward Zachary. As if a jolt had gone through him, he stood and took a step forward, his hand raising slightly as if he would reach for her too. Something fizzled out in Audrey then, like the last bits of an Alka-Seltzer tablet dissolving in a cup of water. As she sang her last lines, she felt as if she was floating on air.

I'm on my way, I'm on my way

I'm on my way to you.

Audrey didn't know this at the time, but her performance would be described by many a fan as the most moving performance of her career. A careful observer may have noticed the way her body transformed as she sang, as if the song was a journey, and every movement she made transported her beyond the next leg.

An especially astute observer (such as myself) could tell you that Audrey's body and soul were aligned in that moment as they seldom had been before.

And so she sang her heart out to her companion from eons ago, and eons to come.

27

"I set sail in three weeks from Orleans Marina."

Audrey and Zachary sat knee to knee on a small couch in her hotel suite overlooking the Miami coast.

Upon emerging from her show to find him waiting at the front entrance, Audrey felt the sudden need to flee from the sound of traffic, to find somewhere quiet and envelop herself in the feeling of safety she had when she was with him. When he asked her if she wanted to go somewhere to eat or grab a drink, she immediately refused.

"I want to be alone with you," she said. Zachary's responding smile was filled with relief.

Relief and hope.

"So soon," she said now, trying to swallow the writhing sea of emotions threatening to bubble up to the surface from her belly. She tugged at the soft fabric of her sweater. "Why does this feel so sudden, Zachary?"

"I'm sorry," Zachary said, running a hand through his hair. "I know it seems sudden. I should have told you as soon as I decided it was time to leave, but you had already started your tour when I made the decision, and it just didn't seem right to tell you over the phone."

Zachary paused, looking down at his bouncing knees as he did.

"And to be fair Audrey, for me, this isn't sudden. I've been planning this for most of my life. I've spent the last decade working eighty hours a week to make this happen before I'm too old to sail around the world. When my Lead Carpenter offered to buy the business, I knew the universe was opening a door, so I walked through it."

"So you knew when you sold it you were leaving this quickly?"

"Not exactly. I thought I would wait a year or so, but..." He grimaced, as if considering whether to finish his sentence or not.

"What?" Audrey demanded.

"Well, shortly after the business sold I had a... a heart thing." He shrugged as he said it, as if he was referring to an especially troublesome pimple.

"A *heart thing*? What is a *heart thing*, Zachary?" Audrey felt panicked.

"It's okay Audrey," Zachary said, his hand darting to her shoulder protectively. "It was a mild heart attack, and I'm fine now. I'm doing everything I need to stay healthy. It just... jarred me a bit. Made me realize I can't wait any longer."

Audrey was silent, considering his words. His tone was gentle, sad, as if he wasn't only saying he couldn't wait to *leave* any longer. He was also saying he couldn't wait for *her* any longer.

"Where will you go?"

Zachary smiled softly. "It depends."

"On what?"

Zachary's knees parted around hers so he could lean closer. When he spoke it was nothing more than an excited whisper.

"Come with me," he said.

Audrey's heart beat wildly, the three words hanging in front of her like a promise. They were a confirmation of all she hoped Zachary still felt for her, and a tantalizing invitation to yet another new adventure, far, far away. With *him*.

"Come with me, Audrey," he said again. "Come *be* with me."

A second part of her desperately tried to dampen her excitement, whispering to her about her career, her family, her propriety. A battle between what logically ought to occur in her life and what she wanted *right now* raged inside her, leaving her torn and at a loss for words.

"I..." she managed, a hesitant smile playing on her lips. She didn't know what to say, but Zachary spoke before she could form a sentence.

"You don't have to decide right now," he said. He brought his hand to her face and cupped it gently, his eyes looking into hers with a sudden intensity. "This is *my* dream. And I know you're living your dream right now. If you can't walk away from that, I won't fault you. But you need to know that since the moment I met you, my dream has always had you in it. And if you come with me, I will sail anywhere in the world you want to go, until the day I die. I will take care of you, always."

Audrey only realized she was crying when Zachary gently wiped the tears from her face.

"I'm leaving on May 13 at sunrise. If you don't show up..." Zachary was silent for a few seconds, unable to finish the thought. "I'll always love you, Audrey. And I'll save that seat forever."

Audrey could only utter one word: "Zachary."

She pulled him to her, desperate for his touch.

Zachary kissed her deeply, his arms wrapping around her waist with a passionate familiarity. Audrey's body responded immediately, recognizing his touch on the cellular level, wanting to move closer, closer.

She moved against him and his hands tucked beneath her thighs. He lifted her easily and carried her to the bed where their hands moved quickly to remove one another's clothes, to become familiar once again with every crevice of each other's bodies.

Zachary whispered his pleas to her with each kiss he planted on her naked form, from the crook of her neck to the length of her bare stomach.

"Come with me."

His head between her legs, he begged her.

"Come with me, Audrey," he said. "Come for me, Audrey. Come with me."

As he moved his body against her, his fingernails dug the requests gently into her skin, and he gasped them into her open mouth.

"Come with me, Audrey," he said. "Audrey. Audrey. Come with me."

And as they fell asleep in one another's arms, his fingers combing gently through her hair, he prayed she would hear his thoughts as they whirled round and round in his head.

Come with me.

Audrey spent the next several weeks agonizing over Zachary's request. She was tossed back and forth, as if on an ocean, between two forces: the force of her love for Zachary, and the familiar pressure of social expectations. The former felt like a wide-open space, or a brilliant burst of starlight. The latter felt like a warm, comfortable bed, its frame prettily preserved with traces of arsenic.

Her feet itched, wanting to run.

It was a feeling she was familiar with. The desire to move on to a new place, a new task, a new adventure. That itch had propelled her forward many times in her life—toward new dreams or goals, or away from danger. The feeling often came with another: a heaviness in her hands, as if they would grasp on to everything safe and near and never let go.

She expressed her fears to Ty the day she arrived home in New Orleans, only two days after Zachary asked her to go away with him.

"What do I do, Ty?" she asked.

"Are you really asking me? Because I'll tell you exactly what I think," Ty said, their face framed in Audrey's iPhone. "But do you really want to know, or do you want to work this out yourself?"

"I *will* work it out myself," Audrey said. "But yes. I always want to know what you think."

Ty let out a sharp breath, as if they had been holding it the entire conversation.

"Audrey, I think you should run away with that man and never look back," they said. "I mean, what else are you waiting for? You're a star. And you can *be* a star from anywhere in the world if you want to. Create a new name for yourself. 'The Sailing Singer.' 'The Sightseeing Soloist.' 'The Voyaging Vocalist.'"

Ty paused to let Audrey laugh, smiling playfully at her. Then their expression grew more serious.

"Or, you can forget about everything you're *supposed* to be, or do, or accomplish, and just go *be* with your soulmate. No plans. No expectations. Stop thinking about what makes sense and listen to your soul." Ty's eyes flickered to the other side of the room, where Audrey knew Seamus would likely be. "That has value all by itself, Audrey. The both of you happen to be in the position to do it. A chance like that comes around once in a lifetime if you're lucky. This is your chance, Audrey."

This is your chance.

Those words echoed in Audrey's mind for weeks as she considered the necessary preparations to leave, her body and soul moving toward Zachary even though she hadn't fully made up her mind.

She repeated the same words to her lawyer, her manager, her neighbors, her mom: "I may be leaving town for a while. Perhaps a long while."

She meditated, and journaled, and made lists of pros and cons, all the while telling herself she must make this decision carefully. She must not jump too quickly.

But one morning, the day before Zachary was scheduled to leave, Audrey looked up and found herself ready to go. The preparations she started as a "just in case" scenario were all in place. All she needed was to pack a few essentials and she could walk through the front door, never knowing when she would return, and all would be well. She could be with Zachary forever, without really losing anything—without losing anything important, that is.

A rush of energy ran through her at the realization, and Audrey let it propel her to her closet, where her suitcase was barely unpacked from her most recent tour. She began pulling her clothes off of the hangers, choosing an array of options for every type of weather, every type of occasion. In a separate bag she packed shoes, toiletries, a few pieces of jewelry, her favorite blanket, and the remainder of the books on her to-be-read shelf.

When she was done packing, as if the wind had gone out of her, she sank down onto her bed. Just as she did, her phone chimed. It was a text from Zachary: a photo of him and his mom at a cafe table somewhere in the French Quarter. Below it was a photo of his boat, and a message:

I'll be at dock slip 4-24.

She hugged the phone to her chest, an elation running through her body that moved her again, from her bed to the dining room. She began emptying the fridge, throwing away anything that would spoil. Then she moved to the cupboards, packing anything with an expiration date shorter than a year into bags to bring to the food bank. An hour later she was headed to drop them off, bound and determined to pick up her favorite local foods on the way home to eat for dinner—a sort of celebratory goodbye.

When she finally arrived home, fresh gumbo and bananas foster in tow, the sun was beginning to set over New Orleans. She went to her backyard where she ate most of her meals when the weather was nice, and sat down in her favorite patio chair.

The sound of birds and the faint hum of traffic lulled her into a calm state as she gazed out at the yard. The flower bed she'd carefully tended last year was now in disarray, the neglect from her most recent tour showing. She had hoped to nurture it back to life when she got home.

She looked around at her covered porch. In the fading light, she could see the splinters that jutted out at strange angles from the wood, the dark brown paint fading or peeling in some spots. A fire pit she had never used sat just beyond the edge of the porch. When she bought the house, she imagined sitting around it with friends, entertaining. In fact, the idea of bringing this backyard to life was one of the reasons she bought this particular home in the first place. The image of settling in, of growing roots—it felt romantic to her.

Audrey took a bite of her food, trying to imagine it being the last time she ate from her favorite restaurant for the foreseeable future. It tasted like ash in her mouth.

She set down her spoon and sighed. "What am I doing?" she muttered to herself.

This home, this place, was the culmination of her success. She'd paid for the house in cash, images of shelves brimming with books and a garden overflowing with food filling her mind. She earned this place of respite. Besides, her career was at its peak. She'd written six new songs for her next album already, and her manager was making plans for another tour—plans she paused only after much protest when Audrey told her she may be leaving.

Yet here she was, ready to discard a well-built life in order to run away with a man she'd spent little more than a day with over the past decade.

Audrey dejectedly ate a few bites more and walked inside, discarding the leftovers with prejudice, as if they were to blame for her change of heart. She walked to her room.

Her suitcases were sitting on the bed, the smaller of the two open, waiting for those last minute items to be packed—toothbrush, make-up, phone charger. Unable to look at them, she tossed them both in the closet and shut the door.

As she lay there in her bed, Audrey thought about crying. But she felt too tired, too stupid, too raw. What made her think she could have this? And just like that, the battle in her mind between what *could* be, and what *ought* to be, was won.

Audrey turned off her pre-dawn alarms and fell asleep.

She dreamed she was on a shore. Tall, rocky cliffs rose behind her. The sea spread out in front of her as far as her eyes could see, but the water was still, the usual noise of the ocean absent. It was eerily quiet, as if she was standing in a painting.

On the water, she saw a sailboat.

Zachary stood upon it, busying himself with something she couldn't see. His back was to her. She called out, wanting to see his face, but her voice was swallowed by the same heavy silence that covered everything around her.

The scene was immutable. Unchanging. Permanent.

Audrey woke in a panic. She sat up straight, shaking her head as if to dislodge the eery image of her dream from her mind, and reached for her phone. It was 5:52 am.

"Zachary."

Audrey leapt from her bed and bolted to her closet where her suitcases lay haphazardly. The smaller one was open, its contents spilling out onto the floor. Audrey shoved them back inside and zipped it. She gathered anything else she could think of as quickly as possible, her hands shaking as she did.

In five minutes, she was throwing her luggage into the backseat of her car. The sun was peeking over the horizon.

"Shit shit shit shit shit," Audrey muttered to herself as she slid into the driver's seat. She pulled her phone from the side pocket of her purse, meaning to text Zachary and beg him not to leave.

It was dead.

"FUCK, GODDAMNIT!" Audrey yelled as she put the car in reverse. She kept one hand on the wheel as she backed out of her small driveway, her other hand feeling in the semi-darkness for her car charger. She found it and plugged in her phone; a cartoon battery with a tiny red line popped up on the screen.

Audrey raced to the marina, her heart beating so hard she could hear it in her head. A feeling of intense dread washed over her as the sun crept upward in the sky.

"No no no no," she said out loud as she drove. "Don't leave me, Zachary."

She fumbled for her phone but her hands were shaking, and it dropped in the crevice next to her seat. Tears escaped from her eyes as she tugged on the charger, yelling at Siri and cursing her when she heard no response. When her attempts to dislodge the phone resulted in the cord detaching and emerging by itself, she screamed in frustration and pressed her foot down on the gas.

By the time she arrived at the marina, the sun was fully in the sky. Audrey threw her car into park, pulled the keys from the ignition, and ran.

She racked her brain to remember the map she'd found online when Zachary told her his slip number. She silently counted the docks as she ran past them.

1, 2, 3, 4.

She turned right, ran down the dock toward the very end where she prayed Zachary would be, her body crying out against the exertion and her mind pushing her to move faster.

Audrey nearly sobbed when she saw sails in the distance. One of the spots at the end of the dock was empty. She stopped, her chest heaving, and stared at the boat, as if it wasn't real.

But it was. Zachary was leaving her.

No, her heart protested.

She opened her mouth and screamed as loud as she could.

"ZACHARY! WAIT! ZACHARY!" Her cries dissipated in the distance between her and the boat, meaningless.

He was too far. Audrey wiped the tears from her eyes and tried to assess the distance. She could make it. She looked around her and noticed a life ring hanging from a wooden stake a few paces away. She *would* make it, even if she had to swim all the way there.

Audrey ran to retrieve the life ring, pulling off her shoes as she did and leaving them strewn on the ground. Then she rushed back to the end of the dock and took a deep breath.

"Don't leave me," she said under her breath, and bent her knees to jump.

"I would never," said a voice from behind her.

Shocked, Audrey lost her footing, but before she could topple into the cold water Zachary's arms enveloped her from behind.

"Zachary," Audrey sobbed, and fell into his arms. "I thought you left me."

Zachary held Audrey tightly, a hand holding her head to his chest protectively. "I didn't leave you," he said breathlessly.

Audrey allowed the tears she'd been holding back to flow, the panic fleeing her body. Zachary loosened his grip in order to meet her eyes. His face was tear-stained, and he looked as if he'd hardly slept.

"I thought maybe you weren't coming," he said.

"I nearly didn't," she admitted. "But as soon as I gave up on the idea of going with you, Zachary, something broke inside me. Like I was walking away from... well, everything."

Zachary smiled in relief, something between a laugh and a sob escaping his lips as he pulled her close to him again.

"I love you," he whispered. "I've always loved you."

"I love you, too. And I choose you. Forever."

Audrey and Zachary stood there for a long time, holding one another in silent bliss, until Audrey broke the silence.

"I don't think I packed my toothbrush."

Zachary laughed, the rumble from his chest reverberating in her ear.

"That's okay," he said, pulling away from her. "I waited in the parking lot this morning, and when I didn't see you by sunrise I went ahead and paid to dock for one more day. Just in case." He ran his finger gently down the line of her jaw, his eyes boring into hers. "I'm sure we can find time to get you a toothbrush."

"Okay," Audrey said, smiling sheepishly. "But what will we do for the rest of the day?"

"I think a very thorough tour of the cabin is in order," Zachary said with a wink.

Audrey smiled wider, taking his hand. "Lead the way."

Zachary stooped to pick up Audrey's discarded shoes, and led her to a double-hulled sailboat with a name painted on its side.

Cherry Bomb.

Audrey squeezed Zachary's hand when she saw it. She looked up to find him staring lovingly at her, his eyes bright with joy.

"I made you a promise," he said. "Where should we go?"

Audrey walked onto the deck of the boat and looked around. The gentle sway of the water beneath her felt familiar somehow, and a rush of excitement ran through her body as she considered his question. When she turned, he was standing close. She put her hands on his chest and ran them up his shoulders, pulling him toward her.

He kissed her tenderly, passionately, and Audrey whispered against his lips, "Everywhere."

Audrey and Zachary spent their remaining time in this life together.

For Audrey, the final chapters of her life felt like one adventure after another. New places and people constantly came and went. Along with them came new feelings and experiences. Yet with each change, she brought with her a home. She got to experience the joy and freedom that came with never being tied down, *and* the unsurpassable gift of a constant, reliable partner whose love grounded her wherever she went.

For Zachary, their adventures were a culmination of everything that came before. The open sea felt more like home to him than Nebraska, or California, or New York ever did; but since the age of nineteen, he'd dreamed of a home more real and true than any other: Audrey. Years of hard work had gotten him there, true. But it was the years of enduring patience, and unwavering respect for the personal journey of his soulmate, that felt like a true labor of love.

For many years Audrey and Zachary sailed around the world, returning every so often to Audrey's cottage in New Orleans—to rest, to celebrate, to see loved ones, and occasionally, to grieve.

They grieved the death of Zachary's mother, and also of Audrey's.

They grieved Ty, who lived a full and wonderful life, won a Pulitzer Prize, and raised two beautiful children with Seamus before they passed away at the age of 73.

When T and Y left the body they shared, they emerged as a moving, twisting, dancing set of spiritual flames, writhing and laughing through the universe. Not one, and not two, but something more—distinct from one another, but never again separate. A concatenate, if you will.

Zachary followed Ty within a year, leaving Audrey with an empty house and a heart full of memories. She sold the house shortly after, preferring to spend her time on the stationary sailboat. There, surrounded by Zachary's wood carvings and worn mementos of their adventures, she felt Zachary's presence most strongly as he whispered to her from beyond the veil, inviting her once again to come with him.

She spent the years she had left enjoying a blissful solitude—reading, writing, and appreciating very good food—and of course, doting on her nieces and nephews. Between Ty and Seamus, Isaac and Ahmed, and Jenni and Ditya, Audrey (and Zachary, when he was alive) had seven children on which to shower attention between those periods of withdrawal.

It was toward the end of her life that an impenetrable peace settled over Audrey. It was a peace that may be difficult for someone like you to imagine just yet. A peace that comes from having lived your life fully—to have had dreams, and chased them, and caught them in your hand and held them there until you are satisfied—and then, to top it all off, to love. To love fiercely, and loyally, and to continue learning about someone until death takes them from you.

It was the peace of a life well lived alongside one's true soulmate.

If this is not something you have experienced, dear reader, there is still hope.

For time is a plentiful thing, though perhaps you cannot see that yet. There is time, in this life or another, or somewhere in between, to love and be loved in exactly the way your heart desires. For this is what it means that the universe is expanding. We are all reaching, whether we know it or not, toward love.

In the winding spirals and branches of the illusion we call "time," the universe itself reaches toward love, too.

When Audrey died, she was in bed, her hand draped across the space where Zachary used to lay. She felt something like sleep wash over her, but instead of retreating further into her body, she felt lifted, as if on air. It was like the small, invisible strings that held her in her human form were finally worn away, and she crossed into a space of in-betweenness.

What followed felt like a single moment stretched into eternity. She woke to find loved ones waiting for her from numerous lives and realities—friends, lovers, parents, and children. She was awash with love and acceptance, her soul stretching its metaphorical legs across infinite space and time in order to embrace them all.

A joy filled her that was so pure, so magnanimous, that in her human form it would have muddled her mind and broken her heart. She could feel the strands of herself that were woven in the life she lived as Audrey Anderson; they glowed with their own particular light. She delighted in feeling the other parts of herself that were so long submerged. It was like the feeling of putting one's feet into an old, comfortable pair of slippers.

Then, as suddenly as it began, the cacophony of souls subsided, and Audrey found herself in a small, quiet space. It was filled to overflowing with the energy of love and anticipation.

I've been waiting for you, said Z.

Hello again, my love, said A, and moved gratefully toward her soulmate.

And they lived happily ever after—again, and again, and again.

THE END

Thank you for reading my debut novel, *Soulmates: A Metaphysical Love Story*. This book is the culmination of a lifetime of dreams and wishes, and sharing it with you brings me so much joy. For an author, there is no greater honor than to know someone was impacted by their book. If you enjoyed *Soulmates*, it would mean the world if you wrote a review sharing your experience. For independent authors like myself, reviews are critical in helping us share our work with more readers.

Book 2 in the Metaphysical Love Stories series, Fated Tides, releases on January 29, 2024.

Visit www.sarahfaethsanders.com to stay in touch, or follow me on Tiktok (@sarah_faeth_sanders) or Instagram (@sarah_faeth_sanders).

Want to hear the original music from Soulmates? Scan the QR code:

To my beloved family, who have always encouraged my dreams. Mom, thank you for always believing I would write that book, even after I tore the first one up. Dad, thank you for teaching me to love books, and for being my first reader.

Thank you to my sister Erin for being my biggest cheerleader, and to Kimberley for being a constant source of support. To Haiden and Jade for being amazing. To Adam for holding it down while I poured my heart and soul into this book. And to Damian, for everything.

To every fellow author who took the time to answer my questions, give me advice, cheer me on, and laugh or cry with me about all the ins and outs of self publishing: I am forever indebted to you. Thank you for the support. To my beta and ARC readers: you're the best. To Kassie, who went above and beyond to partner with me in achieving this dream, I cannot express my thanks and love for you enough.

Finally, to anyone who has felt like the love they desire is simply too much for this world: This book is for you.

Sarah Faeth Sanders has been a storyteller since she was a little girl, when she would sit her parents down and spin new tales on makeshift stages, always ending her narratives with the mysterious phrase "A Duck and a Rabbit" instead of "The End." This tendency of avoiding absolutes followed her into her career as an author when Sarah released her debut novel, a whimsical tale of fated love, found family, and reincarnation that plays with time and avoids absolutes like "the end" by following characters across numerous lives. This initial standalone novel quickly turned into The Metaphysical Love Stories series, an ongoing trilogy set to be completed in 2024.

Sarah received her BA in Sociology in 2012. She attended a private Christian university, inspired by her conversion to Evangelical Christianity in high school. She began the process of deconstruction at this college, and would eventually leave Christianity behind entirely and embrace her more spiritual upbringing. Sarah's process of healing from religious trauma and the impact of Evangelical patriarchal control informs much of her creative work.

After college, Sarah backpacked through Southeast Asia with her best friend for seven months before returning home and meeting her partner, Adam, with whom she now has a beautiful son named Damian. In 2022, Sarah received her MS in Medical Cannabis Science and Therapeutics from the University of Maryland, Baltimore. She currently lives in the Pacific Northwest, where she draws inspiration from her natural surroundings to create new worlds. Sarah aspires to someday become an elusive hedge witch, increasingly one with the forest, communicating with the outer world solely through her increasingly whimsical and cryptic stories and a few friendly crows trained to deliver handwritten messages.